THE CHASE

THE CHASE

by

Jesse J. Thoma

2013

THE CHASE

© 2013 By Jesse J. Thoma. All Rights Reserved.

ISBN 10: 1-60282-859-8
ISBN 13: 978-1-60282-859-9

This Trade Paperback Original Is Published By
Bold Strokes Books, Inc.
P.O. Box 249
Valley Falls, NY 12185

First Edition: March 2013

CREDITS
EDITORS: VICTORIA OLDHAM AND CINDY CRESAP
PRODUCTION DESIGN: SUSAN RAMUNDO
COVER DESIGN BY SHERI (GRAPHICARTIST2020@HOTMAIL.COM)

Acknowledgments

Writing is an odd solitary pursuit in that it requires a huge number of people to get a simple idea to become a book. The story, words, and work may be mine, but *The Chase* would still be a nice little tale I told myself from time to time were it not for the wonderful people, both new and old, who have had a hand in this book's creation. First and foremost, without the wonderful Bold Strokes Books and Radclyffe's leadership, this novel would not be. That thank-you extends to everyone at Bold Strokes, authors and those working behind the scenes alike. I feel a special debt of gratitude to my editor, Victoria Oldham. She was a joy to work with, and I can honestly say this book would not be worth a darn without her insight, guidance, cajoling, and encouragement. A warm thank you to Cindy Cresap for her copy editing and Sheri for a beautiful cover.

I have an outstanding group of friends and family who support and encourage me unconditionally. Thanks especially to Patty, Martha, Alli, Deb, Claire, and Amanda. And Meg, who knew handing me a Bold Strokes book and saying "These are really good, you should read one," would have led to this?

I especially have to thank my parents and my wife's family for being proud of me no matter what I pursue.

And finally, a thank you to my wife. Without you, writing about romance would be impossible.

Dedication

For Alexis
Love Rocks when we're together
Love Rocks, gonna love you forever
Love's got me rockin and I only wanna rock with you

Chapter One

Peanut zigged as Holt zagged.

Holt was incredibly adept at catching her man, but Peanut was smart. And fast. When judges determined flight risk, they didn't consider the hazard presented by a pair of sneakers on the right feet. She leapt over a short garden fence, crossed the lawn, and jumped the fence on the opposite side. They'd been running for blocks, and it didn't look like the teenager she was chasing had any intention of slowing down. At least her gym membership was proving useful.

No one paid the least bit of attention to the baggy-panted teenager running like hell, pursued by a scruffy looking woman. This was Providence, Rhode Island, after all, and there were other things to worry about than the trials and tribulations of two people sprinting down the sidewalk of a busy street.

Holt cursed. Peanut was fearless, and she knew the direction his thoughts were going the moment he glanced across the street to the residential neighborhood on the other side. There were hiding places all over that area, tucked in among the basketball hoops, lawnmowers, and patio furniture of the perfect suburban enclave.

Peanut chose an opening the duration of a blink and darted into traffic. Holt hesitated only a second before charging after him. All around her, car brakes screeched and horns blared, but she kept her eyes on her prey, despite the sweat streaming down her face.

The roadbed was much warmer than the sidewalk, the heat from hundreds of roaring engines turning an otherwise pleasant day into a scorching, paved torture chamber. Peanut was ten feet in front of her and slowed to avoid a speeding car. Holt picked up her speed, hoping she wouldn't need to tackle him in the middle of the street. She saw the BMW speeding toward her and saw the driver yelling at the driver in the car next to him. He turned back and saw her just in time to put his car into an impressive skid. She crouched, knowing she didn't have enough time to get out of his way. His momentum had slowed enough by the time he reached her that she wasn't thrown over the windshield when she leapt onto his hood. Her quads reloaded as she landed and in one motion sprung onto the BMW's roof. A long, striding step brought her to the trunk and she leapt safely to the ground. With so much adrenaline pulsing through her body, she was pretty sure she could run through a brick wall and not feel a thing. *James Bond, take that.*

Peanut stood openmouthed on the curb, looking like he was about to applaud. His amazement was short-lived, however. Holt hit the ground running, determined to get her man before he could elude her in the tree-lined neighborhood directly behind him. With a lunge, she grabbed Peanut's shirt, but the material slid through her fingers as he bolted toward the residential area. She planted her right foot firmly to push herself into a tackle when her left foot unceremoniously collided with the back of her calf. She scraped her hands on the uneven cement, only narrowly missing a total face plant, and Peanut pulled ahead of her again. *So much for James Bond.*

"Fuck! Peanut! Slow your skinny ass down. I'm tired of chasing you."

Of course, he ignored her; she hadn't expected anything else. Fuming at her clumsiness, she scrambled back to her feet and sprinted after him.

The neighborhood they'd entered was standard cookie cutter, the different gardens the only thing to set them apart, and high fences around the yards made it difficult for anyone to find a quick escape route. Holt knew she could react to any trick Peanut tried to escape, though she was less than ecstatic when he settled for fence climbing, no doubt hoping her upper body strength wasn't as impressive as that of her legs.

Holt sighed in exasperation. The first fence Peanut chose to scale was wooden, with an uneven top, providing little leverage for her legs and likely to sting like hell when it came in contact with her road rash-damaged hand. She headed straight at the six-foot barrier, planting one foot against the rough boards and surging upward at the same time. With the grace of a high jumper, she pivoted her body over the top and dropped to the other side.

Peanut obviously hadn't landed quite as delicately and was limping away as fast as he could across a beautifully manicured lawn. Holt caught up to him and grabbed a handful of his shirt as he skirted the impossibly blue pool dominating the backyard. She saw no reason to bring him to the ground since the fight had gone out of him. She relaxed her grip enough to let him know she wasn't going to hurt him as she pulled them to a stop.

Satisfied he wasn't going to take off again, she bent double to catch her breath. Peanut twitched. Holt geared up for another chase, but when she followed his line of sight, her adrenaline surged for another reason. Just before the deafening "boom" and the spray of buckshot littered the house behind them, Peanut ducked his head and drove his shoulder hard into Holt's sternum. They both flew backward, landing with an explosive splash in the cool, refreshing pool, buckshot peppering the water over their heads. Luckily, he had been aware enough of his surroundings to see the hooded head pop up above the fence line and level the shotgun barrel at them. If he hadn't jumped, she never would have looked over. Peanut saved her life.

❖

Isabelle Rochat jumped off her couch. Whatever punk had just thrown a firecracker into her backyard was going to be sorry he ever laid eyes on her. It was Saturday. She was working. And she really hated being interrupted when she was working.

Through the sliding glass door leading to the patio, she could see two individuals splashing in her pool. One, a teenage boy, was being dragged toward the pool's edge by a brunette woman. She knew she sounded too much like her mother, but she really did have to wonder about the lack of respect people showed for each other these days. Who in their right mind would think it was okay to take a dip in a stranger's pool? Readying herself for a showdown, she slid the door ajar and stepped out onto her back patio.

"What do you think you're—"

"Get down," the brunette yelled before Isabelle could finish her question. "Get the fuck down! Look at your goddamned siding! Get your ass on the ground."

Isabelle saw the hooded figure appear over her fence at the same time she registered seeing the small holes littering her siding. She dropped to her stomach a split second before another explosion sounded across the quiet neighborhood, spraying deadly shot where her head had been. Squealing tires registered briefly before her mind was filled with a flash of white somewhere in her peripheral vision and the slap of wet shoes on concrete. The brunette was out of the pool and running in a crouch toward the back fence. The teenager clung to the side of the pool, making no move to pull himself out. The mystery woman stopped at the fence and listened before pulling herself up to look over the six-foot high obstruction. She hung there for a moment, looking around. Isabelle was captivated by the tease of tattooed skin through the shirt as the stranger was suspended on the fence. A colorful blur spread over her tense, powerful shoulders and down her spine. Isabelle had a soft spot for ink, and despite the seriousness of the situation, she felt her body react as the tattooed intruder squelched her way back to the pool and dragged the young man out of the water by the scruff of his T-shirt.

The dripping hair and tight body were something out of a movie, and Isabelle was glad the woman's face was hot too. It would have been a huge letdown if she were ugly. Her wet white T-shirt left little to the imagination, clinging to a dark blue racer back sports bra and a lean, muscled torso that formed an almost perfect triangle from her strong shoulders to her narrow waist.

"Was that one of your crew, you little punk?" Her voice was gravely and a bit rough, perfectly complementing the unrefined owner.

The teenager shook his head emphatically. "Come on, H. You know that's not how I run. I don't know who that guy was."

His face had lost all color, and Isabelle wondered if he was more afraid of the gunman or the tall woman berating him and shaking him like an empty sack.

"You saying none of you idiots have shotguns and ski masks?" the brunette asked angrily.

"Well, I don't think that would be an accurate assessment," the youth admitted carefully. "But if that was one of my guys, why the hell would he be shooting at me?"

The brunette's body relaxed and she seemed to let go of her anger. Her grip on the young man's shirt loosened and she glanced at Isabelle. "Peanut, you kill me. You've run me across the whole damn city, and now I've got myself an ethical dilemma. Get your scrawny ass out of here before I change my mind. If I find out it was one of your guys though..."

"Thanks, H. Been fun runnin' witcha today. I haven't forgotten your offer either. Just got to think some things through." Peanut backed away as he spoke, glancing over his shoulder for the fastest way out of the yard.

When he disappeared through the gate, the impressive stranger yelled after him, "And reschedule your court date." She pulled her cell phone out of a soaked pocket, examined it in disgust, and dropped it back into her jeans. "Damn it, I hate getting fucking shot at." Seeming to remember she wasn't alone, she jogged over to Isabelle, who was still flat on the ground, her elbows propping her up. "Are you okay? Did you get hit?"

Isabelle looked up into the bluest eyes she had ever seen. They were soft with concern, but she imagined they could be cold as steel when anger flashed through them. The blue stood out all the more because of the chin length dark hair framing the intruder's perfect face. From a distance, it had looked angled and androgynous, but up close, the features were refined, almost delicate. Isabelle had been correct in her snap judgment. The woman was gorgeous.

"What? Oh, no. I'm fine, thanks to you. Just a little shaken up. Is it safe to get up?" Isabelle hated how small her voice sounded. She didn't like being out of control.

The woman pulled her to her feet with an ease that gave proof to the muscled outline beneath her wet T-shirt. "Yeah, I think it's safe. Bad guy's long gone. I'm Holt Lasher. Sorry about the excitement." Her eyes were still soft, but she continued looking around cautiously, probably scanning for danger.

"Isabelle Rochat." As some of her fear receded, Isabelle remembered she was pissed. Getting shot at hadn't helped. Neither had being turned on by an indistinguishable back tattoo. The gunman wasn't there to receive her wrath, which left the woman who was dripping water all over her deck. And anger, fear, and adrenaline, combined with soaring hormones, made it one hell of a wrath. "What the hell were you doing in my pool?"

Holt's attention snapped back to Isabelle. Given that Holt was now thoroughly taking in every part of her, head to toe, Isabelle wasn't sure Holt had really looked at her before. Holt's intense stare seemed to pause longest on Isabelle's blond hair and she noticed Holt took her time tracing the line of her curvy torso. It was very disconcerting and a bit of a turn-on.

Isabelle studied her uninvited guest, who was now rolling her eyes and pinching the skin between her temples, looking like she was resisting the urge to slap herself in the forehead. Isabelle wondered if the woman was always this impulsive. Holt Lasher—a name Isabelle suspected was a heap of crap, as it sounded like it belonged to a superhero, thus, annoyingly, making it a tiny bit sexy—had started rocking back and forth from foot to foot almost imperceptibly. If it was a nervous habit, Isabelle thought it gave her a bit of vulnerability she hadn't shown when dragging the kid from the pool. The change in her gaze was disconcerting. Her blue eyes had gone from light and distant to focused and dark gray. Isabelle knew that look. It was probably the same one she was sending back. Some stranger was looking at her with sex eyes on her back deck, and there wasn't a damn thing she could do about her response. Already, her pulse was racing in parts farther south than was polite on a first meeting. She briefly contemplated asking Holt inside and insisting she get out of her wet things. All of them.

The soft ping from her computer reminded her she had work to do. Afternoon sex with a stranger would have to wait for another day.

Ignoring the little voice in her head that pointed out the absence of perfectly fuckable women who'd dropped into her pool before today, she said testily, "You didn't answer me. Why were you in my pool?"

"Your pool…right. I was in your pool because Peanut pushed me into it."

"Peanut, I am assuming, is the kid who went hightailing it out of here once you let go of his neck?"

"One and the same."

"Do I even dare ask why you were in my backyard taking a fully clothed dip with Peanut?"

"I was chasing him. He missed his court date again, and I was trying to convince him to reschedule. He actually saved us both by launching me into the pool with him. He could have let me get shot. I knew he was more than just a little shit."

"Well, in that case, I'm really thrilled that you were able to use my pool to find out a juvenile delinquent is really a criminal with a heart of gold. Please feel free to use my home as your proving ground anytime. Maybe I should give you a key." The adrenaline high she had been riding was wearing off, and her initial anger at having strangers in her backyard had returned. Even if the rational side of her knew Holt probably wasn't thrilled with getting shot at either, she was so calm about the whole experience it was adding to Isabelle's annoyance.

"I'm a people person, so I know you're being sarcastic, but you do have a lovely pool. And you do learn a thing or two about a person by nearly getting shot."

"What can you possibly learn from something like that?" Isabelle asked. "It's happened to me once now, and I can say I never want to repeat the experience. Has this happened to you before?"

Holt hooked her fingers into the belt loops on either side of her narrow hips and hiked her pants back up to a decent level. The water was pulling them farther and farther down the longer they talked. Isabelle thought Holt's pants hitting her deck would be a wonderful distraction to this mess of a day. She knew she was the one looking at Holt with sex eyes now. Holt looked like she wanted to reach out and pull Isabelle close and kiss her. That sounded nice to Isabelle too, but then she recalled something Holt said.

"You're a bounty hunter?"

"Bond enforcement agent."

Isabelle barely heard her. She just noticed the Wonder Woman tattoo on Holt's left bicep. Holt jumped when Isabelle traced the flow of her forearm tattoos.

"Oh, well, that doesn't sound so bad now does it?" Isabelle thought it sounded terrible, but after the thirty minutes she'd just had, Holt's tattoos countered that. It wasn't like she was going to have to see this woman again, so why not enjoy what was in front of her now?

Holt didn't seem to mind the attention. She held out her forearms as Isabelle gently traced the phoenix on the right, and the Japanese kanji on the left. Isabelle was also quite impressed with the nautical stars on both of Holt's wrists.

"What's on your back?" Isabelle asked.

Holt raised her eyebrows. "Oh, I think you would have to wait for at least a second date to find that out. For now, what you see is what you get."

"I'm not sure I'm satisfied with that answer," Isabelle said. "And getting shot at isn't my idea of a first date."

Isabelle stepped in closer to Holt, their bodies almost touching. Holt's eyes were no longer focused, but she wasn't scanning the area for danger anymore either. A look of disappointment flashed across Holt's face as she took a step back. Isabelle wasn't interested in letting her get away. She mirrored her step, and the next two that Holt took. They ended up backed against the edge of the pool, leaving Holt nowhere else to run unless she wanted to get wet again, and not in the good way. Isabelle didn't think Holt looked all that sad to have run out of places to go.

Sirens wailed in the distance, but Isabelle didn't care. Holt's eyes were clearly inviting Isabelle to take anything she wanted. She kissed her deeply, quickly exploring the softest lips she had ever felt. Isabelle wanted more. When the doorbell rang in the house, they stood frozen for a second, then Isabelle pulled away. "And you should have had to wait until at least the second date for that," she said.

Isabelle felt out of control again, but this time Holt was the cause. She hated being out of control. With a slightly cooler head, bond enforcement officer did sound pretty bad, but then there was that kiss. Holt looked awfully proud of herself, and her eyes were full of mischief. She leaned forward on the balls of her feet, perhaps inadvertently thrusting her pelvis Isabelle's way. Isabelle laughed at the not so subtle signs of an alpha dyke celebrating her conquest. Not so fast, she thought. Isabelle planted a hand between Holt's breasts and gave a small push and Holt had no choice but to take another swim. Isabelle headed for the front door, since whoever was there was clearly impatient, but she couldn't help but sway her hips when she heard Holt sputter laughing to the surface.

"The police are here, Holt. Someone must have called them. Shotguns aren't usual for this neighborhood." When she returned to the yard with the police, Holt Lasher was nowhere to be found. A wet trail of footprints led up and over the back fence.

CHAPTER TWO

"Yo, H, what the hell happened to you, man? You take your fish for a walk or something?" Jose Martinez was never one to hold back.

Holt studied her friend and business partner. He was handsome in a working guy kind of way, and at the moment, was ass deep in a messy engine repair. The auto repair shop they co-owned fronted a busy street close to the action of Providence's small "big city" downtown. As far as any of the employees knew, M & L Auto Repair was Jose's business, and Holt was a friend from childhood who rented the back rooms as office space. Plenty of shady characters sought out Jose's services for their legitimate vehicles, and having Holt's name attached would hinder his business. It wasn't exactly a secret that a bounty hunter operated behind the mechanic's shop; news traveled fast on the street. But Holt didn't broadcast her presence since she didn't have any walk-in clientele, and keeping a low profile enhanced her reputation on the street.

Next door to M & L Auto Repair was a tattoo shop, also owned by Holt and Jose. Over the ten years since she'd established herself in the neighborhood, it had been invaluable to be located next to both an auto repair shop and a tattoo parlor. She couldn't count the number of bail jumpers she'd caught simply showing up for work in the morning. There seemed to be no end to the amount of damage a felon could do to his car in the commission of a crime, not to mention the ink needed to commemorate the achievement.

"Do I look like I'm in the mood, jackass?" she asked, trying to squelch through the repair shop in the most dignified manner possible under the circumstances.

The offices housing her operation consisted of a large common area where most of her crew worked and two or three smaller private offices off the main space. She had the largest of those private offices, although she frequently preferred to work at one of the desks placed throughout the common area. Today, however, she was glad for the privacy. As soon as she reached her office, she started shedding clothes. Her T-shirt was off before she opened the door to her private office. Two of her crew, sitting at the desks closest to her office, looked up with surprise written plainly across their faces, but they valued their jobs enough to keep quiet as they glanced at their computers to give her some privacy. Holt was prepared for almost any situation, and it wasn't the first time she'd come back to the office soaking wet, missing clothes, or in an unexpected outfit.

Her sports bra flew into the small dirty window behind her desk, sticking to the glass briefly before slowly sliding down, leaving a muddy trail in its wake. Jose leaned against the doorframe and laughed. "I hear you and Peanut put on quite the running clinic this afternoon. Did you catch the little twerp?"

Holt glared at him. Although she was naked from the waist up, her ribs, chest, and stomach sported a variety of colorful and intricate tattoos, which always made her feel clothed, even if she wasn't. In one hand, she held a clean, dry white T-shirt, in the other, her useless, chlorine-infused cell phone and wet T-shirt. She glanced at him and he ducked the wet shirt she threw at his head. "I'm taking my pants off now," she said.

"Nothing I haven't seen before." Jose followed her the rest of the way into her office, closed the door, and dropped into one of the chairs facing her desk. "You didn't answer my question."

His indifference matched her own. She doubted he had seen any woman naked except her. He was as gay as they came. She dropped her wet jeans and boxers to the floor, kicked them aside, and reached for the change of clothing she kept folded neatly on top of her two large filing cabinets. "That little fuck is going to kill me. I don't know why they keep giving him bail."

Her operation wasn't tied to any particular bail bond agency, and as a result, she chased guys like Peanut all the time. When they got re-arrested, they simply chose someone else if their last bondsman felt they were too big a risk. Peanut wasn't really a huge risk, just a kid who couldn't seem to take getting arrested seriously. His violations were relatively minor, but he made it worse on himself by not showing up to court. She'd come to like the little punk for some reason, even if he nearly got her killed on a regular basis. She had always had a soft spot for troubled kids.

"You've never let him slip, H. You getting soft? 'Cause I hear State Rep. Caldwell is getting bonded soon, and if he doesn't show, they're gonna want you." She knew Jose was teasing, but there was some genuine confusion in his tone. Holt was good, and a little wannabe tough guy like Peanut didn't usually get away from her.

"There was a problem. I had the kid cornered in a yard, but some nutcase with a shotgun started firing at us."

Jose's body tensed and he leaned forward. "Who? A buddy of Peanut's?"

Holt buttoned her jeans, feeling infinitely more human in dry clothes. "Not according to him. The guy was wearing a ski mask and a hoodie. We ended up in the pool trying to stay alive. I couldn't drag Peanut's scrawny butt to jail since he was the one who saved my ass."

"Oh, God, I do love a pool boy," Jose said wistfully.

"I don't think this pool owner employs a pool boy. A hot chick in a bikini maybe…" Holt thought about the kiss and was a little less dry. "Fuck, I get myself in trouble with blondes."

"Excuse me?" Jose looked astonished. "You just chased Peanut halfway across the city, got shot at, and ended up in a pool. I know your crew picked you up ten minutes after you called. Just how the hell did you have time for a blonde?"

"It was her pool," she said with a wink. "And for the record, I didn't 'have' a blonde; she just kissed me. No big deal."

"You know what," Jose said, standing up, "I'm a jealous asshole. Shit like that never happens to me."

"You should try getting shot at. I bet it works just as well on the fellas. Or you could work on a damsel in distress routine and we could find you a strapping hunk to try it out on."

Jose shot her a look, but she decided not to hassle him about the muscle man he had been in love with since high school.

"Speaking of you getting shot. What the fuck? Any idea who wanted you to find God?"

"Find God? What are you talking about?"

"You know, holy? Swiss cheese?"

"Jose, it's a really good thing you're good with cars, man. But to answer your question, I have no idea who was shooting, or who they were aiming at for that matter. I'll have Max look into reports of similar incidents. The whole thing just feels weird. Who uses a shotgun to shoot people?"

❖

Despite the mound of paperwork threatening to topple off her desk, Holt had trouble keeping her mind on her job. There were plenty of open files, but she wasn't interested in any of them. Instead, her mind kept wandering back to Isabelle and her damn pool.

"Are you really this worked up over one kiss?" she said under her breath, glaring at the paperwork mocking her.

The more she thought about the kiss, however, the less she fixated on it. It was an amazing kiss, and she was still a bit turned on, but it was the shooting itself that was nagging at her. The gunman had been above her when the shot rang out, yet almost all the buckshot ended up in Isabelle's siding. That would make sense for the first shot, since Peanut pushed her into the pool and out of harm's way, but why didn't the second shot rain buckshot down into the water?

"Uh, H? You got a letter." Max Winters, her youngest employee, cautiously poked her head in the office. She was only nineteen, and for some reason, seemed to be terrified of Holt. She was incredible with the computer, however, and Holt had her to thank for more than one capture. Jose swore Max's deer in the headlights attitude had nothing to do with witnessing Holt go ape shit on a cop who had tried to play grab ass with one of the female members of the crew. He said she had a case of hero worship. Holt didn't care about her reason; she didn't need Max to shrink from her. The kid was brilliant. That was what she needed.

"A letter?" The mail had already come today.

"Well, more of a card actually. Although I suppose there could be a letter in there too. I don't—"

"Max?"

"Yes, boss?"

"The card?"

"Oh, yeah. Right. "

Holt accepted a bright red envelope and turned it over looking for some indication of its sender. When she found none, she debated the merits of opening it. There were a lot of pissed off convicts in the world, many of whom Holt had tracked down and tossed back in jail. She got hate mail all the time. She was always aware that one day a letter might contain more than just angry words.

This envelope, however, wasn't sealed, which she took to be a good sign. She pulled the card out and had to laugh at the two puppies shown frolicking on the front. The message inside stopped her cold.

I hope you will accept my sincerest apologies for the unfortunate incident this afternoon. I wish to assure you, you were not the target of my overly eager employees. Should our paths ever cross, I will introduce myself at that time. In the meantime, I hope this whole incident can be forgotten, as I would hate for this misunderstanding to linger between us. I have watched you over the years, and I believe we are much alike. Perhaps there is an opportunity for a partnership in the future.

It wasn't signed. Holt jumped from her seat. If she and Peanut weren't the targets, that only left Isabelle Rochat.

"What the fuck is this? Who delivered it?" she asked, her mind filled with images of Isabelle, shot and bleeding on the back deck of her home. Or worse yet, floating in that damned pool.

"I don't know. One of Jose's guys brought it in. Said it was taped on the door when he got back from lunch." Max was stuttering and had gone pale.

"Which guy? Bring him in here now!" Holt's instinct was to rush to Isabelle's house and make sure she was okay, but the logical side of her knew she needed a minute to calm down. That was why she was so good at her job, and she prided herself on being able to keep her head in any situation.

"He didn't know who dropped it off." Max sounded the tiniest bit defensive. "I talked to him for five minutes and he never changed his story. Besides, Jose's guys respect you. Why would he lie about this?"

Holt met Max's determined eyes and was reminded why she'd hired her a few months earlier. Max was small, not more than five foot two, and painfully thin, but she carried herself with the presence of a larger woman. She knew how to project confidence and strength, and her determination was second to none, even if she was terrified of Holt. "I apologize, Max. Of course you would have asked him all those questions." Letters left taped to the door would alert the suspicions of her staff. "Will you do me a favor?"

Max stood up a little straighter. "Of course, anything."

"Find Peanut. Have him here when I get back." She held up her hand, effectively halting Max's next frantic question. "I don't really care how you find him, or how you get him in here. All I care is that he is sitting in front of me when I get back."

"Yes, ma'am." Max almost saluted on her way out the door. She looked decidedly less nervous.

"Moose!" Holt yelled out her door. She took Moose, real name Bobby Petro, with her when she needed muscle. They'd known each other since childhood, and she had offered him a job at a time in his life when everyone else had given up on him. For that, she had his unwavering loyalty, and a trusted confidant and friend.

While she waited for him, she scribbled on a fresh sheet of paper, *Who the fuck are you?* and, *If not me, who?* She folded the note roughly and jammed it back in the bright red envelope.

"Heard you got your ass shot at. You cool?" Moose filled the doorway, his beefy arms crossed.

Holt looked at him. There was a time when he had been waif thin and strung out on heroin, but now his muscles bulged under the dark green T-shirt tucked neatly into his black cargo pants. The entire package was made for intimidation.

"We're going out. Tell the crew they can go home at three." Holt knew if she asked, or if they were worried, her small team would stay all night, so she tried to give them time off whenever she could.

"I'm not taking you to the hospital because you got shot and didn't want to tell anyone, right? You know I hate watching you get patched up." Moose looked Holt over, clearly checking for blood.

"I'm fine. They weren't shooting at me. We're going to find out why someone wants to kill Isabelle Rochat."

Moose looked relieved. "Isabelle wouldn't happen to be the blonde Jose was muttering about? Something about wishing he was straight and could follow you around and pick up your castoffs?"

Moose winked and Holt felt calmer. Moose had that effect on her. Jose might have a big mouth, but he always meant well. She reminded herself, as she had many times, not to tell Jose anything she didn't want shared with half of Providence.

"It's possible Isabelle is blond, yes," Holt said, locking her office door on the way out.

"And willing to kiss your ugly mug. You should definitely try and see her again." Moose tossed her the car keys and deftly avoided the jab to the abdomen he knew was coming.

On her way out the front door of the mechanic shop, Holt slammed the red envelope against the glass door, secured it with a piece of tape, and looked at the angry, bold address she had scrawled across the front: *Dirtbag*. She doubted anyone would be back to pick it up, but it felt good to strike back.

❖

"Decker, I can explain." Gary Capelletti shifted his five foot one and three-quarter-inch frame nervously from foot to foot.

"How about I summarize what you've told me so far, and we will see if further explanation is necessary?" Decker said. "I am out of town for less than twenty-four hours. In that time, my accountant, Isabelle Rochat, calls my office and informs you that the IRS is auditing my tax returns filed last year. She shouldn't have been contacted about this, and you got nervous. We have an understanding with the auditor, but Ms. Rochat does not fully appreciate how our business is run. However, instead of waiting twenty-four hours for my return, you decide to take matters into your own hands and have my secretary send Ms. Rochat our sanitized files when she contacts you looking for a specific piece of information. Am I accurate so far?"

Gary nodded, looking miserable and uncomfortable in his ill-fitting suit with sweat stains spreading under his armpits. Decker knew he had a sterling public reputation as an amiable, upstanding businessman. He also took great personal pleasure in the fact that those who knew him well were terrified of him. The greatest compliment he ever received was from a man who had called him ruthless, calculating, and dangerous.

"In your haste to be a problem solver, you rushed my secretary, who made a mistake and sent the wrong files to Ms. Rochat. And this is the point where I get a little fuzzy on the details, Gary. Because between when the file was sent and right this minute, you decided to try and shoot Ms. Rochat. Do you think you're in the fucking mob? Do you think we operate with gunmen hiding in bushes? And what made you think you had the right to make that decision at all? Because even in your deluded little mind you must realize I'm the boss here, and bosses only keep around those who actually make problems go away. You, on the other hand, have made the problem worse. What the fuck were you thinking shooting at her? Did you ever just think to ask her to *return* the damned file?" Throughout the conversation, this was the first time Decker raised his voice.

"I did ask her," Gary said, sounding hurt. "You know how she is though. She's an overachiever and would do anything for her clients. I told her I sent her the wrong information and we would take care of that part, and she went out of her way to let me know she would be happy to take care of all of the audit. The more I talked, the worse it got. It's the reason you hired her, right? Her sterling fucking above and beyond, best in the business reputation? Well, now it bit us in the ass."

"No, Gary, it bit you in the ass," Decker said. "It cost me. It cost me a headache, and now I have to find a new secretary, someone with a pulse and just enough smarts to follow directions. Thanks to your blunder, my former secretary no longer has those qualifications. You still didn't answer my question about what the fuck you were thinking shooting at Ms. Rochat? You'll have to forgive me for not following your logic leap."

"Diamond and me, we were trying to scare her, make her know she shouldn't talk."

"She can't talk about what she doesn't know, and she wouldn't have had any reason to think there was something wrong. I've seen those books of yours. You have enough fucking coded James Bond shit in there to confuse me, and I know what I'm looking at. Now we're left with a few options: waiting and hoping, stealing that file back, or finishing the job you started."

"Steal? What about the cops? And just for the record, I wasn't trying to kill her. I was aiming for the window. I'm not a monster, and I'm not stupid. I do run your businesses pretty well."

"So not stupid, or a monster, but what about when I need you to be both?" Decker laughed, enjoying Gary's discomfort. "There's plenty of other scum that would take your place, Gary. You're a monster if I tell you to be, and you're stupid if I say you are. As for the cops, I've told you before, the cops aren't a problem. They can be handled. What concerns me is Holt Lasher."

"The bounty hunter? Why would she care about us?"

"Well, you shot at her too. That would piss me off. I reached out to her. If we could bring her into the fold, this idiotic move of yours would prove to be a stroke of genius."

"I'm not worried about some wannabe cop chasing down jaywalkers," Gary said. "Why would you want her on board?"

"Do you know how old Ms. Lasher was when she tracked down her first criminal?" Gary shook his head and Decker continued. "She was eighteen. A year earlier, she witnessed a murder, and the authorities said they couldn't touch the guy, that witness protection was the only way to go. She refused, and as a teenager, she tracked down one of the FBI's ten most wanted men so she wouldn't have to live in witness protection. She finds people no one else can find. Does that sound like it isn't a problem? On top of that, she is ambitious, ruthless in her pursuit of fugitives, and has a fine business mind. She and I could go far together."

"Can't we just kill her? You said the cops aren't a problem. You seem to know everything about her, so let's just drive over to her house and shoot her. You've got plenty of business mind on your own."

Decker smacked Gary in the head. "You've been watching too many movies, and I'm beginning to question your assertion of intelligence. That kind of dumb thinking got us in this mess. We're not the mob. We don't go around killing unnecessarily. That draws unwanted attention. But if the time comes and I ask you to kill someone, use a rifle. Shotguns are for deer. Only the vice president uses them to shoot people."

CHAPTER THREE

Isabelle closed the front door as the last of the police officers returned to their cars. She wasn't used to having large groups of people in her home, and having strangers poking around her life was uncomfortable. Despite the reassurance and safety they provided, she wasn't sorry to see them go.

The officers had been thorough, but she knew there was little they could do. No shotgun shells had been left behind, and there were no footprints on the concrete in the alley outside her fence. They had taken great pains with a pile of old mattresses, long abandoned and probably what the shooter had stood on, but no one was particularly optimistic they would discover the assailant's identity. They had asked a million questions about her life and people she knew. Had anyone ever said, "Oh yes, I know who might want to kill me," when the police asked? Surely, that only happened in movies. She assured them it must have to do with the bounty hunter and bail jumper who had landed in her pool seconds before the shooting. Obviously.

The anger and lust that had carried her through her earlier encounter with Holt Lasher were long gone. Sadness and fear replaced them, and every shadow in the backyard looked like a masked gunman, every car backfire was an attack missile aimed for her head. She slid the door open and ventured onto her back deck. Her personal Eden had become a war zone.

She shuddered as she saw the buckshot in her siding. The repairs wouldn't start until Monday, an eternity away when there were bullet holes in her house. Once the siding was fixed, she hoped she could get on with her life. This house had been her home for five years, and she didn't want one incident, quite outside her control, to ruin her sense of peace every time she opened the door.

Deciding there was nothing better to distract her than the pile of work she brought home with her for the weekend, she closed and locked the back door and plopped down at her desk in her cozy office next to the living room. Sitting down, however, provided a jolt of arousal, one that shot through her too quickly to chase away. It was an annoyingly pleasant reminder that she was feeling vulnerable because a criminally sexy woman had decided to get shot at while taking a dip in her pool. It irritated her that Holt hadn't stuck around. She had figured she would come off like a crazy woman to the police, talking about a bounty hunter with a stupid name. The police, however, had surprised her when they had practically bowed at her feet just for mentioning Holt Lasher. They said they knew where to find her and would stop by her office the next day.

Isabelle wished Holt were there now. She didn't know whether she would strangle her or kiss her, but she was sure either would make her feel better.

"Did Lois Lane have to put up with this?" Isabelle asked her reflection in the darkened computer screen. "Lusting after some stupid superhero trying to save the world? At least Holt wasn't wearing tights." Revisiting what Holt had been wearing when Isabelle met her set off a new pang of arousal. "Oh, honestly," Isabelle chastised her reflection. "Pull yourself together."

She picked up the file for one of her most boring clients, Decker Pence. He was a local well-respected businessman. He owned a methadone clinic, a pizza joint, a gas station, and a sub shop. His financial records had always been impeccably organized, and she felt a little guilty charging him for her services. The man barely needed an accountant. He had a bookkeeper who took care of the daily transactions of his businesses. She largely filed his taxes and advised him on more complicated issues. Every year, she offered a lesser package of services, more commensurate with what she actually did for him, but he refused. He always said she was the best in the state and he was willing to pay for that. He explained that she was on retainer and if anything ever happened, he wanted her available. Now he was being audited and, somewhat strangely, his bookkeeper hadn't immediately sent over all his business files. Wasn't this the kind of big thing he paid her to be available for? She made a mental note to speak with Mr. Pence as soon as she returned to the office.

Armed with work to do, Isabelle tried her best to forget bounty hunters, masked figures, and shotguns. She hoped digging through line after line of business transactions would help calm her. She quickly looked over the business records for Mr. Pence. The first three looked as they always did, organized and profitable. When she got to the methadone clinic, however, she burst out laughing. His secretary had sent a file she needed for part of the audit, but she hadn't had a chance to open it until now. The methadone clinic wasn't part of her initial request, but after speaking with Mr. Pence's bookkeeper, she had agreed to handle a larger part of the audit for him.

As with the other business, it looked neat and well documented, but as far as she could tell, the file was a record for a combination bubble factory/circus/professional sports team. Despite the absurdity, a niggling feeling, one she couldn't pull forward, dug at the back of her mind. Something seemed off. She drummed her fingers on the desk, willing herself to see what had caught her attention. She tried writing it off as anxiety after her stressful day, but the feeling wouldn't go away.

Isabelle's focus was so complete as she stared at the computer screen that she screamed at the sound of a gentle tapping on the glass of her back door.

Her instincts screamed for her to sprint to the living room and dive behind the couch, but she was also tired of feeling like a helpless victim. She settled for shaking legs, rapid breathing, and a death grip on the edge of her desk. But she forced herself to remain calm.

When no shotgun blast immediately disrupted the night and a second gentle knock sounded at the door, she steeled herself, took a deep breath, and boldly poked her head around the corner. When she saw the scruffy hair, baggy jeans, heavy boots, and clean, dry, white T-shirt, her heart leapt into her throat. She had no idea why the sight of Holt was so comforting; she didn't even know her, but after endless police questions and reports, feeling afraid, drained, and aroused, the living reminder of the kiss they shared was wonderful.

An apology from Holt would go a long way to making Isabelle feel more comfortable. She needed to know the buckshot was meant for Holt.

"I have a front door you know," Isabelle said as she opened the door to a sexy creature with a stunning grin. She hoped it wasn't obvious how badly her legs were still shaking.

"Couldn't figure out which house was yours from the front. Never been invited in, after all."

Isabelle hesitated before resigning herself to welcoming trouble into her house. "Consider yourself invited," she said, stepping aside. "If you have any weapons, after the excitement, I don't want them in my house. Check them at the door. How did you get into my backyard, by the way? The side gates are locked."

"I got in your yard the same way I left it earlier. Over the fence. And no weapons," Holt said as she stepped inside. "I don't carry a gun, but if you'd like to search me just in case, I would be very cooperative."

Isabelle was tempted. She really wanted to see that tattoo she'd glimpsed through Holt's wet T-shirt. If possible, she was even sexier in dry clothes. They outlined Holt's frame so magnificently, Isabelle figured her pants were the only place she would be able to hide a gun, and a concealed weapon was probably much safer than Holt Lasher without her pants.

"You're a bounty hunter and you don't carry a gun? How do you shoot the bad guys?"

"Bring them in dead or alive really had its heyday in the Wild West. Today, the emphasis is really more on alive," Holt said, looking over every inch of Isabelle's home.

"But what about when they shoot at you? You could shoot back then, right?" Isabelle wasn't totally comfortable with Holt's scrutiny of her home. It made her feel vulnerable, something she'd had enough of today. She glanced around, trying to see what Holt saw.

"Sure, I could shoot back, if I had a gun, which I don't." Holt seemed to be enjoying herself.

"Wait, you could have shot back at the guy today. You could have stopped him. If you had a gun, he wouldn't have gotten away." She stopped before adding, "And I wouldn't have to be so terrified being home alone tonight." Her legs were no longer shaking, and the anger from earlier in the day bubbled back to the surface, a much more comfortable emotion than fear.

"Maybe," Holt said, "or I could have killed him and then we'd never know why he was shooting at us, or I could have hit someone innocent in the alley, or the bullet could have ricocheted and hit you, or me, or Peanut. I don't like guns." Holt's eyes looked haunted and empty, Isabelle fleetingly noticed before her anger took over once again.

"Shooting at us? They weren't shooting at me. No one shoots at accountants. They shoot at bounty hunters."

"Why would anyone shoot at a bounty hunter?"

Isabelle glared at Holt, who seemed immune to her anger. Isabelle looked over the strong body in front of her. When their eyes met, Holt winked. Isabelle closed the distance between them, grabbed Holt's face, and kissed her roughly. Before Holt could deepen the kiss, Isabelle pulled away and slapped her sharply across the left cheek. Holt grinned even wider, seemingly immune to pain as well as anger.

"Feel better?"

"Not at all." Isabelle felt wretched. She had never had the impulse to strike out at another person, not since she left home. If she was scared before, she was terrified now, and buckshot had nothing to do with it. "I'm so sorry. You didn't even flinch. I've been slapped. It hurts, and you didn't even flinch." In the moment, both kissing and slapping Holt had seemed like perfectly reasonable reactions. How could she have let herself get so out of control?

"You've got decent power, but believe it or not, I've been hit harder in the face. I think I'll survive. How about we call it even for my scaring you so badly by knocking on your back door? Is there anything I can do about the person who has slapped you? I don't like the sound of that at all."

Isabelle shook her head, part rejection of Holt's request, part shame. She couldn't talk about her past with Holt, a stranger who thus far had brought nothing but trouble to her life. She wanted to blame the slap on the stress of the day, her out of control emotions, but those were the excuses she always heard when it happened to her.

Holt seemed to accept her unwillingness to open up. "An accountant, huh?" Holt looked skeptical. "For the mob? CIA? Save the Whale Society?"

"The what? No, I'm an accountant for normal, boring, rich people. *I'm* not a criminal." Isabelle was angry at Holt again, for not apologizing, for asking her stupid questions, and for looking so hot she was having trouble remembering to be angry.

"Neither am I."

"Oh, right, I forgot. You catch criminals, except the one that shot at you today. That one you let scamper away." Isabelle stared at Holt's mouth and thought about kissing her. She chastised herself yet again. The woman in front of her was a bounty hunter, she was dangerous, and she was a jerk. If she wasn't a jerk, she would have come here and done the right thing. She would have made Isabelle feel better. She would have checked on her sooner. Hell, she wouldn't have disappeared in the first place.

It looked like it took a great deal of effort on Holt's part not to bite Isabelle's head off. Her eyes were razor sharp. She took a couple deep breaths before speaking again. Suddenly, Isabelle was nervous. Holt looked like she could be terrifying when angry, yet Isabelle had just slapped her and Holt had smiled in response. Either she had a very tight grip on her temper, or she was more even-keeled than she looked at the moment. In the past, when Isabelle had seen this potential for anger, she had always pulled away. Her normally nonviolent and peaceful nature came from her upbringing. Although she was nervous, Isabelle wasn't frightened of Holt, even with the potential for anger, and that surprised her. Holt was intimidating but also a bit sexy in her powerful emotions. Isabelle didn't know her enough to base this on anything but gut feeling, but Holt seemed like the type who used her power for good and not evil. Something Isabelle found very alluring.

Despite all that, she was still angry at Holt for the earlier gunfire and that Holt had yet to apologize. "You sit your ass on my couch like a civilized person and apologize for getting me shot at or you can leave."

"Apologize? For getting you shot at? What if you got me shot at?"

"We could play what if all day. What if you weren't a bounty hunter? What if I was a firefighter? What if we'd never met? I didn't get you shot at. I don't have stalker ex-girlfriends, creepy people at the gym, or at work. I have boring clients who make lots and lots of money and don't do anything illegal." Even as she was saying that, the same niggling feeling she had had looking over Decker Pence's file returned. "You are an asshole for coming here and trying to blame this on me. I'm tired, I'm a little panicky, and I'm done with you asking dumb questions and scaring me more. I'm sorry for slapping you and for kissing you. Now it's your turn. Either apologize and give me some peace or go to hell." Isabelle suddenly felt exhausted.

Holt looked taken aback. "I'm sorry we got shot at today, and I'm really sorry that you're so afraid. I promise you'll be safe tonight. I have a whole crew of people that work for me, and I have to pay them even if they sit in the office and play poker, so I was going to have them move their card game to your neighborhood tonight. No one in or out without our knowing about it. And definitely no shotguns."

Holt was hard to figure out. Isabelle thought the security detail sounded like blissful overkill, but Holt's apology was lacking. "Not good enough," Isabelle said, pointing to the door.

Holt held out a business card, which Isabelle took and dropped in the trash. Holt fished it out and strode to the kitchen. She secured the card to the fridge with a smiling whale magnet. "Save the Whale Society, I knew it. Call me if you need anything, anything at all. And my crew will be around tonight so try and get some sleep. Your neighborhood will be the safest in the state."

"Go away, bounty hunter," Isabelle said, close to tears. The first woman to turn her completely inside out had to be inappropriate, unmanageable, and unable to make her feel better. All Holt had to do was apologize and not scare her out of her mind. That was the right thing to do. That was what a decent person would have done. But Holt asked questions instead, making it clear no one knew why her house looked like a drunken artist's abstract connect the dots.

Without a word, Holt spun around and left the way she had come, through the back door and into the evening.

"I have a front door you know," Isabelle called after her.

❖

"You gonna tell me what happened to your face?" Moose asked when Holt slid back into the truck after leaving Isabelle's house.

"Not at the moment. Just drive."

While Holt was talking with Isabelle, Moose had moved to the driver's seat of the large black truck. The person left in the car always occupied the driver's seat when they were working. That way, if they needed a quick getaway, they were prepared. Keeping people safe was all about planning ahead.

Holt didn't say a word as Moose drove across town to the boxing gym Holt owned. Moose always understood when she didn't want to talk. They had been working together for ten years and had a level of unspoken communication not many people could replicate.

The encounter with Isabelle had left her cranky, horny, and confused. Her lips still burned from the wild and unexpected kiss, and her cheek smarted from the sudden assault. There was undeniable chemistry between them, but Holt knew nothing about Isabelle except that someone was shooting at her, at some point in her past she had been hit, and she had an unpredictable way of managing stress. Although getting slapped in the face was amusing, Holt didn't like how much it had upset Isabelle. In fact, she didn't like how much *she* seemed to upset Isabelle. No one liked to be unpopular. It really wasn't any of her business who was shooting at Isabelle. She wasn't a client, and if someone was shooting at her, it would be wiser to stay a million miles away from her than try to help her. But the idea of her being someone's target practice made Holt's stomach churn. It pissed her off when nice people got caught in the bad guys' crossfire.

She grabbed her cell phone and dialed her office. Max answered.

"I need a team sitting on a house tonight. I'm sending you the details."

When the call ended, Moose looked at Holt questioningly.

"It's just for tonight," Holt said. "Until I can figure out which fucking way is up. The cops will drive by a few times I'm sure, but I'd rather know our people are watching over her until the morning."

"Does that woman know how lucky she is?" Moose asked.

Holt tilted her head, not understanding.

"Most people who slap you wake up a week later in the hospital. Unless you left her unconscious on the floor, which isn't your style, then not only did she get away with hitting you, but now you're protecting her as well. What's up, H?"

"I need ten rounds. Ask me then," Holt said, already gearing up mentally for the workout her body craved.

As a teenager, Holt found the gym a safe harbor against the turmoil in her life. The men from the first boxing gym she frequented as a teenager didn't care that she was a girl, and they didn't care about her race, her economics, or that she had assholes for parents. When she was in danger, they held her safe for a few hours, allowing her to regain her strength. When she was hurting, they alone understood her need to beat it out. She had gone on to become one of the most feared female fighters in the country, three times winning the women's Golden Gloves amateur boxing tournament. If women's boxing had been an Olympic sport when she was in her prime, she would have had medals hanging on her wall.

When she had told Isabelle she didn't carry a gun, she failed to mention she had rarely needed one. In close quarters, there was no one in New England, male or female, who was more effective with their fists.

While she changed clothes and wrapped her hands, Moose turned on the music and started the round timer. It didn't matter how loud the rap music pounded in the small gym, every boxer could hear the bell signaling the end of a round. He helped her into her well-loved, red, sixteen ounce, lace-up training gloves and tied them off.

"Only give me fifteen seconds rest," Holt said. She needed to reach exhaustion quickly.

For six rounds, she pounded on the super heavyweight bag, which tipped the scales at one hundred and fifty pounds. It hung from the ceiling on a ten-foot chain, and when hit hard enough, started swaying with the rhythm of the punches. The larger men at the gym, Moose included, often struggled to move the bag more than a few inches. Today, Holt had to stay on her toes, dodging and weaving her way around the violently swinging bag.

After the heavy bag, Holt stepped under the ropes and into one of the two boxing rings, her sweat-drenched gym clothes stuck to her body. The old building housing the gym was previously used as a swimming facility, so the boxing rings were sunk deep in what used to be the pool. Holt chose the ring in the deep end. Moose stepped in the ring after her, the training mitts already on his hands.

Moose called out punch combinations and moved his targets, which looked like giant stuffed pie plates, around for Holt to seek and destroy. For three minutes at a time, they worked silently, except for Moose's instructions. During the fifteen second rest period, they talked, one question and answer per round.

"You find out why someone was trying to kill your lady friend?"

"She slapped me, Moose," Holt said, rubbing her gloved hand against her still tender cheek.

"I had noticed that," he said before holding up the mitts again as the round timer chimed.

They danced and weaved around the ring for another three minutes. When the bell rang, they both leaned against the ropes and resumed their conversation.

"It's really none of my business." Holt wiped sweat from her forehead. "For all I know, she runs a terrorist cell and the guys shooting at her were doing us all a favor."

"You really think she's running a terrorist cell? What's your gut tell you?"

"Okay, no terrorists, but she is creating some malfunction in my gut. I'm too damned hot for her." Holt was amused for the first time since leaving Isabelle's. "Fucking blondes."

The bell rang and Moose held up the mitts in surrender. "I'm tired, and this is more important. She didn't have any idea why she got shot at?"

"She yelled at me. She wanted me to apologize for bringing trouble to her doorstep. I was minding my own business, chasing Peanut, when *her* nutcase started shooting. But she's convinced I'm the one the shooter was going for."

"You were trespassing, but that's beside the point. Look," Moose said seriously, "you dug me out of the gutter when everyone said I was a worthless excuse for a man. You've got a pretty good sense of who needs saving. Let's keep a team on her house for a while, see if anything strange turns up."

"I don't know if that's good enough. Even if someone had been right outside when the shooting started, they wouldn't have been close enough to do anything except call a rescue. Besides, she says it's unrelated to her. Unless she's lying, she's probably not going to sneak off in the middle of the night and lead me right to the shooter's door."

"Why don't you just go out with her then?" Moose asked. "You said she's hot, and she likes you enough to slap you. I think you have a future."

"She's an accountant, Moose. I'm a bounty hunter. What kind of future could we possibly have? And is that even right? Sometimes I don't even know where the line is anymore."

Holt was feeling dejected, but her statement on their possible future wasn't one of self-pity. It was an observation born from experience. Women like Isabelle didn't have long-term relationships with women like Holt. Everybody wanted to sleep with a bad girl, but no one ever settled down with one.

"Besides, I give it three dates, which would officially be my second longest relationship. If it's not my job, it's my temper. You know how much I hate putting up with women who love the idea of dating a superhero until they realize I work all the time, spend a lot of time doing paperwork, get pissed off at the wrongs in the world, and don't own a cape."

"Hey, she's got balls enough to slap you. Seems like she can handle you better than most. If not, she sounds feisty, and at least the sex will be good. And how can she be mad at you for wanting to keep her safe?"

"Please don't ever think about my sex life, me having sex, or anyone I might sleep with, ever again."

Holt was laughing, but thinking about Isabelle as simply a quick hookup was uncomfortable. There was something different in the way she felt about this particular blonde. Although a part of her knew it was probably best to leave well enough alone, the idea of Isabelle in danger, or worse yet, riddled with buckshot, was more than she could take. What kind of self-respecting bounty hunter would let an accountant die by any means but a thousand paper cuts? She would never be able to live with the guilt if Isabelle got shot. Obviously, a peace offering was in order, and maybe another conversation about her wealthy clients. Rich people hid things, and if they made up Isabelle's client list, she could know more than she thought. Holt hoped she was making the right decision. Particularly since she probably wouldn't get paid for being a good guy and saving the maiden. She was also fairly sure if Isabelle ever found out she had thought of her as a maiden, a damsel in distress, a princess in peril, or any other such term, she would do more than slap Holt.

With as much bluster as she could manage, mostly for Moose's benefit, she said, "Fuck it, you're right. What do I have to lose? At least she's hot."

❖

"Mr. Pence? Hello, it's Isabelle Rochat, from CSP Financial." Isabelle was surprised when the businessman answered her call on the first ring.

"Ah, Ms. Rochat, what can I do for you?"

Isabelle had always liked Pence's voice. It was strong and professional, but had a gentle quality to it. Today, it didn't. He sounded surprised to hear from her. Isabelle wished she were meeting him in person and could see his face. Decker Pence was one of her clients that was much easier to read in person, although even then he kept his expression neutral most of the time.

"One of your employees sent over a file earlier in the week. I spoke with your bookkeeper, Gary, I believe his name is, and I offered to take over a larger part of the audit, but I am afraid the file must be a mistake. It doesn't make sense. I tried to call your secretary, but she was unavailable." Isabelle had pored over the files after Holt left, and she still couldn't rid herself of the feeling something was off.

"Ms. Rochat, I am sorry for the inconvenience. I will make sure the proper file arrives this afternoon. My secretary unfortunately no longer works here, and perhaps this incident gives you an indication why. I will take care of it. Thank you for calling me," Pence said a little too quickly.

"Do you know what the file was? It was full of silly line items like sports teams and bubbles, but it looked like very technical accounting."

"I do not know, Ms. Rochat. I can't say I've ever seen a file quite like that. Perhaps it is one that Gary was using to train his new assistant. If you wouldn't mind deleting that file, I'll make sure this is the only time you are bothered by a mix-up."

Pence sounded relieved.

"Mr. Pence, I'm happy to provide any additional services you need. I know you have a bookkeeper, but if it's easier, I can take over a more active role in the finances of your company. Or my company offers many other services such as financial planning and business management, precisely for clients such as yourself." Although what she said was all true, there was something about Pence's voice that was unsettling her. She wanted a closer look at his total finances.

"Ms. Rochat, I am satisfied with our current professional arrangement and the services you offer. Please delete the file and continue to work on whatever parts of the audit you and Gary have discussed. I will ensure you receive the correct file this afternoon."

Pence's voice had lost any of the charm Isabelle had once detected. He sounded cold and more than a little scary. Isabelle had a flash of Decker Pence in a ski mask with a shotgun, but she pushed it away. The man was well known in the community. He was probably just embarrassed by such an error by one of his staff.

"Of course, Mr. Pence. If your bookkeeper has further questions about the file I requested, please have him give me a call." She wasn't ready to delete the file. There was something that still didn't seem right.

After she hung up the phone, she wandered to the kitchen and stared at Holt's card on the fridge. Was this the kind of thing she could help with? Isabelle quickly shook off the thought. Help with what? She had no idea what she was looking for, or if there was anything to find. She couldn't explain to herself the cause of her concern, much less to Holt. The file was made-up names and gibberish. Besides, they hadn't parted on the best of terms. She wasn't even sure she wanted to see her again. She decided it was best if she kept this to herself. If anything changed, she could call then.

"Gary, you stupid fuck," Decker yelled into the phone at his moronic underling. "She thinks your bookkeeping code is as stupid as I do. You could have gotten those files back, or let her keep it and she would have forgotten about it, but you shot at her instead. Now she's asking questions."

"What did you tell her?"

"I told her I didn't know, but that it was probably a file you used to train your assistant. I told her to delete it and get back to work. I wish I could delete you."

"Did she figure it out? Does she know anything?" Gary's voice had taken on a quaver, most likely from visions of what Pence would do to him if Isabelle was going to expose them. Decker was picturing them himself.

"I don't think so. She said the file made no sense. I guess it's good you still use those inane codes. They're finally paying off."

"I told you an extra layer of security was a good idea, Decker. She'll never crack that code."

"Security is a password or encryption, Gary, and before you congratulate yourself on your Fort Knox of bookkeeping, I don't think she is going to do the smart thing and rid herself of that file. At the first sign of trouble, you will have to get it back, carefully."

"I'm always careful. But computer files aren't like paper files. She could have copies in twelve different places, not to mention her e-mail. I'm not a hacker."

"Yes, the police tape and buckshot attest to your discretion." Decker had his voice under control again. "I don't care how you recover those files, if and when I ask you to. That is one of the reasons I pay you as much as I do, and we both know how well my money was spent last time you thought for yourself. But if she thinks she's being targeted, she's going to dig deeper."

"I trust my code. The code's safe. She can't break it."

"For your sake, I hope so."

CHAPTER FOUR

Holt shifted from one foot to the other. Once again, she was standing at Isabelle's back door, this time ready to knock and fall on her sword. Isabelle needed an apology, and Holt was willing to give her one, even if she hadn't done anything wrong. Lying as part of her job wasn't something she enjoyed, but it was necessary from time to time. She had debated for three days the best way to get Isabelle to like her again and was shocked to realize just how much it bothered her that she cared about it at all.

"No guts, no glory," she said as she tapped gently on the sliding glass door.

Anxiety oozed from Isabelle as she peeked around the corner. Holt felt bad for startling her again. Quickly though, the fear was replaced by exasperation. The sliding door grated open and Isabelle dragged Holt by her shirt collar into the house, through the living room, out the front door, and deposited her on the front stoop.

When the door slammed in her face, she assumed Isabelle wasn't in a forgiving mood, until she heard her shout from inside the house. "Use the damned doorbell like a normal person."

"Really?" Holt asked. She could see Isabelle through the glass side panels flanking the front door. Isabelle pointed at the doorbell. She was surprised to see Isabelle jump when she complied.

The door opened quickly and Holt and Isabelle stared at each other. Holt could see how conflicted Isabelle was. Her body language was guarded, but her expression was more relieved than irritated.

"May I come in?" Holt asked, ready to duck should Isabelle decide to slap her again. After Isabelle's reaction, she got the feeling that would never happen again. In her line of work, it never hurt to be prepared, though.

"Oh, damn it all to hell," Isabelle said. She grabbed Holt by the hand and pulled her inside.

"Hi," Holt said, liking the way Isabelle's hand felt in hers. She gave herself a few luxurious seconds to stare at her. She saw Isabelle's warring emotions and took strength from the fact that Isabelle seemed to be having a hard time disliking her. That had to count a little in her favor.

"Can I help you with something?" Isabelle asked, dropping her grip on Holt's hand and rubbing the exposed skin as if she had been shocked.

Holt took a deep breath and plunged ahead. Now was her moment. "I wanted to see you." She had meant to say she wanted to see how Isabelle was, but her mouth betrayed her. "And apologize," she added quickly.

"Did you stop and consider that maybe I didn't want to see you? It's so much easier to pretend you're some kind of scary monster when you're not around. When you're standing in front of me, you're cute, and nervous, and sweet, and only a little scary."

"I did consider it, and that's where the apology comes in. I'm sorry I make you miserable."

"You don't make me miserable, but you do scare me a little. I need you to tell me those bullets were meant for you, that I'm safe in my own home. I know I was a bitch a few days ago, but I'm not used to getting shot at. I told you what I need, and if you didn't come to offer me that, then honestly, why are you here?"

Holt hadn't realized how frightened Isabelle was and instantly felt bad she had spent three days debating how best to get back in her good graces, even if she was still having the house watched and knew she was safe. "I came to invite you out. To a party. With me. Tomorrow?"

"A party? You do remember I'm an accountant, right? We're math nerds, paper pushers, bean counters. I've been to a bounty hunter party exactly never. Boring people tend to date their own kind.

Will there be strippers and orgies? I get most of my information from movies. Aren't most mob parties in strip clubs?"

"You need to watch different movies," Holt said. She was hurt and didn't try to hide it. She didn't say another word. She simply turned and slammed out the front door. If Isabelle wanted to think of her as the kind of scum who took advantage of people, there was clearly no common ground for them to work from. She was tense with anger, making her gait jerky as she stormed down the street in the direction of her truck. She couldn't believe she had tried to invite Isabelle to her godson's party. Even worse was how upset she was over Isabelle's joking about it being slimy. She was more upset at her overreaction to the joke than the joke itself.

Most of the people she considered family would be at this party, and Isabelle had inadvertently sullied the goodness she felt when in their presence by questioning the nature of the party. She was by no means celibate, but she didn't sleep around as much as her reputation suggested, and strip clubs had never been her thing. But being a supposed Casanova was actually good for business. It was amazing what women would tell her while trying to get her in bed. Although she did have a weak spot for blondes, she hated that Isabelle thought so little of her. What kind of insensitive monster would use Isabelle's fear and vulnerability to get her in bed?

"Holt, stop. I'm sorry. What did I say wrong?"

Holt stopped, but she didn't turn around. Isabelle had to come around to face her.

"Why did you walk out? I was only joking."

"Do you really think I'm that much of an asshole? I mean, I know you don't like me, and fine, you have your reasons, but you think I'm that much of a dick? Really?"

Holt knew she wasn't doing a very good job of hiding her hurt, and Isabelle looked taken aback by the display of emotion.

"I don't think you're an asshole. The last time I saw you I kissed you, then slapped you. Today, you show up and ask me to a party. You'll have to excuse my confusion. I don't understand what bounty hunters do. And I don't fully understand why you make me act like a crazy person."

Isabelle looked supremely frustrated, but she never broke eye contact with Holt. It felt like Isabelle was searching for every last kernel of Holt's makeup, maybe hoping to find some redeeming aspects. It was unnerving. Holt felt even more exposed and vulnerable.

She could feel the muscles in her neck bunch as she tried to get control of her emotions. The unintended effect was to distract Isabelle completely. Holt had a tattoo that started on her chest and snaked its way up her neck in thin, delicate vines, and she had been told that when she got angry, the vines rippled and danced with the movement of her muscles. Isabelle seemed to be enjoying the show. She also looked a little intimidated by Holt, but mostly, she looked like she wanted to trace the vines with her tongue. Holt took a step closer. Isabelle didn't step back.

"My neighbor is really nosy, Holt. If she's not wrapped up in something on TV, you're going to make her worry her rosary beads down to sawdust. I'm going to take a step back so I don't do something rash. Why don't you tell me what I did to make you look so incredibly sad?"

Holt let Isabelle take a step back, but what she really wanted to do was kiss her. So far, they had kissed twice, at totally inappropriate times, and it was sort of fun. Isabelle was certainly not predictable. "First, you didn't give me much time to explain my invitation before you jumped to conclusions. Second, exactly what kind of things do you think bounty hunters do? Rape and pillage? Sleep with every woman in the village, sow our seed, create an army of bounty hunters? I was asking you to an adoption party. For a two-year-old. If you can make that sexual, then skip bail sometime and I'll be happy to show you how I feel about it." Holt stepped around Isabelle and continued toward her truck.

"Did you grow a penis in the past three days?" Isabelle asked.

She had to raise her voice since Holt was a few feet away. Holt figured the nosy neighbor had probably just dropped dead.

"Excuse me?"

"A penis. Have you acquired one that I don't know about? 'Cause without one, sowing your seed would be a tad bit difficult." Isabelle walked into Holt's personal space, stopping just short of locked lips. "The pillaging part, now that's another matter. I could imagine you quite capable in that area if you put your mind to it." Isabelle ran her hands up and down Holt's biceps, squeezing her still tense muscles.

"So I'm not a sex fiend as long as I don't have a penis, but I'm still a Neanderthal brute because of my job?" Holt couldn't remember why she had been so angry.

"Are we still fighting, or have we switched to dirty talking foreplay?"

"I have no idea," Holt said, blowing out a breath.

"Is the offer of a party still on the table?" Isabelle asked, backing up a step.

Holt figured she didn't want to once again confound the issue of adoption party and sex. She appreciated it. "I'll pick you up tomorrow. And this time I'll ring at the front door."

CHAPTER FIVE

Isabelle felt ridiculous. She had already burned through three outfit options getting ready for a two-year-old's adoption party. She was confident he wouldn't care what she was wearing. The problem was Holt and how much she had thrown her world into chaos. What if Holt thought this was a date? Clearly, casual Sunday afternoon attire was out. But if gunfire erupted, she was not interested in being shot because her high heels prevented her from hauling ass.

She decided over breakfast to call Holt and cancel, but procrastinated long enough that by midmorning she had changed her mind. She had wished over and over since Holt asked her to the party that she could rid herself of the specter, real or imagined, of potential violence oozing from every aspect of Holt's life. She had lived like that for long enough, and had sworn to never go back. Once again, the problem was Holt. In the time Isabelle had known her, Holt had not once done what Isabelle expected her to. She was effectively refusing to be placed in the neat box Isabelle desperately wanted to cram her in.

When the doorbell rang an hour later, she chided herself for jumping. Her heart was racing as she let Holt in. Her fifth and final outfit choice matched Holt's casual, yet well put together style. Holt kissed her on the cheek by way of greeting and held the door for her as they headed for the truck.

Isabelle thought this was probably one of the crazier things she had ever done, but when Holt smiled at her, she was happy she said yes. She worked all the time, hadn't been on a date in months, and had spent most of the time since the shooting frightened out of her mind. But Holt was quite possibly the hottest woman she had ever seen outside the movies, and they were going to a party for a two-year-old. She doubted the child's mother would have invited Holt if gunfire were a regular part of her days.

At least for today, Isabelle was content to take advantage of the only positive she could see in Holt's job—airtight security—and Holt's smoking looks. If it turned out she really was a jerk, at least Isabelle would know for sure. Her sister was constantly telling her that her standards were too high. Two weeks ago, Isabelle wouldn't have stayed through a first date with Holt, even if they'd been speed dating. Her sister was going to be very proud.

On the way to the party, Holt's phone rang. She held up a finger to keep Isabelle from commenting when she answered it. "Now? After four days, you pick right now to finally bring him in? No, Max, it's fine. Be there in ten."

Holt sighed when she hung up. "Do you mind if we make a quick pit stop? I wanted to forget work for today, but one thing you should know about bounty hunters, we're always on the clock."

"Doesn't your phone have an off button?"

"Not if you own the company," Holt said, looking at Isabelle apologetically.

Isabelle was surprised to hear Holt owned her own business. For some reason, it didn't seem to fit with how she imagined her life. "Where are we going?"

"My office. You don't have to come in. I'll just be a minute, as long as you promise not to bolt while I'm inside."

"No, I want to come in," Isabelle said. "I want to see where you work. I really don't have a clue what you do day-to-day, except manually remove the off button on all your employees' cell phones. And push teenagers in pools."

"Just don't expect guns blazing and bad guys lined up in rows. The reality is nothing like the movies."

Isabelle laughed and was quiet for a moment. "Are you sure your friend won't mind the extra person? At the party?" Isabelle asked.

"She won't mind at all. The more hands on deck to keep the kids entertained, the better. Hope you like rugrats." Holt grinned as she opened the door and led Isabelle into her building.

Max jumped to attention when Holt burst through the door. Most of the crew had left for the day, but Max was still manning her desk. A few other people were spread out around the room, but it looked like a skeleton crew. If Max was caught off guard by the presence of Isabelle, she didn't let on. "Uh, ma'am."

"Max." Holt stopped her, putting her hand up to keep her from continuing. "Stop calling me ma'am. You make me feel like my mother."

"Or course ma—boss. Peanut is in your office. I'm sorry he's a few days late. We also got a new jumper. This one's big."

Holt raised her eyebrows. "Max, I chased Peanut across half the county. Where the hell did you find him holed up? And who's the new jumper?"

"State Rep. Parker Caldwell is our new jumper, boss. And I found Peanut at his cousin's house. The idiot can't help buying things for his truck. Next time he should use cash."

Isabelle and Holt looked up sharply at Max's news. Isabelle was surprised to hear the well-known and, until recently, well-respected state representative hadn't shown up for his court date. His handlers must be going crazy. There was a time he had aspirations for the governorship.

Holt looked annoyed. "Max, he's not in court until Tuesday."

"Yes, ma'am…sorry, yes, H, I know. Seems he wants to give you a head start." She held out an envelope, bright red, like the previous one taped to Jose's shop door.

She grabbed the envelope, ripped it open, and looked at the scrawled message that looked like it had been written in crayon. It simply said, *I won't be in court, find me if you can. P. Caldwell.*

"No return address I see. Think anyone will answer this time if I leave a response?"

Max shook her head.

Isabelle was fascinated by Holt's business headquarters. If she didn't know better, she would mistake it for any computer or paperwork based business. Except that anyone sitting in front of a monitor had biceps that could crush metal.

"If that little shit has anything to do with this…" Holt said as she strode purposefully to her office, swung open the door, and slammed it loudly behind her, making Isabelle cringe.

Max and Isabelle could hear her yelling from where they were. Bits and pieces drifted out to them, mostly cursing. They both jumped at the large bang and leaned toward the door at the silence that followed.

"She has a bit of a temper," Max said.

Isabelle nodded mutely. The anger from Holt was startling. Isabelle wasn't sure if she should be anxious. She had guessed that an angry Holt was terrifying, but when she slapped her, Holt had laughed. Isabelle knew if she worked with the kind of violence and depravity she imagined Holt did on a daily basis, she would be full of rage. Thinking about the violence she experienced as a child usually angered her for hours.

"Doesn't she scare you?" Isabelle asked. Max looked a little afraid.

"She used to," Max said. "Sometimes she still does, I guess. The thing is, I've never seen her get mad at anyone who doesn't deserve it. She went ballistic once because a cop tried to feel up one of the female staff here. It was my second or third day, and she was just screaming at this cop. I thought there was going to be a fight, or she was going to hit him. Now I know better. She never loses it like that, you know? She was plenty pissed, but she wasn't out of control. Me, I probably would have hit him and gotten shot since he was the only one carrying a gun, but not H. She knows if she goes down, there's no one to run this place, keep doing the work, take care of all of us."

Isabelle wanted to ask if Max checked her drinks for mind-altering worship powder but figured it wouldn't do any good. It did help to know that Max seemed to have no fear of Holt or her temper. Although she was still aware of what was transpiring in Holt's office, Isabelle was curious about the rest of the space. She looked around, gathering information, trying to put together the puzzle that was Holt.

Though the décor wasn't what Isabelle would have chosen, the office space seemed like a perfect extension of Holt. This was her bat cave, and she was in full command. It was easy to feel confidence in Holt's ability to do just about anything when you were standing in her command center.

When Holt's office door slammed open against the wall, Isabelle and Max both leapt back. It would have been comical to see Holt holding Peanut by the scruff of his shirt, dragging him from her office, his feet barely touching the ground, if they weren't so startled and sheepish getting caught eavesdropping.

"I'm still thinking about your offer, H!" Peanut shouted as he practically flew out of the office. Clearly, spending the afternoon handcuffed to Holt's desk wasn't his idea of a good time.

"Wasn't Peanut," Holt said grumpily as he shot from the building. Isabelle felt the chill spread through her belly as reality set in. She didn't realize she had been hoping the shots were meant for, or instigated by, Peanut. If the young punk wasn't involved, then it was someone she didn't have a face for. Someone who most likely wanted Holt dead, or even more terrifying, wanted her dead. Thinking it was Peanut made the whole situation less scary. Peanut seemed like a punk, but of the goofball variety, not the scare your pants off type. She needed to get back on steady ground, feel connected and safe. Her first thought was to run to Holt, snuggle against her strong, steady body, and let her protect her. Her second thought was a string of curse words her father would have been proud of. She wasn't the weak damsel in distress, running for the cover of strong arms at the first sign of trouble. And if she were to run to anyone's strong arms, they would be related to her, just like they always had been. Rochats took care of themselves.

"Max, I appreciate your getting Peanut in here so fast. I'm sorry I had to just let him go."

"Couldn't you have at least trumped up some reason to keep him a couple hours?" Max said. "I chased him all over town."

"And you have my eternal gratitude," Holt said, looking at Isabelle.

Isabelle appreciated the question in Holt's eyes. She appreciated that Holt was aware enough to notice that Isabelle was upset. She wouldn't appreciate it if Holt asked her about it. She doubted she would though. Isabelle had long ago perfected her "leave me alone;

don't ask questions" stare. It had come in handy with nosy teachers thinking they were being helpful, drunken frat boys, and overeager women looking for a good time.

"I'll keep you safe. I'll protect you, if you let me."

Isabelle needed to work on her death stare.

"I don't need it. I still think they were shooting at you, remember?" Isabelle said quietly.

"Me? Why would anyone want to shoot me? I sit behind a desk all day, shuffle some papers, go home. Very boring," Holt said playfully.

"Smart ass," Isabelle said, happy to let it drop for the moment.

"You ready to go?" Holt asked, rubbing Isabelle's shoulder as she moved past her. It wasn't a movement that looked natural to her, but Isabelle was grateful for the attempt, however awkward. "I need to finish up with Max, but then it's all party, until about seven when all the kids have to go to bed and the adults fall asleep on the couch."

❖

An hour later, Holt parked the truck in front of a neat two-story house. It was a light yellow, and the yard was simply, but nicely, landscaped. The driveway was full of minivans and Subarus, and Holt's truck looked odd next to all the cars representing a life neither she nor Isabelle led.

"You ready for this?" Holt asked.

"Just don't leave me to the wolves or little children," Isabelle said. "How long have I known you? Three hours? Five? A week at most?"

"Seems like longer to me too," Holt said seriously. "Here goes nothing," she said sounding happy as she rang the bell. "I've been looking forward to this day for two years."

"HOWT, HOWT, HOWT!"

A red blur streaked into view when the door opened. Holt barely had time to brace herself before a small child launched himself at her. "Superman!" Holt yelled, scooping him up and over her head.

Superman giggled and straightened his arms flat in front of him and made loud, cute flying noises as she rocked him from side to side. The Man of Steel in flight.

"God, you spoil him." An athletic looking woman with wavy dark brown hair just tinged with gray, approached Superman and Holt, his flying machine.

Holt pulled Superman into her arms and reached her arm back in Isabelle's direction. Isabelle couldn't tell if she was going for intertwined fingers, a protective hand on her back, or if it was simply an instinctive move. Regardless, Isabelle wasn't ready for hand-holding, and she still couldn't decide if she wanted or needed Holt's protection, so she stepped forward, around Holt's outstretched arm and cooed at the cute kid wiggling in her arms. For the second time in less than an hour, Holt was left with no option but the awkward pat on the shoulder.

Although her initial intent had been to embarrass herself making silly faces at a baby, now that she was so close, Isabelle was lost in Holt, this energetic, softer, happy Holt. Her body language, bearing, and the look on her face were polar opposites to what they had been back at the bounty hunter office. Isabelle was spellbound, a feeling that quickly disappeared when the athletic looking woman leaned in and kissed Holt on the lips. She looked like she had done it a hundred times before, and Holt didn't seem surprised by the greeting. Isabelle had only one thought as she saw the possessive way their attractive host kissed Holt: run. Her emotions were already too jumbled, her nerves too raw. She didn't need an ungodly sexy woman screwing with her mind and her heart. She should have trusted her instincts and stayed as far away from Holt as possible.

Holt had said she didn't have a girlfriend, and Isabelle had stupidly believed her. No one as good-looking as Holt was single. She just couldn't understand why she would have brought her to this party knowing her partner would be there.

As Isabelle was plotting her exit strategy and Holt looked like she was trying to disentangle herself from squirmy Superman and affectionate friend, the woman looked at Isabelle.

"You didn't tell me you were bringing someone." She slapped Holt playfully in the stomach as she took in Isabelle and Holt's protective stance.

"I knew you would harass her. Better to catch you by surprise and give her time to breathe." Holt let Superman finally squirm his way to the ground.

"How far into this date are you?" the woman asked.

Isabelle was confused and annoyed that Holt seemed to have read her mind and was blocking her only escape route.

"An hour," Holt said.

"How cute. An hour in and you're already in over your head." The woman held out her hand to Isabelle. "My name's Amy." After fifteen minutes being led from room to room by Amy, Isabelle had met everyone at the party, and the idea of Holt having a girlfriend was no longer an issue. Amy had introduced her as Holt's guest, and to a person, the other partygoers had reacted with shock and a few gentle jokes. She also noticed a look or two of jealousy and grudging respect. Isabelle liked the feel of the group of women. She had always been a believer that the best indication of a person was who their friends were. So far, Holt's spoke well of her.

Eventually, Amy returned Isabelle to the company of Holt. She was in the kids' playroom, sprawled on the floor, surrounded by hundreds of toys and six kids, ranging in age from just crawling to three or four. Superman had her pinned on her back. He was sitting on her stomach and bouncing up and down until she surged forward and tickled him. The game probably could have gone on forever except Superman was laughing so hard he fell to the floor every few tickles. Holt didn't notice the adult presence right away, and it gave Isabelle a moment to study her without worry about getting caught staring.

She was beautiful, in an androgynous, female Adonis kind of way. Her shaggy hair framed her face perfectly, and the crisp white T-shirt she wore had been pulled up her torso by the bouncy toddler. Underneath was a sight to behold. She was all taut muscle and smooth skin. Isabelle was reminded of what it felt like to touch her, and she was immediately on fire.

The passion was tempered by how damned cute she looked, sprawled carelessly on the floor, surrounded by little children, all clamoring for her attention. When Holt did finally notice Isabelle, she stood up, tucked Superman under one arm, and another stray child under the other. Both were laughing hysterically, enjoying the game. The more they wiggled, the tighter Holt held them, rocking back and forth so their legs waved around behind them. She finally let them free.

"Hi," Holt said, looking suddenly shy. "I'm assuming Amy introduced you to everyone? She's not my…I'm not…There's no one. Amy's just a lip kisser. Be prepared next time you see her, because you'll get one too. I figured that's what made you look like you'd changed your mind about staying before she took you away."

Isabelle had seen Holt trying to follow her after Amy had led her away, but another party guest had shooed her away.

Isabelle stepped forward, feeling a calm, steady attraction. Her face must have shown what she was feeling, because the usually unflappable Holt looked decidedly, well, flapped. Isabelle could understand how her change in attitude could be surprising.

"I know. I'm sorry I doubted you," Isabelle said softly, touching her index finger to Holt's lower lip. She laughed as Superman tried to climb up Holt's leg.

Holt scooped him up again, this time throwing him over her shoulder like a sack of potatoes. Looking pensive and altogether too serious for the situation she replied, "I would never lie to you, especially not about something like that."

The moment of solitude from prying adult eyes was interrupted when half the party trekked into the playroom a moment later. The noise level picked up, and it was hard to tell who was more giggly and loud, the children or their moms.

Isabelle noticed almost all the women greeted Holt in the same manner as Amy had. Not everyone kissed her on the lips, but everyone was physically affectionate, a stark contrast to Holt's solid boundaries and powerful presence when she was working. The women were also staring surreptitiously at her, a fact that made her want to squirm as much as Superman.

"Come on. Let's leave the monsters to their parents for a few minutes. They usually lock me back here with them so they can all gossip about each other without worrying what their kids are eating behind the couch. Better grab some food while we can."

"Lead the way." When they were out of earshot of the other women, Isabelle put voice to the question that had been nagging at her since they arrived. "Why is everyone staring at me? Are they like this with all your dates?"

"All my dates?" Holt looked shocked.

"Come on, a girl like you? That looks like you? Those tattoos and blue eyes, the shaggy hair. You must have a new one every month."

Holt still looked like she wasn't comprehending.

"Every week?" Isabelle asked.

"I've never…I don't," Holt was stammering. "I'm surprised the whole party didn't tell you. I never bring anyone here."

"Why did you bring me?" Isabelle asked.

"I don't know," Holt said. "It's nice having you here though, very nice."

Isabelle felt the same but was prevented from sharing that thought by a banging on the front door.

"Uh oh, this is definitely not going to go well," Holt said, moving quickly and intercepting the angry woman stomping into the hallway.

"She's not here," Holt said forcefully. Isabelle recognized Holt the bounty hunter.

"The fuck she's not. I saw that stupid bitch's car out front. Thinks she can just waltz in and steal my girl," the stocky, angry invader said, trying to push her way past Holt.

"You're talking about a friend of mine, so you best be watching your language," Holt said, her voice even but her tone deadly serious. She had stepped a bit closer as well, appearing in the small hallway to be much larger than she actually was. Isabelle was torn between rushing to Holt's defense and watching the scene unfold. It seemed like something from a movie. She half expected the front door to transform into swinging saloon doors with both women itching to pull their six shooters. If someone had described this exact scenario to her three days ago, she would have held it as a shining example of why she and Holt would never work.

She had lived this scenario as a child, her father storming in, angry and accusatory, but she wasn't feeling what she felt then. Although her anxiety level was high, the adrenaline making her right leg shake uncontrollably, she didn't feel nervous in the way she would have imagined. Holt was solid and comforting and seemed so damned capable of handling anything this woman threw her way. Maybe it was the conversation with Max, knowing that Holt wasn't the loose cannon she had initially thought, but it was hot watching the knight defending the honor of her friend.

Despite Holt's efforts at calming the intruder, it didn't take long for the shouting to reach the living room, and more women began cramming the narrow hallway. One of them shoved her way through the crowd and stood just behind Holt.

"You can't come in here shouting like this," the woman said, obviously upset.

"You think you can just walk out on me and end up with that stupid bitch?"

"Hey!" Holt yelled into the invader's face, catching her off guard. "There are children here, and like I told you before, you're talking about one of my friends. Ashley is free to date whoever she wants. As are you. Now go home." Holt stepped closer, forcing her opponent to take a step back.

"Who the fuck do you think you are, H? I don't care if either one of them are your friends."

The angry woman leaned back and did the unthinkable. She spit directly in Holt's face. The offending projectile hit Holt square across one cheek and slid disgustingly down and landed with a plop on the floor. The room was silent as death.

"Well, that was dumb," someone said quietly behind Isabelle.

Lucky for Amy, no one had bothered to close the front door during the confrontation or it would have splintered as Holt drove her shoulder into the spitter's abdomen. She attacked with such thrust that they cleared the two steps leading to the front door and landed on the cement walkway below. Although winded, the offensive newcomer seemed to know she was done for if she didn't put up a fight. She started flailing and managed to land one solid punch to the side of Holt's head.

The blow was enough to make Holt pause, and before she counterattacked, she had a boot to the gut and was flung onto the lawn. Unfortunately for the other woman, Holt's reflexes were well honed, and she sprang to her feet before her assailant could land another blow. Once Holt was standing up, the fight was over. Holt couldn't lose and everyone knew it. Everyone except the newcomer, who resembled a bull charging recklessly at the closest target. She should have stopped to think just who it was she was fighting. She swung wildly a few times and then took a seat as a left hook connected solidly with her temple.

Holt didn't say a word as she looked down at the loser sprawled in front of her on the grass. The stranger was conscious but wouldn't be able to drive for a while. Holt's fists were still clenched, and she didn't relax them as she turned and walked back into the house. Someone else would have to pick up the woman stupid enough to spit in Holt's face.

Isabelle saw the offender's ex-girlfriend put her hand on Holt's shoulder and thank her as she walked by. Isabelle trailed in after Holt who stopped in Superman's room after grabbing a towel from the bathroom and wiping off her face. Somewhere between their quest for food and the fight, the little man had gotten quite sleepy and had curled up on the floor to play with his toys, his little head resting on his arm. The other kids were similarly tuckered and asleep in portacribs, or on the floor like Superman. Holt held him tightly to her, rocking gently back and forth. He nestled happily into her neck, relaxing into her so easily it suggested he had fallen asleep this way many times before.

"How do you know them?" Isabelle asked, noticing the easy way they moved together.

"He's my godson," Holt said quietly, not turning around, continuing to rock the sleepy bundle. "I've known Amy since high school. She was there for me at a time when no one else was, and always has been."

"I can see that's his favorite place to fall asleep," Isabelle said, finding herself irrationally jealous of the toddler's proximity to Holt. "Lucky bastard."

Superman grunted unhappily when he was shaken from sleep by Holt's laughter. Her shoulders shook, and despite her obvious efforts not to laugh aloud, she failed. She kissed his head and laid him in his crib. He nestled into the blankets and was back asleep in a matter of seconds.

Isabelle wasn't prepared for the hungry look in Holt's eyes when she turned to face her. Holt was still chuckling, but her grin was feral and looked dangerous. Dangerous in a very exciting way. Isabelle wanted to rip her clothes off and let Holt eat her alive.

Holt moved to her, with confidence and determination, and Isabelle thought she should check her mouth for drool. Without touching her, Holt walked Isabelle backward out of the baby's room.

Their bodies were six inches apart, eyes locked, breath mingling. She didn't say a word, but her presence was so commanding and the desire in her eyes so easy to read, that Isabelle was held captive. She found it exciting how in control Holt was and she knew she was wet from the look Holt was giving her.

Before Isabelle could up the ante, she was jolted back to reality by a literal splash of cold water against her face. She heard Holt sputter and saw her eyes flash with anger. Holt had her back to the rest of the house and couldn't see Amy standing behind them with an empty cup of water. The anger eased from Holt's face when Isabelle smiled and Amy started laughing.

"Sorry, young lady, you'll have to forgive my friend here," Amy said, handing a towel to Isabelle but giving Holt nothing but a stern look.

"You just can't seem to help but get wet around me," Isabelle said quietly, never taking her eyes off Holt's, for the moment ignoring Amy and the other women who had gathered in the hall.

"You have no idea," Holt said, before turning and putting herself between Isabelle and her friends, perhaps in a futile attempt to protect her from the teasing that was sure to come.

"You've never looked at me like that," one of them complained.

"And we know it wasn't because you weren't trying," another teased the first woman.

"Come on, Amy. What did I do to deserve that?" Holt asked, her eyebrows rising dangerously in question, although her angry glare was diminished by the fact that her hair was sopping wet and water was dripping in her eyes.

"Uh oh," someone muttered, although the rest of the group laughed. Isabelle liked that Holt's threats were falling on deaf ears. It was comforting to know they all trusted the temper Isabelle had seen displayed earlier wouldn't be directed at them.

Isabelle wrapped her arms around Holt's middle, thrilling at the feel of sleek muscle and power. She rested her head against Holt's back, taking in the feel of her. Truth be told, she was glad Amy had doused them and put a stop to what she was sure she would have regretted in the morning. That being said, Holt's body was unreal and she didn't mind the quick moment to touch it. She pulled away quickly since she didn't want Holt to get the wrong idea. She hoped she hadn't already, whatever that was.

"You ready to go?" Holt asked.

Isabelle nodded and went to get her bag.

As she walked away, she heard Amy say, "If you really like this girl, you shouldn't be trying to fuck her in the hallway of my house. I thought I taught you better than that."

Isabelle wondered how many people could get away with talking to Holt that way. She figured probably about as many as had seen the softer side of her, or even knew one existed.

Chapter Six

S ince I dragged you to a kid's party and got you all wet, I hope you'll let me buy you dinner," Holt said. "Have you ever had hot wieners?"

"Is that some kind of sex thing? Can't say I'm familiar with that one, and I've gotta tell you, it didn't feel like you were equipped back at the party. And I know what we were getting geared up to do back there, but I think I need things to slow way down."

"No slow down needed. I was picturing a hairy, sweaty Greek guy with a hot dog, not so much, well…what you might have been picturing. But I can take you home if you're tired, or aren't interested in the Greek guy."

"Would this be a date?" Isabelle asked.

Holt wasn't sure. "Would it change your answer if I said yes?" She wanted to keep Isabelle safe, and casually dating her had seemed like the way to do it. But now her hair was wet because she lost control of her emotions, and she wasn't sure she should be mixing business with pleasure. Although there weren't many better ways to ensure someone's safety than keeping them in your bed. If it got messy, and it probably would, protecting Isabelle would be out the window.

"I might be willing to go on a date," Isabelle said. "But to recap, my choices are either hairy, sweaty man with meat or home alone? Is there a write-in option?"

"Not tonight. Hot wieners is the best offer I've got. Still in?"

"Are you trying to show me your softer side? That you really are a regular gal, one who likes to go on dates, take long walks on the beach, and curl up with a good book?"

"My plan exactly. How am I doing?" Holt was glad to hear the teasing in Isabelle's voice.

"So far, you're verging on decent. I think a sweaty Greek guy and a hot wiener will push you right over the edge."

Isabelle looked gorgeous framed against the sun setting magnificently behind Providence, and the butterflies in Holt's stomach flew into overdrive.

They pulled up in front of a square concrete bunker-like building with an aggressively bright 50s style drive-in food marquee. Isabelle grimaced. Holt ordered for them and handed Isabelle her favorite guilty pleasure food. "Just try it," Holt said, "you'll love it. Every kid in Rhode Island grew up on these things. Hasn't killed anyone yet."

"That you know of." Isabelle looked down at the hot wiener, piled high with mustard, meat sauce, onion, and celery salt, closed her eyes, and took a bite. She clearly resisted the urge to hold her nose while she did.

"Oh my God. This is delicious. How do you keep your body looking like that if you've been eating these things since you were a kid?"

"Well, I started late in life, since I didn't have my first one until I was eighteen, but I'm making up for lost time. I'm glad you like them. Isn't this better than whatever fine dining on Federal Hill you had in mind as your write-in option?" Holt ducked in time to avoid the meat sauce covered napkin aimed at her head. "Okay, not quite as good."

"Okay, bounty hunter, since you won some points with your greasy, heart attack in a bun, tell me about your big, bad, scary job."

Holt almost choked on her second hot wiener. She frantically searched for a way to make her job not scare-your-pants-off scary. Isabelle didn't need those stories, although Holt knew ignoring dangerous situations wouldn't make her think they didn't exist.

"You don't need to tell me how many times you've been shot at, or how many rapists and serial killers you've caught. Just tell me about your day."

"Seems a little normal, me telling you about my day," Holt said. "Today was pretty slow. Lots of paperwork, some background work with Max. I arrested a guy, and Moose and Tuna sat surveillance for eight hours."

"Do you work with anyone with a normal name? You've told me about friends of yours that are named for food products and animals, and now you tell me about one who qualifies for both."

"Hey, my name is normal, and there's Max. Not an animal, mineral, or vegetable."

"Your name isn't all that normal, and Max doesn't count. For one, she's too young. You haven't had time to sink your nickname claws in her yet, and her name is only normal if you yelled for her and either a teenage boy or golden retriever appeared."

Holt was encouraged. Isabelle looked like she was enjoying their time together.

"I've always thought of Max a little like a puppy. Maybe that's why she hasn't gotten a nickname. You can't name a puppy until you really get to know them, understand their personality."

"How long has she worked for you?" Isabelle asked.

"Less than a year, but she's really fitting in well. Might have to get my nickname claws in her soon."

Isabelle rolled her eyes. "So tell me more about the guy you arrested. Did you have to go in guns blazing?"

"I don't carry a gun, remember? Up for a walk?" Holt asked, rising to leave. "The gentleman today, he might have been my easiest arrest. I knocked on his door, told him I was the cable guy, got invited in and offered a beer. I sat on the couch, watched the Red Sox game for a few innings, and arrested him when he flopped, passed out drunk as a skunk in my lap. He even thanked me for waiting to catch the end of the game before I dragged him back to jail. When he woke up, he wanted to make sure the Sox held the lead."

"Does that sort of thing happen often?" Isabelle was laughing. "That sounds pretty tame."

"That exact scenario, no. That was a first, but you would be surprised how many people come back in the fold willingly. People have all sorts of reasons for missing court. They're not always trying to avoid justice. Some just need more time to finish up whatever pressing business they're dealing with. Some forget, some don't care enough to show up, and then some really are trying to hide. The number in the last group is surprisingly small."

"But you do chase the really bad baddies, right? Murderers, rapists, drug dealers?"

"Yes, those high value criminals usually come to us. The reason they do, though, is because we are the best. We're the most prepared, the most highly trained, and best able to handle people who really would rather not go to jail. Safety is always my number one concern for everyone who works for me."

"Do you realize you're talking about safety concerns and high value criminals, and it all sounds so normal? At my office, we prepare for safety concerns by having fire drills twice a year. The worst I have to deal with is an IRS audit flustering a secretary into sending a bookkeeper's training file instead of the real thing and my client being upset about it."

"Does that happen a lot, people getting angry?"

"No, not often at all. A little more with the economy the way it is, but that's just frustration. Perhaps angry isn't the right word. I don't know how I would describe that conversation." Isabelle's focus was elsewhere. She seemed to be trying to remember her earlier discussion.

"Try me. What did he sound like? What were you talking about when he got upset?"

Holt tried hard to avoid switching into work mode, but something in Isabelle's voice triggered her instincts. Isabelle looked off-balance at the change.

"Holt, it's fine. He was annoyed. I'm just a little spooked after you got us shot at." Isabelle softened the accusation by squeezing Holt's shoulder.

"What's his name? His bookkeeper is the one who sent over the training file by mistake? No, you said the secretary sent over the bookkeeper's file. How did you know it was a training file?"

"He's a local businessman, owns a few stores, a methadone clinic. It really wasn't a big deal. I'm just on edge. Besides, it was obviously a training file, or some fake records. All the names were ridiculous, animals, sports teams, bubbles. It was nonsense. Don't worry."

"If you change your mind, or feel weird about this guy again, you'll tell me, right?"

"Stop worrying, bounty hunter. I'm fine. In fact, I'm great. Certainly better than that poor woman over there."

Isabelle pointed across the street to where a woman was being questioned by three police officers. The woman was obviously upset, yelling at the officers and struggling against one of them who was holding her loosely. A small crowd was starting to gather.

"Fuck," Holt said, looking completely dejected. "Now, of all fucking times? Things were going so well."

"What's going on?" Isabelle asked.

"I have to make a phone call. I'm so sorry." Holt looked miserable.

When Holt got off the phone, she turned to Isabelle and kissed her deeply, intensely, and thoroughly.

"Holt, what's going on? You're scaring me a little." Isabelle was sure she would have been less freaked out had Holt started ranting and raving. The kiss was weird. It felt a little desperate and strangely like a good-bye. "What just happened?"

Before Holt could explain, a black truck similar to the one Holt drove skidded to a stop, a giant of a man behind the wheel. He hopped out and stood waiting for instructions. For the moment, Holt ignored him.

"The brother of the woman across the street is someone I'm looking for. He's one of those bad baddies you talked about. I need to speak to her." Isabelle was surprised at the pain on Holt's face.

"So talk to her. I'll wait." She didn't understand. Even the silent man looked uncomfortable.

"She's being arrested, and she's suspicious of anyone tied to the police," Holt said, like that explained everything. "The arresting officer is my cousin. It presents a unique opportunity. One I don't think you're going to like, but one I don't think I'm going to get again. I'm sorry. I have a feeling you're about to see the parts of my job you file in your head under 'worst case scenario.'"

"They're moving, H. Time's up. You want me to get Isabelle home safe?" the man said.

Holt nodded but didn't take her eyes off Isabelle. Her expression was tender as she took Isabelle's face in her hands. "This is Moose. He works for me and he's going to get you home safe. Whatever you decide after this, I had a wonderful night with you. Everything I felt and said was real, whatever else you believe." Holt kissed her once more and loped across the street without looking back.

"Mr. Moose, what's going on? She's acting like she's dying." Isabelle's heart was pounding and she felt slightly nauseous.

"It's just Moose. I'm sorry we have to meet under these circumstances. To answer your question, I think she's afraid. I've rarely seen Holt act like that, but if I had to guess, I think she's worried that after today, you won't speak to her again. Get in the truck. I'll drive you home."

"Afraid? In the truck? I'm not going anywhere until you tell me what the hell is going on." Isabelle couldn't help her volume and frustration. She was upset, and all the secrecy and odd behavior was making her anxious. She had no idea where the perfect evening she had been enjoying had gone or why Holt would think she wouldn't speak to her anymore.

Before Moose could answer, Holt's gait changed and caught Isabelle's attention. Instead of the confident, strong woman she was used to, Holt was now walking like a falling down drunk. She wove her way into the crowd on the sidewalk, shoving onlookers aside.

She honed in on the largest of the three officers and moved directly into his personal space yelling and gesturing at the woman they were arresting. The officer yelled back and the situation escalated quickly.

Isabelle watched in horror as Holt recklessly shoved the officer and then pulled her arm back, wound up, and threw a wild punch aimed at his head. It caught him on the chin. Isabelle wasn't sure if it was her that screamed or the woman standing in handcuffs next to Holt, but all was silent when the officer retaliated and dropped Holt to the sidewalk with a punch to the left eye. Isabelle's first reaction was worry for Holt's safety. That punch looked solid, and Holt lay on the sidewalk clasping her hands to her face.

But worry was replaced with dismay and bewilderment that left her near tears and trying not to vomit as the large officer shoved his knee into Holt's back and cuffed her hands roughly behind her back. When he pulled her to her feet, Isabelle took off across the street. She ignored the apology and sadness in Holt's eyes, or at least in the one that wasn't swelling closed, and for the second time, raised her hand to slap Holt. The three officers stepped in to ensure Holt's safety, but didn't try to contain Isabelle. They didn't need to. She had been ashamed of reacting with violence when she had slapped Holt before, but it had been pure surging emotions. There was no turmoil now. She was sad and she was pissed. Holt wasn't worth the slap and how bad she would feel about herself after. Maybe Holt reacted impulsively to things, but she didn't.

She couldn't believe the strange, twisted turn the evening had taken. How the hell would getting arrested help Holt talk to that woman? And how could Holt let her believe her workday had been so normal, and then do something like this? Was work really more important than the wonderful night they'd been having?

"How could you do this? How could you be so stupid?" Isabelle was so furious her hands were shaking. She had shoved aside her fears about Holt, but now they were hitting her full force, and it was a shock to her system. "You know how I feel and you still do this? When they let you out, lose my number."

Angry at Holt and embarrassed by her own lack of judgment, Isabelle turned silently, crossed back to the other side of the street, and let Moose guide her to the truck. "You're just going to let this happen?" she asked Moose. He didn't answer. She climbed into the passenger seat and fastened her seat belt. She didn't look back. She had no desire for her last glimpse of Holt Lasher to be the moment they loaded her in the back of a police cruiser.

She could chastise herself later about ignoring her instincts, but for now, she was exhausted and wanted to be at home, in her bed, and, sadly, alone.

"Please take me home, Moose. There's nothing left for me here."

Chapter Seven

Decker, the accountant is still a threat." Gary briefed him at their weekly meeting.

"It's been over a month since you sent her that file, Gary. There's no indication she's cracked your code. Holt Lasher hasn't been seen near her, and our business is running smoothly. What has you spooked?" Decker had forgiven, if not forgotten, Gary's mistake dealing with Isabelle Rochat previously. Luckily, his idiocy hadn't cost them. It hadn't netted him a partnership with Holt Lasher either, but in this case, a draw seemed like a good outcome.

"She hasn't cracked the code, but she's been digging around. She called your new secretary, and she's been in touch with the auditor."

"And he called you?"

"Yes, we pay him enough. It's the least he can do."

"Any idea why this woman won't let that damn file go?"

"I told you already. She wants to help out on the whole audit. She says you pay her for full financial services but only utilize a small part of what she offers, blah, blah, blah. We're gonna get nailed by Mother Teresa."

"Shut up, Gary." Decker was quickly losing his patience. He didn't tolerate talk of failure. "If she has so much free time on her hands, perhaps we can add something to her life to keep her busy. Do you know anyone who is up for a little B and E?"

"Won't she get suspicious if we toss her house?

"Who said anything about her house? I want you to hit her office. Her firm has about ten employees. Plenty of office supplies and paper for your boys to play with. Leave her office alone. I want it spotless. Spook her a little, and if we're lucky, for a while, the cops will think she did it."

"I don't see how that's going to work, boss. Why would she destroy her own office?"

"This is not the part where I pay you to think," Decker said. "I don't really care if it will work. I have a few cops who are well paid too. We can keep Ms. Rochat busy for a while, too busy to worry about taking on an extra audit for a client who doesn't want her services anyway."

"You got it, boss. We'll be real secretive. Nice and subtle. It will never get traced back to you." Gary looked excited by the chance to atone for his past mistakes.

"Forget subtle. Subtle takes too long to notice. Destroy the place."

❖

Holt was usually energized around the time of the annual fundraiser she sponsored. This year, she felt disinterested in the frivolity, lonely when she returned each night to her empty apartment, and even more short-tempered with her mother than usual. The gym smelled just as comfortingly fetid as always, like stale sweat air freshener. She knew the three rows of gym clothes hung to dry on clotheslines after people's workouts didn't help the smell, but it always made her smile to see the boxers strip down to their underwear after a hard workout and carefully, neatly, hang their clothes on the line to dry the sweat from them for next time.

Only when the shorts could stand on their own was it time for a wash. No matter how many times she reminded herself that Isabelle was a woman she barely knew, and they hadn't exactly parted on good terms, it upset her when thoughts of Isabelle invaded her day, which they continued to do with alarming consistency. It felt as though she had lost more than a casual acquaintance. It wasn't enough to know her crew was ensuring Isabelle's safety, watching over her house every night. Holt wanted a second date. Preferably without any arrests or angry endings. She could see the regret she felt in her own eyes anytime she looked in the mirror, and unfortunately for her, boxing gyms were wall-to-wall mirrors. She was, whether she wanted to be or not, in the midst of self-reflection hell.

As was true anytime Holt was upset, she reverted to the physical. She trained her body with such intensity that by the time she collapsed in bed at night, she was too tired to think. Too tired to realize she was alone, and that for the first time, that was bothersome.

She should have been happy for the excuse to train more. The only remaining link between her and her parents was an annual gala they threw together. This fundraiser benefited the same charity the gala did, the only cause for which Holt was willing to spend an evening with her parents every year. The fundraiser took place at her boxing gym and pitted her against a team of five challengers from the ranks of her employees. Two treadmills stood black and stark center ring, contrasting with the vibrant red ring mat.

Holt chose the pace, evening the playing field some, and the team of five tried to outlast her in a running competition. She was allowed one pace change during the competition if she desired. It was a strategic nightmare for her employees. They could train to run fast, but risk burning out too quickly, and if Holt chose a relatively slow pace, seven- or eight-minute miles, they would never be able to match her stamina. However, if she felt like sprinting, training for a marathon was a serious mistake. Usually, individuals on the team specialized and hoped the ones who trained for the wrong event could hold on long enough to be useful. They had to switch runners on the fly too, which was harder than it seemed. Jumping on a treadmill moving at six-minute mile speed was difficult. She knew they practiced their handoffs at every speed imaginable.

In five years, no team had come close to beating Holt. Last year, the challengers had held on for fifteen miles, but her punishing pace of six and a half minute miles had worn them down. This year, she was even faster. She was embarrassed by Isabelle's rejection and upset that her worst assumptions about Holt had seemingly been proven true. Emotions had fueled her training once before, and the result was Holt standing alone atop the pyramid of the best female boxers in the country. Moose was the only one on the other team who had seen her train, and he had admitted they didn't have a chance.

The gym was crowded, filled with friends and sponsors. Since it was a fundraiser, people donated based on varying criteria. Some chose to donate per mile run, others by how long the challengers lasted before calling off the battle. Every year, one man offered ten thousand dollars if Holt's team could beat her. The money never tempted her to throw the event. The integrity of the fundraiser was important to her, but more than that, she really hated losing.

Holt scanned the crowd as she stepped on the treadmill and readied herself. She knew almost all the faces looking back at her, eager with anticipation. What hit her like a sack of bricks, however, was that there was no one in the crowd for her, just her. No one was watching her every move, enjoying the feat of athleticism, and offering, without words, to take care of her aches when they returned home. Everyone wanted to see her challengers win. No one was there to watch her win. She always won, but eventually, cheering for the winner gets boring. Until her one date with Isabelle, she had never noticed. She wasn't saying Isabelle was the one, but every jock likes a hot girl spurring them on. And she really would have liked having Isabelle there cheering for her.

"Speed ten point four," Holt announced, enjoying the looks of dismay that crossed the faces of three of her five competitors. If she ran fast enough, maybe she could outrun the loneliness eating at her.

Five minute forty-five second miles weren't ones she could maintain for more than about ten miles, but after an hour of running her opponents into the ground, she wasn't sure anyone would be left to challenge her if she chose to slow down. She was ready.

"Letting your emotions get the better of you?" Moose asked quietly from the side of her treadmill.

"Trash talking, Moose? Not really your style." When he didn't say anything, but stared at her with his arms crossed, she rolled her eyes. He was only looking out for her. "I'm fine. Let's get going."

In her business, failure to control emotions could be deadly. In her athletic pursuits, especially in the ring, the idea was the same, even if the scale of consequences was different. Too much fear made you overly cautious, too much anger made you sloppy, and too much excitement burned you out too quickly. The treadmill would keep her paced, and if she lost a few minutes to adrenaline and emotion, she didn't care.

After thirty minutes, Holt's clothes were soaked through with sweat and she had eliminated two runners. For the past two miles, she had gone head-to-head with Max, who despite a jerky gait and clear fatigue, seemed to be running on sheer force of will. Holt guessed she was one who had trained for distance, not speed. She was impressed by her determination. Max was dwarfed by the treadmill but was proving her mettle. The crowd was responding to her heart and actively cheering for the underdog.

Two miles later, Holt wasn't sure how Max was still upright. Holt was beginning to feel some fatigue as well and was plotting her speed strategy when she heard the door to the gym open. Isabelle slipped in, looking timid and unsure. She was scanning the crowd and finally settled her gaze on Holt.

Holt did the only thing she could do; she slammed her hand against the stop button on the treadmill and nimbly jumped off the moving belt, giving Max the victory of a lifetime.

She was only vaguely aware of the roaring crowd as she patted Max on the shoulder, walked to the edge of the ring, ducked under the ropes, and picked her way through the crowd. She hoped Isabelle didn't move, because once she was engulfed in the masses, she lost sight of her.

When she popped out the other side of the celebratory group, she resisted the urge to wrap Isabelle in a hug, not sure of the reception she would get and not really wanting to anger her. Not to mention being soaked in sweat.

"I'm sorry for the way we left things. I know I have no right to be here, but I didn't know where else to go." Isabelle was clearly struggling to keep her emotions in check. She was pale and thinner than she had been a month before, dark circles highlighting her eyes.

"Of course you should have come here. I'm glad you did." Holt didn't let on how wonderful it was just to see Isabelle. She would tell her that later, if and when a time arose when Isabelle didn't look like she was about to burst in to tears.

"But the way we—"

"It doesn't matter. If you need me, I'm here." Holt realized with a jolt those words would always be true. "We can figure the rest out later. You want to go somewhere a little less noisy and tell me what's going on?"

"Only if you tell me why Max is being carried around the gym like a conquering hero." Isabelle looked around, as if she were truly taking in the surroundings for the first time.

"She just raised ten thousand dollars for the fundraiser we're putting on here today," Holt said.

"Money for your legal defense fund?" Isabelle asked, clearly realizing too late how that sounded.

"Just couldn't help that one, huh?"

"Apparently not. Sorry."

Holt smiled and was rewarded when Isabelle relaxed her shoulders, letting them return to a position below her earlobes.

"You look just like the first time we met, all sopping wet, focused, and worried. Skinnier though."

Holt led her to an office tucked in a tiny room just outside the entry doors to the main gym. It usually smelled at least marginally better, although with Holt currently occupying it, there were no guarantees. Isabelle sat in the offered chair. She looked close to tears.

"You're looking at me so kindly right now, and I'm still furious with you," Isabelle said quickly.

"Setting up ground rules?" Holt asked.

"I don't know. You're…perplexing. I came here because you once offered me help, and I thought, as a professional, you could loan me some of your unique skills. I think I might be in trouble."

Holt was surprised to feel a pang of hurt at Isabelle's impersonal description of the parameters of their relationship. She wanted to search Isabelle's eyes for signs that she felt the same way, but now wasn't the time. Isabelle needed her work self.

"Tell me what's wrong."

"I will, but first, how did Max just win ten thousand dollars? What were you guys doing in there?"

"We were running, and she outlasted me."

"Max outlasted you? Little Max? Tiny, skinny Max?" Isabelle looked incredulous. Suddenly, she seemed to understand. "You quit. I walked in and you quit. That's why she beat you?"

Holt hoped it wasn't her imagination that Isabelle seemed to be leaving a lot left unspoken.

"Like I said, it's for charity, a good cause. There are no losers today. Now, what's going on?"

"Holt, I didn't mean…" she trailed off when Holt reached for her hand and squeezed it.

"Tell me everything, from beginning to end, even the details you think aren't important." Holt pulled out a notebook and pen, ready to work.

"Four days ago, I arrived at work to find the building full of police officers. The offices of the firm I work for had been turned upside down. Computers were on the floor, file cabinets emptied and the files thrown around. Chairs were overturned, shelves and paintings pulled from the walls. It was a horrible mess."

"Was anything stolen?"

"At first we just assumed robbery was the motive, but it was so hard to tell if anything was missing with the mess. The computers were all still there, which seemed odd to me. The other strange part was my office was untouched. It was completely pristine."

"Where is your office located in relation to the main door? Can you draw me a quick sketch of the layout?"

"My office is one of three along the back wall, farthest from the main door. I have the middle office. The other two were a mess. Mine was untouched."

Isabelle's eyes filled and Holt could tell she was fighting hard not to cry. Even if she needed a shoulder, Holt's probably wasn't the first one she would choose. Holt knew that was largely her job's fault.

"Who called the police? Obviously not you?"

"I don't know who called, but that's the part where I think I become a suspect. A woman called nine one one, during the robbery, from my desk phone. That was the only thing in the room they touched. After she made the report, she left the phone off the hook. One of the thieves apparently yelled my name and the caller responded. I wasn't anywhere near work. I was at home, but I don't think they believe me. Why would I ransack my own workplace?"

"I'll be right back. Sit tight."

Holt edged out of the small room and headed back into the gym. She waded back into the crowd, hoping to find her cousin quickly in the throng. Luckily, he was near the perimeter. She motioned for him to follow her, and they returned to the office together.

"Oh man, I never got to tell you how brilliant you were. I was pissed that this brute had just punched me in the head, but I really thought I was going to have to protect her from you. Wicked good acting," he said to Isabelle when he stepped into the office.

"Shut up," Holt said, giving him a shove in the back.

Isabelle looked like she had just stepped into an alternate reality. Of course she had no idea that this guy was her cousin, or that he thought she had been in on Holt's plan the day she got arrested. Holt hated that she needed to remind Isabelle of that day.

"She punched you. You arrested her," Isabelle said.

"Of course. How else was she going to get that lady to talk to her? Did H tell you about the mean fucker she pulled off the streets because of the information she got from his sister? The show you put on, man—"

"Shut up, Danny," Holt said more forcefully, giving him another shove, this one verging on assaulting an officer territory.

"But, H, I just wanted—"

"I said shut the fuck up, Danny. It's time for you to listen." Holt turned back to Isabelle.

"Isabelle, this is my overly talkative cousin Danny. He's a Providence cop and might be able to help out. Do you mind telling him the story?"

While Isabelle talked, Holt tried to get her anger back under control. It wasn't Danny's fault that he had stumbled onto a hornet's nest. She couldn't think about that night, when her job had come before Isabelle's feelings and her own desire. Not right now, not when Isabelle needed her to focus.

"What do you need from me, H?" he asked when Isabelle finished her story.

"Do you mind doing a little digging? Don't get in deep. I'm just curious what the police have cooking. It seems strange that they would be trying to pin this on Isabelle so quickly."

"Sure, no problem. Anything else?"

"Yeah, actually, there's a bank across the street, ATM in front, facing Isabelle's building. Think you could get me the ATM camera footage for that morning?"

"I'll see what I can do."

"Good man, thank you."

Holt walked him back to the celebration still raging in the main room of the gym. This was a party to rival one following a winning penalty kick in the World Cup final. Holt was amazed everyone still had their shirts on. Max was going to be a hero for a long while.

"I'm sorry for whatever I stepped in back there. You know I always got your back, right?"

"Don't worry about it, Danny. The problem is that she wasn't acting. I haven't seen her since that night."

"Oh fuck, I'm sorry, H. That sucks. She's back now though. She got in deep and came to you. That's gotta count for something."

Holt clapped him on the shoulder and returned to Isabelle. It was true. Isabelle was scared, in trouble, and she had come to Holt. The knot of anxiety in Holt's stomach started to unravel.

"So," Holt said when she and Isabelle were alone in her office. She was completely unprepared to face Isabelle, who utterly mixed her up. One minute, she was pissed off with her for being so innocent and prudish, the next, she wanted to protect her and keep her innocent. She envied her black-and-white views of right and wrong.

"Holt," Isabelle said, her voice soft but laced with warning.

"I know. There's a lot to talk about. But not tonight. Dinner? It's family night."

"I'm having dinner with my sister tonight," Isabelle said, sounding disappointed.

Holt took that as a good sign and carried on. "It's family night. Bring her along. Amy will be there too. It can be a double date."

"Holt, my sister is married and straight. With kids. You can't be setting her up with your—Oh. That's not what you meant is it?"

"No setup. It's family dinner. There will be plenty of familiar faces. You bring your sister; I'll bring Amy."

Holt felt like the volatile energy from a few moments ago was gone. Even Isabelle looked more relaxed. There was no denying they had chemistry.

"I'm not going to meet your mother am I?"

Holt knew she hadn't successfully contained the Pavlovian grimace of pain that always accompanied the mention of her mother.

"That's biology. This is family. Starts at seven. Give me a call if you and your sister can make it."

Holt retreated with a nod and joined the revelers in the gym. She felt Isabelle's gaze on her back. Her tattoo tingled across her shoulders as though Isabelle's fingers were caressing the lines. As she turned the corner, she heard Isabelle on the phone.

"Hey, sis, mind a change in dinner plans tonight? I've got someone I'd like you to meet."

CHAPTER EIGHT

Isabelle was uncharacteristically fidgety as she and her sister approached Holt's door. Life would be simpler if Holt didn't exist, but she did, and although she wanted to insist they keep things strictly professional, she spent the afternoon turned on and cranky after seeing Holt at the gym.

Not unexpectedly, her sister, Ellen, had jumped to conclusions about Holt. Explaining exactly who Holt was and the bizarre circumstances around their meeting had taken fifteen minutes of storytelling and another half an hour of apologizing for not telling her sooner. She had conveniently not found the time to tell Ellen about the shooting or Holt. Isabelle wasn't sure why she had kept it all from her, but she had ended up angering the person she trusted most in the world.

Ellen had seen Isabelle through heartbreak, first love, family trouble, and had even been known to hold her hair while she regurgitated the spoils of a late night of partying. Isabelle should have called her sooner, a fact that Ellen was eager to point out. Despite her anger, Isabelle could tell Ellen was dying to meet Holt Lasher, Bounty Hunter. It was possible the terms Isabelle had used to describe Holt had Ellen expecting a caped superhero decked out in colorful spandex, wearing her underwear on the outside, not an ordinary, though hot as hell, woman.

The building Holt had directed them to was in an active, but decidedly rough, neighborhood. It was a converted mill building and didn't look like much on the outside. However, when the door was flung open and they were ushered inside, Isabelle was floored.

The space was completely open, with dining room, living room, and kitchen occupying the front of the loft and also taking up the most space. Strategically placed bookcases toward the back hid what she guessed was Holt's bedroom. The urge to run back and take a peek at Holt's bed was strong, but she hushed her inner child and continued to look around. She took in the soft leather couch and matching armchair, the flat screen TV, and marble topped kitchen island. The loft was impeccably clean and decorated in a strong but understated style. It was Holt to a tee, and Isabelle loved it.

"Hi. I'm glad you could make it." She leaned in and gave Isabelle a kiss on the cheek. "You smell like lilacs. I like that."

Isabelle realized too late her expression likely screamed, "I want to eat you for lunch; you are the sexiest woman I have ever seen." Holt looked like she wanted to drag her to the bedroom, but instead, she turned her attention to Ellen. Isabelle knew they looked remarkably alike. Sometimes they were mistaken for twins even though Ellen was older and, Isabelle thought, looked decidedly straighter.

She half expected to see interest in Holt's eyes while she took in Ellen, but there was nothing but cool evaluation and cautious welcome. Hot and smoldering seemed reserved for her alone, a fact she had to admit pleased her.

"Holt, this is my sister, Ellen. Ellen, Holt."

"Nice to meet you, Ellen. Thanks for coming."

"Well, I simply had to meet the bounty hunter who saved my sister from a shotgun blast."

Holt grinned slightly. "You give me too much credit. I have to warn you, though, if you're looking for a lot of action and excitement tonight, you might be disappointed. I'll consider tonight a success if I don't fall asleep before eleven and you both have a wonderful time. Shall we?" She motioned to the living area where most of the guests were. She introduced everyone, and Isabelle felt right at home amid the noise and laughter.

Dinner was a raucous affair. Aside from Isabelle and her sister, Moose, Max, Amy, Superman, Jose, Danny, and two other members of Holt's team from work, Tuna and Lola, filled out the table. Isabelle was largely quiet, just taking it all in, but Ellen seemed to be reveling in the experience.

"So," Ellen said, "at what point in the evening do you all get a call on the bat phone and have to run out and save Gotham City?"

"I'm more of a Spider-Man fan myself," Jose said. "And I'm not part of the Holt save-the-world crew, just a lowly mechanic. I stay and do the dishes while they save the world, and when they get home, I tune up the Batmobile."

"You do the dishes while we're gone?"

"Hey, Alfred was Batman's butler. Someone has to make sure things run smoothly. How did you think all the dishes got done while you all were out running around town?"

"Housekeeper," Moose suggested.

"A bored Flash?" Lola said.

"I always assumed elves," Holt said, nudging Jose lovingly.

"Anyway," Amy said, apparently knowing when to bring the teasing to an end, "I think Moose qualifies more as the Incredible Hulk."

"More like Incredible Hunk," Jose whispered loudly enough for the table to hear.

Moose turned beet red and coughed up whatever he had just attempted to swallow. The rest of the table roared with laughter.

"Did Isabelle tell you about Holt's latest high profile capture?" Jose asked.

"Jose." Holt's tone was filled with warning, but Jose ignored her.

"If Miss Ellen thinks you're a superhero, I see no reason to disappoint her with boring tales of your boxing exploits," Jose said. "May I continue?"

"Like anyone could stop you," Holt said. She sighed and settled in.

"I saw you put on your big girl Captain America Underoos this evening, so you can handle a compliment. Now, where was I?"

"The beginning," everyone said, rolling their eyes.

"Oh, right. Okay, so there's this really bad dude, arrested for not nice crimes against kids. He jumped bond, and because everyone knows Holt's outfit is the only one worth its salt in this city, she got to chase him. He's a douche bag and a pretty good ghost, so it took our fearless leader a couple weeks to get a bead on him. The only one he's ever been close to is his sister." Jose paused for a breath and Danny jumped in.

"His sister used to be a pretty bad girl herself, stolen cars, a few fights, but she's been clean the last few years except for court fines. Those she just can't seem to pay off. So every couple months, she gets tossed in the can for a couple nights to pay off her debt to society, or some such crap. I was arresting her on a warrant when Holt spotted us. It was the night she was out with Isabelle, eating those hot wieners that are going to kill her some day."

"Hey, lay off the hot wieners," Holt said, looking like she was warming to the story. Isabelle liked the sparkle in her eye as they relived the chase.

"Anyway," Jose picked up the story again, "Holt clocked Danny boy here, and of course, what is a good cop to do when assaulted, but arrest the punk who punched him?"

"I barely hit him," Holt said. "You make it sound like I knocked him cold."

"Nah, I wouldn't have woken up for a week if you had really hit me," Danny conceded.

"Didn't stop you from hitting her pretty hard," Isabelle said, surprised by the anger in her voice. Why she was defending Holt was almost beyond her comprehension.

"Don't worry," Danny said, seemingly oblivious to Isabelle's anger. "She's got a hard head."

"Can I get back to my story?" Jose asked. When no one answered, he continued anyway. "So rumor has it, something transpired that made it appear as though Holt had a girlfriend, who thought she was cheating on her with our bad dude's sister. This rumor perhaps had to do with a certain blond guest of ours being a little upset that she had just been forced to eat hot wieners, and to top off the night, Holt was going to ask her for bail money. H, was the plan all along to pretend you were this woman's super secret lady love? Anyway, see, this sister has a new squeeze, and is cleaning up her act for this chick. Rumors about cheating can kill a relationship. During their time in the clink, Holt was able to talk some sense into the sister, and when Danny, our hero, decided not to press charges, Holt got out and arrested the douche bag."

"You got arrested for your job? That's dedication," Ellen said. "Are you that dedicated to everything you do?"

Isabelle elbowed her, not amused with the implication behind the question.

"Like a Boy Scout," Moose said. He wiggled his eyebrows and laughed, clearly understanding where Ellen was headed with her question.

"What happened to the sister and her girlfriend?" Isabelle asked, worried that she had torpedoed a stranger's chance at happiness while wrapped up in her own emotional turmoil.

"Oh, this is where it gets good," Max said, still looking freshly victorious after her big win at the gym.

"Hey, pipsqueak, one victory at the gym and you think you can roast me too?" Holt asked.

"Oh shit, sorry, ma'am." Max looked ready to jump out of her chair to stand at attention.

"Holt," Amy said, "quit scaring the poor child. Max, look at the big lump. She's teasing you. You kicked her ass fair and square today. Strut a little."

"Well, technically—" Isabelle said.

"Max beat me, like Amy said. Revel, Max. You earned it."

"Finish up the story, dragon slayer," Jose said.

"When Holt got out, she found the lady's girlfriend and told her the rumor was bull. And I hear she paid off the court fines too, so the two could start over fresh. No more arrests. Not that Holt has confirmed any of that."

"One of the problems of working with the best talent in Rhode Island is that you never have any secrets," Holt said, shrugging.

"A superhero indeed," Ellen said, clearly impressed.

Isabelle was stunned. Her imagining of that night was so different from the reality as recounted by Holt's friends. Holt hadn't been reckless or impulsive or stupid. Isabelle still didn't like the methods she employed to get the information, but some of the fury over getting ditched in the middle of a date dissipated. It almost sounded like Holt had done the right thing. No wonder she felt like she was always a step behind all the time around Holt. None of her friends had girlfriends who got arrested because it was the right thing to do.

"Like I said, a Boy Scout."

Across the table, Holt's eyes held questions Isabelle didn't have answers to. Holt still looked scruffy and outrageously hot, but the air of vulnerability she showed around her loved ones was just as alluring.

Was Isabelle ready to accept this kind of danger and intrigue into her calm, ordered life? Or at least into a third date? Before dinner this evening, the answer had been a firm no. She could still feel the hurt and betrayal as Holt put her job first and was arrested. How could she ever explain to her colleagues why her girlfriend wasn't at the annual firm picnic? After hearing the tale of bravery and self-sacrifice, she was less sure of her answer. Holt was still the bad girl, and Isabelle still wasn't. That complicated matters, as did the attraction Isabelle was unable to quash. Bravery and attraction still didn't solve the firm picnic problem. Perhaps they could at least be friends. Until the mess at her office was figured out, she anticipated seeing much more of Holt.

During dessert, Max's cell phone rang. The office phone had been forwarded to Max, and the call was for Holt. Isabelle saw the professional mask cloud Holt's features as she listened to the caller. She did most of the listening, with minimal inquiries for information. The table that had moments earlier been light-hearted and loud, was now quiet and tense. All eyes were on the boss.

"Is that the bat phone?" Ellen whispered. Isabelle shrugged.

"C.B. Sixty," Holt said and ended the phone call.

When Holt turned and looked at Isabelle, her eyes were filled with unease. "Is it your birthday? Anniversary? Special holiday?" Holt asked.

"No, my birthday is in January. What's going on?"

"Someone delivered flowers to your door about fifteen minutes ago. Normally, that's not something I would care about, but events surrounding you haven't been particularly normal lately. And the deliveryman said the flowers were from Parker Caldwell. Do you know him?"

Isabelle shook her head. She didn't know the state representative. She felt a little queasy.

"How did you know they were at her house?" Ellen asked.

"I've had someone keeping an eye on the house since, we, um, since the unique circumstances that caused our meeting."

"You're still having me watched?" Isabelle asked. The thought of someone invading her cherished privacy, particularly without her knowing, made her stomach turn.

"What? No, I promised to keep you safe." Holt looked shocked at the accusation and everyone else at the table looked uncomfortable. "They drive by a couple times a night. No one is sitting on your trash can with binoculars. But I can't keep you safe if I can't see who might be hanging around your house."

Holt held out her hand as the phone rang again. It was exactly sixty seconds since the first phone call had ended. "Do you mind if the flowers are delivered here?" Holt asked Isabelle before she answered the phone.

Again, Isabelle shook her head. Why not? She clearly had no control over her surroundings anymore. Holt hung up again and sighed.

"Well, next time the superhero phone rings, I would prefer it not be about my sister," Ellen said, staring intently at Holt.

"As would I," Holt said, holding Ellen's stare.

"Are you sure you don't know Caldwell? Never met him at a function, lunch meeting, coffee shop, the post office? Rhode Island is small; it could have been anywhere."

Isabelle shook her head. She knew she had never met the man.

"Okay, what about your clients? Do any of them deal with him that you know of? Have you done business with his office or anyone related to him on their behalf? Do you think anyone may know him?"

"Holt, I have no idea if anyone knows him. Like you said, Rhode Island is tiny. I don't ask for a list of everyone my clients have ever met when they hire me. I can only tell you I have never met him, and I have not done business with him, his office, or as far as I know, anyone connected to him, either on my own or anyone else's behalf."

Isabelle didn't like being grilled. She didn't like being made to feel as though she were hiding something or had something to feel guilty about. She was sure this wasn't her fault.

"Honey," Ellen said, rubbing Isabelle's hair just like she had done since they were little, "this isn't the same as back home. Holt's just doing her job. No one thinks you did anything wrong."

She knew all that, of course, but it felt the same as it always had, like being interrogated. She slumped into a dining chair and wrapped her arms around herself. "I'm sorry, Holt. I just can't think of any connection. I'll keep trying." If all of this was happening because of something she had done, or someone she knew, that was terrifying.

Five awkward and tense minutes later, there was a knock at Holt's door and the flowers were brought in and deposited in the middle of the table. Everyone gaped at the lavish display of lilies, orchids, and three kinds of roses. Whoever sent them spent a fortune. There wasn't a carnation or overabundance of greenery to be found.

"There's a note here," Isabelle said, reaching for the bright red envelope.

The sight of the note seemed to anger Holt. Her shoulders bunched, and she looked ready to do someone physical damage. That alone increased Isabelle's apprehension. She was glad she had seen Holt angry before and had an idea of how she would react.

She opened the envelope, addressed to her. As she read the note, it felt as though someone had injected ice water in her veins.

You aren't safe. I'm coming soon. We need to talk.

The ten seconds it took to read those words was all the time Isabelle needed for her world to come crashing down around her. There was no denying the shooting at her house was directed at her, the ransacking of her office building wasn't a random crime. Now she had an on the lam drug addict coming for a chat. It wasn't exactly a visit to look forward to.

In the moment of realization, she reacted on emotion and sought comfort from the only person in the room who seemed stronger than the demons scratching at the door. She flung herself into Holt's ready embrace and buried her face against her strong, secure body. Tears squeezed their way from her tightly closed eyes and fell onto Holt's shirt.

After ordering all but Ellen and Moose from the room, the only words Holt spoke were ones of gentle reassurance. Isabelle knew they were just words, and the promises Holt was making couldn't be guarantees, but she felt safety and gratitude in equal measure as Holt whispered into her hair.

"How do we keep her safe?" Ellen asked, clearly worried.

"I would prefer she stay here, or at a hotel, but—" Holt didn't have time to finish before Isabelle made a sound of protest. "I'm guessing she won't agree to either of those conditions."

Isabelle shook her head. She wasn't going to be forced out of her home. She had stayed after the buckshot had ruined her back siding, and she was going to sleep in her own bed tonight. Granted, it was significantly more scary thinking a wanted criminal might come barging in to shoot the breeze at any time, but she wasn't going to give in to her fear. The tears were gone. Holt still had her arm protectively around her shoulders, and Isabelle was still leaning into the embrace, but she knew she needed to stand tall alongside Holt, not hide behind her if she wanted her world to right itself. She refused to be a damsel in distress, waiting for rescue.

"In that case, with your permission, Isabelle, I'd like to set up a security patrol and develop an escape plan."

"A security patrol? Like guys with guns pacing in front of my house? My neighbors are nosy as hell. Remember the woman with the rosary beads I told you about? Do you know how fast the cops would be at my house?"

Holt shrugged. "My guys, the cops, either way, Caldwell won't come near you with us around."

Isabelle looked at Holt thoughtfully. "You need to catch him don't you? Why not wait for him to come to me and then get him?" Lying in wait, helping to catch a bond jumper would give her some semblance of control of an out of control situation. It sounded crazy coming out of her mouth, but it also seemed crazy that someone had shot at her and that Caldwell wanted to meet her. Maybe she should embrace it.

"No," both Holt and Ellen said forcefully and in unison.

"Why not? It makes perfect sense."

"I absolutely will not, ever, use you as bait. I know you think I'd do anything for my job. When it's me on the line, perhaps I'm more reckless, a little looser about crossing the line, but not with you."

"There are other ways of protecting you, without using you as bait," Moose said. "Let's set up the escape plan first, just in case. We like to over prepare, so humor us."

The rest of the group was recalled and Max pulled out her iPhone. She pulled up a perfect blueprint of Isabelle's home and Holt and Moose began arguing the virtues of different points of exit.

"Where did you get the house blueprint?" Isabelle asked.

"I'm working on an app. It pulls information from the tax assessor website, aerial views of the building, building permits, and any other information about the property from public records and comes up with a reasonable guess as to the blueprint," Max said. "I'm still working out the kinks, but recent testing has found it to be pretty accurate, especially for the newer buildings."

"Okay," Holt said, "the guest bedroom closet is your hiding place. It gives you equal access to two windows and the back sliding doors if an exit is possible. We also know where to look for you if you're not able to get out of the house." No one in the room looked all that excited about the idea of Isabelle needing an escape plan, and although they were all on the same page, it made Isabelle want to puke.

"Fine, I'll go back in the closet if I have to, but no guys with assault rifles roaming the neighborhood."

After a bit of arguing between Holt, Ellen, and Isabelle, they compromised on Holt setting up camp inside the house. A security detail would do twice-hourly drive-bys, but the bulk of the protection was left to Holt. Lola, Moose, and Max had offered to take the point duty, but Holt refused them all. Isabelle felt safer knowing Caldwell would have to get through Holt if he wanted to talk. She had no idea when she had gotten so damned popular.

CHAPTER NINE

You've known all along the gunshot on the day we met was meant for me, haven't you?" Isabelle padded into the kitchen and shuffled to the coffee maker. It was four a.m., but she knew she wouldn't be sleeping any more. She hadn't slept past four in the morning for the week Holt had been staying at her house. During the day, Holt's employee, Lola, stayed in the house with her, followed her to the grocery store, the post office, or anywhere else, and Holt left, only to return looking a bit more exhausted every evening for another sleepless night on duty. Isabelle sat next to Holt on the couch and hugged her coffee cup to her chest.

"Yes," Holt said, her eyes laser focused but weighed down with deep circles and heavy bags.

"Why didn't you tell me?" Isabelle had lost the anger she had once felt toward Holt since she had been protecting her. It was harder for her to see what Holt did as just a job when her dedication, focus, and ferocity were for her benefit. Every night as Isabelle walked down the hall for bed, she looked back to her kitchen and was treated to the sight of strength and solid protection in the form of a scruffy haircut and well-defined muscles sitting at her kitchen table. While they had plenty of meaningless conversations at random hours when Isabelle couldn't sleep, they had yet to regain some of the closeness they had developed, and Isabelle missed it desperately. She had learned about Holt's predilection for comic books and spicy food, and shared her own interest in trashy pop music, but so far, they hadn't breached the walls they had both so carefully cultivated. It made Isabelle feel more alone with Holt in the house than she had felt without her there before her world turned upside down.

"In case I was wrong. I didn't want to scare you." Holt's voice was weary, her posture more slumped than usual.

"Are you wrong often?" Isabelle knew the answer. Holt's job was to be right, and every indication pointed to her being very good at her job.

"Why are you up? Can I get you anything?"

"Holt," Isabelle scolded her affectionately, "you're in my house. No waiting on me, or I'm going to dress you in a butler's uniform."

"I do look pretty good in a morning suit." Holt sat up straighter, puffed out her chest, and looked at Isabelle with the playful glint that had been missing since their aborted date.

It was the first time the flirtation was back in Holt's eyes, and Isabelle could have wept at the sight. She hadn't realized just how much she had missed the fun in their exchanges.

"Is that similar to a birthday suit?" Isabelle asked.

"Don't you just wish you could see me in my birthday suit?" Holt said, standing and stretching provocatively.

It was clear from the grimace as she unkinked the knots that seduction wasn't her intention. Isabelle's body didn't care what Holt's purpose had been; seeing the white T-shirt stretched tight across Holt's chest and the sleeves pulling taut to reveal another delicious inch of tattooed skin was all she needed to remember exactly why Holt had been so alluring the first time she laid eyes on her.

"Please don't look at me like that," Holt whispered, letting her arms drop to her sides.

"Why?" Isabelle felt like she was seeing Holt in all her glory, anew, and she just wanted to stare.

"Because I'm too tired to not tell you you're beautiful."

"I don't mind hearing it," Isabelle said quietly, moving closer to Holt.

"Everything that has been complicated since the beginning is still complicated. Hard to ignore that."

"We could for a night." Isabelle was so close she could taste Holt's essence on the air.

Holt froze. Isabelle could tell how conflicted she was, and how tired. She could see it on her face. If she pushed, she was sure Holt would give in. But seven days of this intimate living arrangement and she was seeing Holt differently. She wasn't just a hot woman to fuck anymore. Holt was putting herself on the line to protect her and she deserved better. She kissed Holt gently on the lips, took her hand, and led her to the couch.

"Tell me a story. How did you become a bounty hunter?"

"I can't tell that story tonight. You want to see a big bad bounty hunter cry?"

"Telling me would make you cry?"

Holt looked uncomfortable. "If I say yes, will you pretend I never mentioned it?"

"Um, no, definitely not."

"Then no, it won't make me cry."

Isabelle was wildly intrigued, but just as she did when the topic of sex arose, Holt looked too vulnerable to push. "Okay, no bounty hunter origin story. We'll save that for another night. What about your family?"

Holt visibly recoiled. "Can't do that one either. Besides, it's pretty much the same story. Why don't you tell me a story? How did you become an accountant?"

Isabelle was a little hurt that Holt didn't trust her enough to share important parts of her past, but she tried not to let it show.

"It's not that I don't trust you," Holt said, as though she could read Isabelle's mind. "I trust you too much. I want to tell you everything, but I'm too damned tired tonight to deal with what comes next. Emotional regulation isn't always a strength of mine."

"Okay, mind reader Holt, sit back and enjoy the story of Isabelle the accountant. It all began back in elementary school, where I'm sure almost all accountants begin. It really is a tale as old as time, the hopelessly nerdy math geek gets teased mercilessly throughout school and figures the best way to exact revenge is to forever control the monetary wealth of the people who tormented her. In the back of every client's mind is a tiny shred of worry that they went too far in high school and their accountant is secretly making them irreparably poor, a realization they will come to much too late. All of this is of course accompanied by ominous music."

"Oh, that's cold. Are you really holding high school tormentors hostage? I never suspected this side of you," Holt said.

"Me? No, alas, my revenge is only a figment of my imagination. I grew up in a small town in Nebraska, far, far from here and moved long before I became an accountant. As far as I know, I'm the only one from said town living here now, except my sister of course, and I would never torture her like that."

"I liked your sister. She looks just like you, but somehow not as hot."

Isabelle leaned back into the curve of Holt's arm, her head resting on Holt's strong chest. "Ellen hasn't stopped talking about you since dinner. If her husband wasn't the most laid back, sweetest man alive, I would imagine he'd be mighty jealous."

"How did you both end up in Rhode Island from Nebraska? I love my home state, but most people would have blinked and missed us on the way to New York or Massachusetts."

"My parents got divorced when I was fifteen. Ellen was seventeen. My mom said as soon as we were out of the house, she was moving to Florida. So one night, Ellen and I got out a map of the US. She spun me around about a hundred times and told me to point. I fell over an ottoman and my index finger punched right through Rhode Island on the way to the floor. Ellen applied to schools here, got into Brown, found an apartment, and we both moved. I finished high school just before we left. The best and only advantage to being the nerd I described before is you can finish high school really fast. I followed her to Brown a year later, and then went on to accounting school."

"And your mom moved to Florida? What about your dad?"

"My mom is about as happy as I've ever seen her in St. Petersburg. She has a boyfriend and a bridge club and a much better tan than me. My dad's dead." Isabelle saw the shocked look on Holt's face and rushed to explain. Once she started, it all spilled out before she could stop to think about how much she wanted to disclose. "Well, that's not technically true. He's remarried and lives in Arizona the last I heard, but it's easier to say he's dead. I haven't spoken to him since the day my mother said the word 'divorce.' He has no idea he has grandkids. Ellen says he never will."

Isabelle sighed as the memories cascaded over her. Sharing them with Holt felt natural, but they didn't hurt any less. "I came out when I was fifteen. Just plopped down at the dinner table one night and announced that I was into girls. My mom and sister hugged me and said it didn't matter to them, but my father slapped me so hard he knocked me out of my chair. He came around the table, put his knee in the middle of my chest, pinned my arms over my head, and said no child of his would be a homosexual and live under his roof, and then he broke my jaw. I couldn't breathe because of how he had his weight on me, but he stood up after he hit me so he could start kicking too. He pulled his foot back to kick me, and my mom hit him in the head with a frying pan, which, unfortunately, still had our dinner in it. It was all very soap opera. He started raging again, my mom said 'divorce,' packed us up, and I never saw him again. I presume she had to see him in court, but that was the last time for me.

"He'd hit my mom before, although she tried to hide it from my sister and me. There were a few times he would be dissatisfied with Ellen for her grades, or that she didn't have a boyfriend, and he would shake her too hard to 'get her attention.' I broke my arm when I was twelve because my father cuffed me when he caught me looking at a ladies' underwear commercial too intently during his football game. I tripped over the cord for the window fan. He made me stay and cry on the floor for twenty minutes until the quarter was over before he got my mom to take me to the hospital.

"He was an angry and miserable man. Even when he wasn't hitting someone or something, the threat was always there. We never could figure out what it was that set him off. To this day, I don't know why my mom stayed as long as she did, but I think the bravest thing I've ever seen is her standing up to him."

Isabelle felt at loose ends having told Holt as much as she did. On the one hand, it felt wonderful to share such a personal story and open up to Holt. On the other, she was a bit embarrassed at her emotional vomit.

"I'm really good at finding people," Holt said, rubbing Isabelle's hand and forearm. "I would love you to tell me it was okay to track this guy down and give him a piece of my mind. I can't fathom someone treating you or your sister so cruelly. If I knew your mother, I'm sure I would feel the same about her."

She should have known Holt would want to right the wrong and come to her defense, even years after the fact. It was one of her most endearing features. It also provided a bit of relief, since Holt didn't seem to think she had over shared. "He actually tracked my mom down in Florida a few years ago to invite us to his second wedding. My invite was addressed to 'the homosexual,' so I didn't think it was worth the trip."

"It seems shocking to me that someone else would marry him, and yet, your mother did, and he is part of you, so there must be something redeeming about him," Holt said. "No wonder you aren't thrilled with my job."

"I appreciate you saying that. Most people just trash him as an ass, which he is, but he's also my father. I just hope his particular brand of horror isn't genetic."

"If anyone is going to understand about complicated parental relationships, you're looking at her. I promise the full story another night. Thank you for telling me about your dad and your childhood."

"Hey, in the end it worked out for the best. Ellen and I moved here, started over, and now I get to spend my nights with a sexy woman, hoping desperately that a deranged man doesn't break in and try to kill me." Isabelle needed to get back on emotionally lighter ground.

"Well, I don't think your mother was the only one in your family to display a whole lot of bravery."

Even though Holt was listening intently and laughing at her jokes, Isabelle could tell she was tired. She was probably awake on willpower alone.

"When was the last time you slept?" Isabelle asked.

"I'm not entirely sure."

"Have you been working during the day? Lola always tells me you're at home sleeping, but I don't believe her. The amount of ground espresso she buys every day while I'm working at my rotating coffee shop interim offices is a giveaway."

Holt nodded. "We've got other cases, and Lola is with you while you're working from home, so we're down a man. I mostly just push paper around my desk and catch a catnap or two at my desk or on my office couch."

"Catnaps aren't enough, Holt. I'm assuming you have to work today?" Holt nodded again and Isabelle continued. "After work tonight, you go home. You can't stay here another night without some sleep. When you're rested, you can come back."

"I'm responsible for your well-being."

"Not tonight you aren't. Besides, you need sleep to be in tip-top baddy-repellant mode. Right now you look like Mickey Mouse could bowl you over." Holt started to protest and argue her fitness for duty, but Isabelle surprised them both and shut her up with a long, lingering kiss.

"You can send everyone from your office to stay here tonight. You can have people do walking patrols and park a tank on my front lawn, whatever you need."

"Then Lola goes to work with you today," Holt said. Her eyes lingered for a moment on Isabelle's lips, but closed slowly as she fought exhaustion.

"It's my first day back at the office. She might stand out."

"I'll leave the tank in the garage if you let Lola go with you today." Holt dragged a hand through her hair, looking bemused at having to negotiate someone's protection.

"Deal." Isabelle pulled Holt to her and rested her scruffy head on her lap. Holt was asleep instantly.

Holt walked through the door to the bounty hunter office still seething at her own carelessness. As wonderful as it had been waking up on the couch, curled up in Isabelle's arms, she had left Isabelle unprotected while she slept like the dead. It was unprofessional and unacceptable. Her mind was filled with "what ifs" and that in itself was so unusual it was adding to her general bad mood.

As had become rather routine, Max was sitting at a desk in the main office, staring intently at a computer screen, tapping at the keyboard and clicking away with the mouse. She didn't notice Holt's arrival.

"Report," Holt barked. "Anything else on the flowers? Have you found Caldwell?"

Max jumped out of her chair, knocking over three empty coffee cups in the process. Holt noticed five more scattered around Max's workstation.

"Um, good morning, boss." Max looked frazzled as she scooped up the empty cups and dumped them in the trash. "How's Isabelle, ma'am?"

"With Lola," Holt said. "Report, please."

"Superman is on his way over. Amy asked if you could watch him for a couple hours. Something about a shift change problem. Two new cases for you to look at. Neither look too high profile or difficult. One drugs, one domestic." Max counted things off on her fingers as she ran down the morning report.

"The flowers came from the shop listed on the card, paid for by Parker Caldwell. It seems his office had an open purchase order with the flower company, and he used that to send the bouquet to Isabelle. I guess if someone else knew about the open account, they could have made the purchase. It's almost as tough as if he'd used cash. But Danny came through with the ATM video. Nothing cooking on the break-in though."

"Max has been working on it all night," Moose said, strolling into the room, two cups of coffee in his hand. He deposited one on the desk in front of Max and took the other to his own desk. "We should probably force Max to sleep once in a while, but, damn, she's doing fine work."

"I'm right here," Max said, her face pinking.

"What'd you get from the video?" Holt made her way quickly to the computer screen, feeling anxiety and hope in equal parts.

"The footage isn't great, and parts are blocked by bank customers, but we did get this shot." Max pulled up a blurry picture of a person, probably a man, across the street from the ATM.

"Max, I can't tell a damn thing about him. This could be me." Holt wasn't really upset with her, and she regretted the harsh reprimand as she watched Max recoil. Max's eyes were red and it looked as if she had been getting makeup advice from a raccoon.

Moose glared at Holt and came over to lean on Max's desk. He put his hand protectively on Max's shoulder and encouraged her to continue. "Ignore the dragon lady. Show us what you were able to do with that picture."

Holt appreciated Moose's protectiveness. He didn't choose his friends casually, and if he was willing to put Holt in her place for Max, Holt was smart enough to get the hint.

"Max, please show me what you have."

"Well, I was able to enhance the quality and I ran it through a program I've been working on. Do you want to know the details?"

"No," Holt and Moose said simultaneously.

"Oh, okay, well, here's the final product."

Max tapped a few keys and a mid thirties, bald man with dark eyes and a long face appeared on the screen. He was holding a ski mask in one hand and seemed to be motioning to another person, out of the camera sight line.

"He was the only one to look at the camera. By my count, there were a total of three people, two men and a woman by the body shapes. They were in the building for twenty minutes."

"Who is this guy?"

Max looked at Holt, panic across her face. "I don't know, ma'am. I haven't been able to find him, although I haven't run his face through all possible databases."

"Print his picture and have some of the crew show it around. I want to know his name. And, Max," she said, remembering something Isabelle had mentioned to her a while ago, "find the names of all the local methadone clinic owners." Before Holt could intimidate Max any more, a flurry of tiny redheaded action distracted her.

"How's my favorite guy?" Holt asked Superman, scooping him up and flipping him upside down. He was the best bad mood killer she had ever found.

Superman only giggled in response. After a few minutes, he began squirming, and one, "Down peas," was all he needed to be on his way. He made the rounds, tapping all Holt's employees on the leg and then grinning before yelling "Hi!" as loudly as he could. Two-year-olds were ridiculous creatures.

While Superman was working the room, Holt greeted Amy and deposited Superman's diaper bag and mountain of toys in her office. She never minded the days her office turned into a playroom.

Eventually, Holt trailed after him and checked in with each of her employees, a normal routine to begin each day. This was a job she loved, and the people who worked for her were competent and loyal. Hers was an empire she had built over time and with great effort. Some of the tension of earlier relaxed. She trusted that this group, and the ones on patrol, or off work, would help her find Isabelle's attackers. And she wasn't doing anyone any good being a grumpy ass.

"Hey, Superman!"

He stopped mid climb, almost halfway onto Max's lap and looked at Holt. "What waydee?" he asked with typical two-year-old attitude.

"Oh, your mother and I are going to have to have a talk," Holt muttered under her breath. "You ready to go play?"

Superman jumped down from Max's lap and ran, as well as a two-year-old can run, full speed at Holt's knees. "Fissy chair, fissy chair" he squealed as Holt scooped him up and carried him toward her office. For some reason, her office chair was his favorite toy. He never tired of spinning himself around and around until he was so dizzy he could barely stand.

When Superman was comfortably settled in her chair and contentedly spinning away, Holt stretched her aching legs in front of her on the floor and leaned against the wall. She pulled her cell phone from her pocket and flipped it from one hand to the other wondering if she would seem like an overbearing stalker if she called Isabelle.

After waking in Isabelle's gentle, sure arms, she couldn't get images of Isabelle from her mind, and if she were honest with herself, she didn't really want to banish the slide show that was making her belly flutter. It had been much easier to see Isabelle as a client before Isabelle had briefly kissed her and before Holt had unromantically fallen asleep on her.

She groaned when her phone rang and her mother's number flashed on the screen. Just when she was starting to snap out of her bad mood.

"Hello, Mother."

"Is that any way to greet your mother?"

From hard-won experience, Holt didn't say a word, just waited for an explanation for the call from the other end of the line.

"The gala is coming up. You must be there."

"Fuck!" Holt said under her breath since Superman was five feet away. She had forgotten all about the event her mother spent a year planning. How could she have forgotten?

"Language!"

"Sorry. Shit! Better?" Holt didn't know why needling her mother came so easily, or provided so much perverse pleasure. Sometimes she felt guilty about it until she realized her mother probably got the same joy from hassling her. It was really all they had in common.

"Marginally. Have you produced any grandchildren yet?" It was a standard question during these chats. Holt hated it.

"Those take about nine months last time I checked. You saw me two weeks ago so I think you would have noticed."

"Don't be silly. I wouldn't expect you to carry one." Holt ignored the dig at her sexuality. "Why can't you procure one like that Thomas Christopher boy?"

"Who?" Holt reached out and steadied Superman, now lolling happily and dizzily in her chair.

"The boy your friend adopted, the one from foster care." These last words were said in a whisper as if saying them aloud meant you were somehow in support of such a radical idea as child services.

"Superman? It took her almost two years to adopt him. For now, you're out of luck."

"Huh, well, at least bring a date this time. I get tired of introducing you as my gay single daughter. It is bad enough you insist on seeing women, even worse that you don't even bother to bring one as a date. It makes it seem like something is wrong with you. You know how that reflects on your father and me."

Holt knocked her head back into the wall after she hung up the phone. Talking to her mother was the only time when self-inflicted bodily harm seemed like a reasonable stress relief.

"Uh oh, you've been talking to your mother. I know that look." Jose was appraising her from the doorway. "What did her high holiness have to say for herself this time?"

Jose could be a pain, but Holt didn't feel like punching the wall anymore. Jose had that effect on her, and he was one of the only people she knew that wasn't afraid of her mother. He had been there when her true nature had shone through and had made it clear he had no use for her. Holt felt the same way, but was unfortunately bound by blood.

"The charity gala is upon us again. I don't know why I ever agreed to this. She's upset I don't have children yet, and even worse, that I don't have a date. It makes my parents look bad you know." Holt knew her voice gave away her hurt and bitterness.

"Sweetheart, having you as a daughter is the only way that old troll will ever look good. Date or no date, she's lucky you will pose for pictures with her. That said, are you going to take this opportunity to get the new office favorite out on a date? I know your weakness for blondes, and Isabelle is hot enough to make me consider batting for your team."

Holt rolled her eyes. "You already bat for team gay. If you want to play my particular game, you're gonna have to cut off your dick." She laughed when Jose's hands shifted to his groin protectively.

She would have shot down the suggestion if she hadn't already decided she was going to do just that. Perhaps if Isabelle could see her in a different light, being a bounty hunter wouldn't be the only thing that defined her. "I'll ask Isabelle if you finally put us all out of our misery and ask Moose to go with you."

Jose turned red and looked horrified. "What are you talking about?"

"I can't stand another year of you moping around because he doesn't ask you, pouting when he goes with someone else, and then ignoring him for three months after. It confuses the hell out of him you know."

"Do you need me to watch Superman this afternoon?" Jose quickly changed the subject, still quite red. "And you really should watch your language around him."

When Holt had to work on her days to babysit, the rest of the crew, and a few guys from Jose's shop, looked after Superman. Amy never minded when he came home happy and exhausted from a day of twenty babysitters.

"Crap." Holt jumped to her feet. The bright red note that had come with Isabelle's flowers was currently under assault from Superman's green crayon.

She pulled the card from under the crayon and almost dropped it again when she saw what Superman had uncovered. Clearly outlined just below the layer of crayon was the beginning of an address. The indentation of the writing had formed through whatever page the address was written on.

"Keep coloring, buddy," she said, giving the card back to Superman, who was none too happy to have had his masterpiece snatched away. "Max," she hollered out the door, wondering as she did, how the office had run without her.

Max materialized quickly. "Yes, boss?"

"Stop with the boss," Holt said distractedly, still watching Superman's progress. "Find me everything you can about this address."

❖

As the day dragged on at her first day back at work since the office had been ransacked, Isabelle became more and more overwhelmed with the reality of her life. Despite being confident that kicking Holt out for the evening was the right decision, her choice meant spending the night without her superhero, protector, and rock of sanity. That was something she wasn't looking forward to. It was much easier to pretend all was fine with the world tucked away safely under Holt's vigilant guard. It was also far easier to fall asleep dreaming of Holt's outrageous hotness sitting right down the hall. There was a definite advantage to that line of distraction, even if it meant wild, sweaty dreams that left her tired and frustrated.

Wanting to regain some illusion of control, Isabelle put work aside for the afternoon and began digging through her client list. She had no idea what she was looking for, but somewhere, maybe, there was a clue to the craziness that had overtaken her. Her first perusal was of the goofy file Decker Pence's secretary had mistakenly sent. Despite his assurances, she couldn't let that one go.

Three hours later, it was time to head home for the day, and Isabelle still didn't understand the erroneous file, but after scouring her client profiles, she had a list of five potential threats, as she had begun to think of them. Two had connections to Representative Caldwell.

One had a son who had been in and out of rehab, although that was based on rumor alone; one was a pharmacist, and the last one had a job description that just screamed fake. Isabelle had never known what a "product analyst and distributor" was, but now it seemed like just the sort of title that might hint at something shady. She printed the list to give to Holt in case any of the potential threats actually did have merit. She was fully aware as she shut down her computer and followed Lola out the door that paranoia was now once again a part of her daily life. It wasn't a comfortable thought or feeling, and it was made worse by the wary glances and furtive whisperings of her coworkers as she walked past.

Lola steamrolled out the door and cleared a path of all oncoming pedestrians as they made their way to Holt's truck. Holt had insisted Lola drive, taking Isabelle to and from work and anywhere else she wanted to go. Isabelle didn't mind. The truck smelled like Holt, and she found the feel of it reassuring, as if the truck belonging to Holt would keep her safe.

"Where to, ma'am?" Lola hadn't spoken much more than three sentences all day. But that wasn't unusual. Lola was always quiet when Isabelle was working, and while it should have been reassuring, there were times when it felt too much like being babysat.

"Lola, you have to stop calling me ma'am. Are all of Holt's employees this polite?" Isabelle was exhausted after an emotional day.

"I don't know, ma'am...sorry...Isabelle. I'll try to remember. Where would you like to go?"

Isabelle sighed. She should go home, unload the dishwasher, do laundry, and finish the two tasks she hadn't managed to finish during her workday, but she wanted to see Holt. Where she really wanted to go was Holt's loft, but she asked Lola to drive them to the bounty hunter offices instead. Being scared witless most of the time made it easier to see the sides of Holt that were often masked by the bounty hunter bravado. In the middle of the night, when Isabelle woke up, thinking she heard a noise in the house, Holt was incredibly tender, gentle, and kind. It was getting harder for Isabelle to see the monstrous vigilante she had originally made Holt out to be so she could keep her own heart safe.

Jose's repair shop was quiet when Lola eased the truck to a stop. Isabelle and Lola walked around back and pushed through the doors to Holt's hidden kingdom. That too was quiet, but there was an air of tension that was difficult to ignore.

Max sat hunched over a computer screen, intently focused on the monitor, absently clicking the mouse from time to time and glancing nervously at the phone every few minutes. She didn't seem to notice Isabelle and Lola.

"Max?"

Isabelle wanted to hug her when Max almost jumped out of her chair in surprise. Her eyes were bloodshot and she looked like hell. Her hair was tousled from running her fingers through it too many times. She was the picture of exhaustion.

"Max, you were wearing those clothes yesterday," Lola said, sounding concerned.

"She's not here right now," Max said, ignoring Lola. She looked pained as she unfolded herself from her hunched position and stretched.

"Walk with me," Isabelle said, taking Max's hand and leading her away from the computer. "Can you tell me where she is?" She wasn't sure she wanted to know.

"She said to tell you she's working on keeping you safe and for you not to worry."

"'Cause that's not a pile of poo big enough to try and block something really scary. Are you going to tell me where she really is?" Isabelle opened doors and poked her head into offices trying to find a good place for Max to lie down and sleep.

"She found an address indented on the back of the note that came with your flowers. She wants more information. She said it wouldn't take long, and I think she wanted to be back before you got off work."

Isabelle nodded, having already suspected Holt was out trying to save her world. Her worry for Holt was momentarily blunted by her worry for Max. There was something Max wasn't telling Holt, but it wasn't her place to get in the middle. She was shocked when she opened a door—to a broom closet no less—and found a sleeping bag and camping mat crammed in a corner. The look on Max's face was all the confirmation Isabelle needed that they belonged to Max.

With minimal protest from Max, Isabelle removed the secret sleeping quarters and dragged the sleeping bag, mat, and Max to Holt's office. She laid them neatly on the floor next to the crib Superman was currently sleeping in and pointed Max into them.

"Sleep for a while," Isabelle said. "I'll get you if anything happens," she added, countering the protest she could see building.

"You aren't going to tell the boss about this are you?" Max asked, sounding like a small child hoping desperately her secret misdeed wouldn't make it back to her father. She crawled into the sleeping bag and her eyes were closed before Isabelle turned to leave.

"No, but you have to." She flipped out the lights and shut the door to Holt's office.

Isabelle sent Holt a text, sat down with Lola and the one other woman still working, and waited.

❖

Holt approached the three-foot high chain link fence. She wasn't rushing, but she also didn't want to appear cautious. Pacing was everything when walking up to a house, business, or person without wanting to attract attention. You had to look like you knew what you were doing and belonged. People only noticed others when they were moving too quickly or too slowly, or looked rushed or lost.

She was dressed as she normally was, blue jeans hung low and baggy, this time accompanied by a long sleeve T-shirt. She blended in, and that made life a lot easier when sneaking around other people's houses.

The house she was targeting was nondescript, a little shabby with a scraggly lawn, surrounded by a low chain link fence and matching gate, but no different than any other on the block. The white paint was peeling in places, but the windows looked new. The blinds were drawn tight. No one had come in or out in the two hours she and Moose had watched.

Although Moose had complained, Holt moved down the street alone. She didn't have her bat with her, and a woman walking down the street with a baseball bat wouldn't have gone unnoticed, nor would a woman walking down the street with a brick house of a man at her side. Except on rare occasions, she didn't believe in carrying a gun, so for this jaunt, she was unarmed. Guns, she found, gave you an overly comfortable view of your safety.

She pushed through the gate and walked confidently to the backyard. She climbed the three cement steps, pulled open the squeaky screen door, and held it ajar with her hip. She made a small show of fumbling with what would look to the casual observer like her keys, and had the door open in less than fifteen seconds. She tucked her lock pick tools back into her pocket and closed and locked the door behind her. She was in.

The back door opened into a small, dirty kitchen with peeling, well-worn linoleum and puke green Formica countertops scarred by burn holes. A small table was shoved into a corner and covered in newspaper. Lined up in neat rows were small empty bottles, only slightly larger than the ones doctors usually drew from when giving shots. The screw tops were laid neatly beside the bottles. She snapped a quick picture with her phone.

Holt moved forward cautiously, not wanting to be surprised. She was relatively sure no one was home, but she also wasn't in the mood to get stabbed or shot. Beyond the kitchen was a small, untidy living room with the saggiest, dirtiest couch she had ever seen. It was brown and one of the cushions was missing. The coffee table held a piece of thick elastic tubing and a spoon, nothing else.

The rest of the house was down a short hallway off the living room. A quick glance revealed two doors off the hall, one presumably the bathroom, the other a bedroom. Holt moved slowly, listening for sounds of life from either room.

The bathroom was the first door she came too, and luckily, the shower curtain was pushed to one side, showing it to be empty. The bathroom looked like it should be contained in a biohazard tent, and Holt was happy to not have to check behind the curtain for bad guys. A razor sat on the edge of the sink next to a brown toothbrush. A single bar of grime-smeared soap sat in the soap dish in the tub.

When she got to the bedroom, she was saved more unpleasantness, as there was no bed to look under. A full size mattress, sheetless and stained, was tossed in one corner of the room. Cinderblocks spaced about two feet apart held a piece of plywood next to the bed. On the makeshift bedside table was another spoon, four cotton balls, and a small bottle of water, filled halfway. A box full of clothes sat in the opposite corner. At the foot of the bed was a pile of copper bits and pieces, and close to twenty cans of baby formula.

Feeling she had stayed about as long as she dared, and pretty sure she had seen all this dwelling had to offer, Holt made her way carefully back to the kitchen. The sound of a car horn blaring loudly from down the street set her on high alert. The sound of a key in the front door made her glance back into the living room where she noticed a cashbox, the kind that children often carry, that locked in the front and had a slot for change in the top, under the coffee table. Cursing her carelessness at missing it the first time through, she hurried as quietly as possible to the back door, pulled it open, shoved her way through the screen door, and groaned as it squeaked loudly in protest.

She didn't wait for the shout from the house to get moving. She was off, running through the small yard, hurdling the fence, and tearing off down the block by the time the alarm was raised. She cut through a driveway, ran half a block up a perpendicular street, then cut back and ran back down a street parallel to the one the shabby house was on. She moved quickly and soon turned onto Thayer Street, a popular, well-populated, and bustling main drag a few blocks from the Brown University campus. She slowed to a walk and joined the crowds flitting in and out of the many restaurants and shops. She called Moose and told him to sit tight. He was pissed but did as he was told. She didn't blame him for being mad. His loyalty had saved her life more than once over the years.

She pushed into a small market, hoping they would already have a few back to school items. She purchased a cheap backpack and a Red Sox baseball hat. Farther down the street, she found a pair of baggy shorts, complete with cargo pockets, and a baggy hooded sweatshirt. Although she could call anyone from her crew and they would come get her, she wanted to have a look at the house and what firestorm, if any, her B & E had set off. The change of clothes was a precaution. She had no way of knowing if whoever had been opening the door got a look at her, although she doubted it since they didn't seem to see her until she was almost out of sight.

She changed into the new clothes, shoved her jeans into the backpack and the ball cap on her head. She tucked her hair up as best she could knowing that with the backpack, hat, and baggy sweatshirt, she would look very much like a young boy on his way home from summer school or the library. She had been called "son" enough in her life to know how she was perceived. It was that kind of quick assessment she was counting on. Rhode Islanders kept their heads down and didn't make eye contact, the perfect situation to advance a cover.

To test her new persona, she purposefully bumped a passerby, mumbled something that sounded like "sorry" and was rewarded with a "s'okay, son, just watch where you're going." Most people just didn't look that carefully.

She walked quickly back toward the house she had fled, her shoulders hunched, her face set in a defiant scowl. Her baggy shorts hung well below her knees, and she walked with a bit of an exaggerated swagger. She looked like half a dozen other teen or preteen boys in the neighborhood. They all worked hard to set themselves apart, but beneath clothing color, skin color, or hairstyle, their actions and mannerisms were the same.

When she turned the corner and approached the house once again, she slowed her pace imperceptibly and fiddled endlessly with her cell phone. Although it appeared as though she wasn't paying attention to anything but the tech toy in her hand, Holt was hyper aware of her surroundings.

Sequestered behind the chain link fence, hunkered down on the saggy front porch, a young man was talking animatedly into his cell phone. The front door was ajar, and a quick glance didn't reveal anyone else inside, although she couldn't see much of the room. A large dog stared at her from the porch next to the man on the phone.

Holt was glad the dog hadn't been in the house. He looked like he could do some damage if properly motivated. As if reading her mind, the dog stood and leapt off the porch, barking loudly as he rushed at the fence. Cell phone man yelled at the dog to shut up, snapped his phone closed, and glared at Holt.

"What the fuck you looking at, kid?"

She made the decision in a split second and, although risky, the chance to learn the man's name was too enticing to pass up. This guy looked similar to the man in the picture from the ATM. Holt answered.

"That Jimmy's dog?

"Jimmy? No, it's not fucking Jimmy's dog. I don't know no Jimmy. Go away, kid."

"Looks like Jimmy's dog. He used to live around here. Maybe you took him. What's your name? I'm gonna ask him."

Anger blossomed in the young man's eyes. Holt knew she was pushing it. Her voice was deep for a woman, but not so much that you couldn't tell if you listened carefully. Luckily, this guy seemed preoccupied and wasn't paying attention to much except his cell phone, which he was glancing at every few seconds.

"I didn't take no dog from no fuck named Jimmy. Dog's mine. Now seriously, kid, go away."

While she was trying to figure out how to continue the conversation and learn the man's name, she felt Moose slide up beside her. He put a possessive hand on her shoulder and gripped hard. She felt the silent message and stood quiet.

"Bobby, where the hell have you been?" Moose was looking directly at her. "You're an hour late, and I swear, I should kick your scrawny ass right here." For effect, he slapped her across the side of the head, knocking the baseball hat askew.

She fixed it defiantly but slumped her shoulders even more, silently giving in to the abuse.

"Sorry 'bout him," Moose said, turning to the stranger. "Always sticking his damn nose where it don't belong."

The young man looked up from his vibrating cell phone and nodded to Moose.

"I'm Mike Tate. If you need a paint job on this house, look me up. I got my own business, and it looks like you could use my services."

Moose held his hand out and looked at the man on the other side of the fence, daring him to not shake. Holt kept her head down, looking and acting like a chastised, sulking teen.

"Diamond, like the jewel," the man said, leaving out his last name, probably figuring either Diamond was a unique enough first name that he didn't need it, or subtly telling Moose to go to hell. "I just rent here. Thanks for the offer though."

Moose nodded and replaced his hand on Holt's shoulder, this time closer to the scruff of her neck. He got a good grip on her sweatshirt and jerked her violently away from the house. She stumbled and then fell in step just ahead of him, letting him lead and push her around all he needed.

"If you change your mind, look me up. I'm listed," Moose said as way of good-bye.

The man with the phone didn't look up again. He pressed send and looked worried as he listened briefly before going in the house, yelling for his dog, and slamming the front door.

Holt stumbled along in front of Moose a while longer, keeping up the charade, even letting him shove her roughly into the passenger seat of the beat up, ancient Crown Vic he had borrowed from Jose.

They waited until they were out of the neighborhood and headed back to the shop before they both started laughing.

"Damn, H, you're getting good at sullen teenager. It took me almost a full minute watching you walk up the block before I made you. With Isabelle back around, I wouldn't expect you to look so angry." He absorbed the playful punch to his arm with a smile.

"Bobby? That's the best you could do? Of all the names in the world, you had to go and assign me yours?" Not many people knew his real name.

"Speaking of which, what the hell were you doing talking to that guy? He's the one that almost busted your ass you know."

"Kinda figured," Holt said. "We got his name, didn't we? You getting soft in your old age? We used to do shit like that all the time."

Moose ignored Holt's challenge. "I think I got the name actually, assuming he's telling the truth. What the fuck were you going to do when you were done with accusing him of stealing someone else's dog?"

Holt faltered, but only for a second. "I hadn't quite worked that part out yet."

Moose laughed. "Does Isabelle know what a pain in the ass you are to be around and care about?"

"Not yet, and don't you dare tell her."

CHAPTER TEN

"Good Lord, are my attackers middle schoolers?" Isabelle asked, lighthearted teasing in her eyes.

"Someone here decided to go undercover and..." Moose trailed off when Holt turned away from Isabelle and glared at him.

"Is it too domestic sounding if I ask you how your day at work was?" Holt asked, trying to redirect Isabelle's attention.

"I thought my coworkers were going to faint at the sight of Lola. Other than that? Business as usual." Despite her smile, Isabelle sounded vulnerable and a bit anxious.

"I'm going to change. All done with the school boy look. I need to meet with some of the crew and then we can get Superman and I'll take you home. Is that okay?" Holt squeezed Isabelle's hand as she moved off. She could see the strain of current events more and more clearly on Isabelle's face. She had to find Caldwell soon.

She was also sure she saw Isabelle's gaze lingering on the crotch of her baggy shorts and the half smile on her face when Holt made eye contact. Had she just been checking to see if she was packing?

She tripped once and had to shake her head to clear it three times in the fifteen feet to her office door. She realized the bad guys she tracked down every day were the least of her worries.

When she flipped on the lights to her office, she was greeted by a field of land mines in the form of race cars, stuffed animals, an empty portacrib, and Superman sprawled, sound asleep, across the chest of an equally tired Max. They each had an arm thrown above their heads, Superman's covering Max's eyes. They were actually quite cute. If Holt had any idea what the hell was going on, she might have stopped longer to appreciate that fact.

She backed out the door, flipped the lights off, closed the door, and turned around. Surprisingly, it was Isabelle who leapt forward.

Holt held up her hand, not needing Isabelle to explain. "Clearly, Superman can get out of his crib, and I think perhaps Max and I need to have a chat."

Isabelle nodded. "You do, but I put her in your office. I forgot, sorry. I didn't know about Superman."

"Never apologize for taking care of people I care about. She looked like hell earlier, although I was too busy yelling at her to really notice."

"You're a public menace. Women as sexy as you, with a bleeding heart and a conscience shouldn't exist," Isabelle said. "It's not good for my blood pressure when you look at me like that."

"I felt like this the first time I saw you, you know."

"I do know. You were looking at me with your big melty sex eyes then too. Don't you have work to do? People are starting to stare." Isabelle looked amused. They were talking too quietly to be overheard, but Holt figured the look on her face needed no explanation. A week on Isabelle's couch was a long time.

A short time later, Holt had cooled off and gathered those of her crew she either trusted unquestionably or had been working on keeping Isabelle safe from the beginning. Someone had woken Max so she was there as well, looking disheveled but less like she was on death's doorstep than she had earlier. Against Holt's better judgment, Isabelle was also present. She had insisted, and Holt couldn't tell her no.

These staff meetings weren't unusual when they were tracking a particularly high profile or difficult bail jumper. It helped to have everyone on the same page, and despite how good she was at her job, Holt knew she couldn't see or think of everything. They were a team in the truest sense of the word.

Besides that, most of the time, she didn't lead the hunts. The smaller cases were farmed out to her crew, and they only met with her for a briefing and with questions as they arose. Since her business had grown, she had taken a more managerial role unless the case was particularly interesting. Despite her best efforts, she couldn't stay off the streets. She had been working them for ten years. It was a hard habit to break.

"We've got a name to track now. Diamond. There can't be too many of those in the state. I have no idea how he's connected, if at all. His house was that of a user, not a criminal mastermind or big time dealer. He doesn't have the resources to be coming after Isabelle, so there must be a reason we aren't seeing for the address being on that envelope."

"How do you know?" Isabelle was focused and taking notes.

"He had drug paraphernalia, rubber tubing, spoon, cotton, water." Isabelle clearly still didn't understand.

"Heroin users cook the heroin in a spoon to melt it, and then pull it up through the cotton to filter it. The water is for rinsing and dissolving the heroin, usually before cooking, but sometimes cooking isn't even needed. The tube is to tie off to get a good vein. This guy also had baby formula and copper shreds, both of which can be sold on the street for a bit of extra money. My guess is he's breaking into houses, busting up the walls, stripping the copper, and selling it to make ends meet." Holt felt in her gut that Diamond was connected, even if she didn't know how.

"Oh."

Holt guessed this was a world far outside the realm of anything Isabelle could imagine.

"I also saw a lockbox, like a kid's cashbox, bright red, under the coffee table in the living room. The kitchen was the strangest part. Table was covered with little plastic bottles, about this tall." She held her thumb and forefinger about three inches apart. "There were probably fifty of them, all empty, screw caps sitting next to the bottles. It was the neatest thing about the house. Here's the picture I got."

"They look like the bottles the methadone clinic hands out. Makes sense with the IV works and the lockbox. To get a take-home dose at a clinic, you have to have a container that locks. Lots of people use those red cash boxes," Moose said.

Holt looked at him. She was the only one at the table who knew what sharing that information meant to him. Although the rest of the people sitting at the meeting probably wouldn't realize how he came by the information, she knew that his recovery from an almost fatal addiction wasn't something he shared lightly. He wasn't ashamed of what he went through, but it was still something difficult to make public. She knew his love for her and her desire to keep Isabelle safe trumped his own desire for privacy, and he would stand on the rooftop yelling about his heroin addiction if it would help.

"Is it possible all those bottles were for him?" Lola asked.

"Nope. First of all, there weren't labels on them. They're labeled like prescriptions when they leave the clinic. Second, you can't get more than fourteen doses at a time. I've heard of clinics that give take-homes for longer, but they don't tend to stay in business. The state isn't fond of unregulated narcotics."

"Could he be a dealer? Maybe selling to Caldwell and that's why the address was on the envelope?" Lola asked.

"He probably is dealing, given the number of empty bottles around. He may even be dealing to Caldwell, but it's got to be more complicated than that. A simple drug user-dealer relationship doesn't explain the first red note, why Caldwell thinks Isabelle isn't safe, and where the hell he is." Holt ran a hand through her hair.

"First note?" Isabelle said.

"Someone tried to scare me away from you when we first met," Holt said. "I probably should have told you about it, but you were already mad at me for not being the one getting shot at. I didn't think hard evidence was the way to win you over."

Isabelle looked like she was trying to decide if she wanted to take issue with Holt never mentioning the first note.

"Seems like it would be helpful to talk to Diamond. He might have information we want," Moose said. "Maybe we can run some kind of scam to get him to talk? We know where he lives, but it might be more useful to see what he's up to with those bottles. We could try to find his clinic."

"Isabelle, you said one of your clients owns a methadone clinic, right? We could start there. Moose, you could get me looking like a heroin addict in withdrawal, right? I could learn more if I was inside," Holt said. She was in planning mode, thinking only of keeping Isabelle safe. Diamond had seen her, but as a teenage boy, and she doubted he would remember.

"Aren't there other people at the clinics?" Isabelle asked. "If I were them, I wouldn't want you tromping all over my privacy just to talk to some dude you could just as well confront in the parking lot."

"I think we could get Holt looking like a heroin user pretty easily," Moose said with a wink. "Problem is, there are a lot of clinics in the state. We don't know where he goes, and we don't want to blow this by guessing wrong. Methadone patients are a chatty group. If we start asking around, we'll probably spook him. Plus, if he has his works at his house, he's probably relapsed so he might not be in treatment any more, or he could have switched to Suboxone. If we want to take a guess, we should start with a clinic closest to his house, or Isabelle's client's place. There are two in Pawtucket. I'll ask a buddy of mine if he knows Diamond. He's been to just about all the clinics in the past few years. If that doesn't work, we can put a car on him, but we gotta be subtle. I bet he's on a pretty short leash by whoever he's working for, especially if he's using. We might want to explore other options for getting to know Diamond."

"If she does this will she be safe? If she gets into the clinic, or greets him in the parking lot I mean?" Isabelle asked, concern distorting her delicate features. "I don't want you doing this if you might get hurt. We'll get him some other way."

"Oh, now you're worried about my safety? You weren't too concerned when you were getting me all hot and bothered," Holt said so only Isabelle could hear.

Not to be deterred, Isabelle persisted. "So? Danger?"

"Some," Holt said. "We track criminals. It's part of it." She shrugged and looked away.

"The clinics have security guards, but there are a lot of people moving through a small space in a short amount of time, and most of them are in some stage of withdrawal until they get dosed. There's a lot of waiting in line until you reach the dosing window. Tempers can flare. Most of the clinics limit the amount of time you can spend milling around the lobby and have pretty strict rules about entering and leaving the line," Moose said.

"You'll be careful?"

"Always," Holt said.

"Okay, good by me. Let's catch the bastard."

"Diamond doesn't own that house, boss." Max had been tapping away at her computer while the others talked. "It's owned by a guy by the name of Gary Cappelletti. No record that I can find. He's owned it since two thousand and four."

"Cappelletti?" Isabelle stared at Max.

"You know him?"

"The name sounds familiar, but I can't pinpoint why. Damn it! I made a list of my clients with any ties to Representative Caldwell, so maybe that's why it sounds familiar. If they are after me, my business is the only reason I can think of." Isabelle handed the list to Max, who went to work on her laptop, typing in the names and cross-checking the results. "I also got a strange file from Decker Pence's secretary. It's all on the list."

"Speaking of Caldwell, we need to find him before he comes and visits Isabelle. We've been looking for three weeks. Where the fuck is he?" Holt asked.

The meeting ended without an answer.

When the rest of the group dispersed, Holt loitered at the table to talk to Moose. It was completely out of character for her to suggest infiltrating a methadone clinic. It felt wrong coming out of her mouth. Perhaps there were one or two less than upstanding citizens seeking treatment, but she didn't feel it justified breaching the confidentiality of the rest of the patients. Most bounty hunters wouldn't think twice about lying their way into any situation that was beneficial to finding the bad guys. She understood the sentiment since it was her job to get the criminals off the streets. On the other hand, innocent bystanders should have their privacy respected and their lives uninterrupted. She had always felt that way and done her best to run her business by those principles. Protecting Isabelle was making her crazy, or maybe it was the job finally wearing her down. She wondered how many other times she had stuck a toe over the line and not even noticed.

"How do you guys know so much about the streets and live so comfortably in this world?" Isabelle asked, interrupting Holt's chance to talk to Moose privately.

"You never get used to it," Moose said. "But I lived in the gutter as a young man, so the street seems like an upgrade."

"The gutter?" Holt said, not sure that was an accurate description. "And had you even started getting facial hair yet? I don't think you were any kind of man." Holt had trouble remembering the creature Moose had been when she had bailed him out of the intake center in the state prison ten years earlier. He was like family to her, and remembering him in so much pain made her heart ache.

"Gutter, jail, whatever. You bailed me out, and that's all the detail I need to remember. Although I would rather have stayed in jail for the torture you put me through. She handcuffed me to a radiator for three days in the dirtiest apartment I've ever spent a night in." Moose was laughing, nothing but devotion and love on his face.

Holt searched Moose's face, willing to change the subject if he didn't want to disclose his past to Isabelle. He smiled and nodded so she defended herself.

"Hey, I stayed with you through all of it. I fed you, when you would eat, and I listened to you call me every name you could think of the whole time. It was good practice for the creeps we pull in since they can't come up with anything he hasn't already called me. Besides, I used all my money bailing him out. I was a kid too. That shit hole was the only place I could afford. He was delirious. I was the one that had to deal, in a completely lucid state of mind, with the rats and cockroaches."

"I remembered every curse and degrading word in the book, but couldn't remember my own name. She kept calling me Moose, and it made me so mad. I had no idea what she was talking about," Moose said, looking at Isabelle.

Thinking of the pain Moose had endured made Holt sad. "He hit a Moose on his motorcycle when he was sixteen. I probably told him the story about ten times during those first few days. He was a legend and couldn't remember a thing about it," she said.

"That accident is when all the drugs started. I got addicted to the pain pills and switched to heroin when I ran out of the others. I was shooting within a year. After I cleaned up, I told H if she ever had to detox someone again, for their sake, get them some meds to help with the withdrawal. I swear if she didn't have me cuffed to that radiator, I probably would have killed her."

Holt felt a little guilty about her rough treatment of Moose, but she wasn't about to let him get away with teasing her. "It worked out all right for you, big man. Besides, I was eighteen. What did I know about heroin withdrawal? At least I was pretty sure it wouldn't kill you."

She remembered the day he was coherent enough to ask to go to rehab. She unlocked the cuffs and drove him herself. He had been clean ever since. Moose had told everyone that would listen that Holt had saved his life. In truth, he had done the same for her. She had watched a good friend get his head blown off, and when the man who shot him skipped out on court, she became his target. Aside from the people at the boxing gym, she had no other support. Her parents were useless. When Moose cleaned up, they became an unbeatable team. Their business had started with tragedy and the determination to be more than anyone around them believed they could be.

"It worked out all right for both of us. H got me as a business partner. Really, what more could she have hoped for out of that situation?"

"And you've been doing this ever since? How did you get into bounty hunting from heroin addiction?" Isabelle asked.

"That's a story for another time," Holt said. She wasn't ready to share that much of herself with Isabelle. It was a simple question with a very complicated answer.

CHAPTER ELEVEN

Isabelle leaned against the doorway to Holt's office. Holt didn't notice her, so she took a moment to watch as she packed up Superman's belongings. Holt looked exhausted, and Isabelle noticed the uncertainty and questions in Holt's eyes. They had been spending more and more time together, and the line between genuine feelings, fear, and forced closeness was blurred. Based on the increasing number of opportunities Holt was finding to be close to her, Isabelle suspected Holt was struggling with the same thing. As Isabelle watched, Holt took a moment to enjoy the snuggle Superman seemed to reserve just for her.

"I think I might be getting in trouble here, little man. I just don't know what kind," Holt said softly.

"Are you talking to yourself and using the baby to cover it up?" Isabelle asked.

"I would never use an innocent sleeping child as my fall guy." Holt rocked Superman lightly as she turned around, diaper bag and toys stowed on her shoulder.

"Give me your keys. I think it's time to get Sleeping Beauty in his car seat."

"Why are you taking my keys? Are you going to drive me into the woods and have your way with me?" Holt asked, but even that sounded tired.

"That's the best you can do?" Isabelle teased her. "As much as I'm sure you would enjoy that, no, I'm driving Superman home, then I'm taking you home, cooking you dinner, tucking you in, and checking in with my minders for the night. You aren't going to argue."

"Oh. I'm not used to being bossed around, but it's also kind of a turn-on. Dinner sounds nice."

"When you start taking care of yourself at half the intensity you're trying to take care of me, I'll stop handling you." Isabelle was concerned about Holt but didn't want to scare her by showing just how worried she was.

"You can handle me all you want," Holt said, looking a little perkier.

"And I see someone is feeling a little better. Get in the truck."

Holt obeyed and they were soon on their way to Amy's house. There was so much Isabelle wanted to say, how afraid she was, how overwhelming the situation was, how much she was enjoying Holt and her care, but she stayed quiet. Her independence was important to her, but more importantly, she thought she might have actual feelings for Holt, and that was scaring the hell out of her. Holt was, despite everything else Isabelle had learned, a bounty hunter, and she was still in tremendous danger.

Whatever the outcome between the two of them, she refused to build something based on Holt always taking care of her. Holt was already carrying too much of the burden alone. She realized that each hour that passed that Isabelle's attackers weren't caught wore on Holt in ways she was only just coming to recognize. Isabelle felt bad she was so quick to point out the invasion of privacy of the other methadone clients. Holt and her team knew the job better than she did. Maybe that sort of thing was routine, but the looks on the faces of the group when she suggested it made Isabelle doubt it.

"Why was Max asleep in my office?" Holt asked, looking half asleep herself.

"I honestly don't know why she was so tired. I could tell she needed sleep, though, and I knew your office was safe. Sorry. I forgot to warn you." Isabelle didn't tell Holt about the contents of the broom closet.

"Where did the sleeping bag and camping mat come from?"

Isabelle rolled her eyes. Of course Holt would pick up on that.

"I think you might need to talk to Max about all this, sweetie."

Holt nodded and was asleep before they came to the next intersection. She didn't wake even when the truck stopped in front of Amy's house and Superman was passed back to his mother.

"She okay?" Amy asked, looking worried. "Maybe she should just stay here. I'm sure she won't mind you keeping the truck."

"Thanks, but I'm going to take her back to her place and let her sleep in her own bed for once. She's done so much for me these past few weeks, I want to repay her in this small way until she lets me take care of her for real after all this is over."

Amy looked at Isabelle intently, studying her a moment before she responded. "I see the way she looks at you. Please be careful. I love her too much to see her get hurt."

"What do you mean the way she looks at me? What about the way I look at her?"

"I don't know you well enough to judge how you look at her compared to others. I can only tell you what I know about Holt, and what I know is that she doesn't look at anyone else like she looks at you."

"She's very dedicated to her job, Amy; you know that. Right now she's made it her job to protect me. I'm in danger. Of course she looks at me differently than she does her friends or family."

"If you believe that, you're a lot stupider than you look," Amy said with a half smile.

"Good night, Amy." Isabelle didn't know what to do with the new information that Holt reserved a special look just for her. She had liked thinking that Holt's smiles or quick glances were special, but it felt different now that she knew Amy could see a difference too.

❖

"Gary, this better be pretty fucking important. It's two a.m. You woke up my wife."

"I'm sorry, Decker, but Diamond just called me. Caldwell's gone."

"What exactly do you mean by gone?"

"Well, you know how they've got him stashed at the empty house in Cranston? They keep him chained up and drugged, but they let him up to take a piss and he got away."

"Holy shit, how incompetent are the guys you had watching him? What did he do, crawl out the bathroom window?"

"Um," Gary's voice was quiet and stilted, probably from panic.

"Don't even tell me. I don't want to know. Have you figured out who broke into Diamond's house a few days ago? I don't like the coincidence."

"He didn't know, boss. He didn't see him. He opened the front door and heard the guy hauling ass out the back. He was gone when Diamond got out the back door."

"Get everyone you can to the accountant's house. That's where Caldwell's going. I'll bet you it was the bounty hunter you said not to worry about that was at Diamond's house. Diamond was probably too high to tell if he was seeing a man, woman, or alien. It would be just like her to stick her damn nose where it doesn't belong. Was our supply there?"

Gary sounded relieved as he was finally able to pass along some good news. "No, boss. The supply is locked up tight, just like you told me. The only things there were the empty bottles. Diamond's on methadone, and if they check on him, it looks like he's got a little side business going."

"Get to Isabelle Rochat's house. Fix this mess. Call me when it's done."

"Won't he go to see the bounty hunter?"

"No, that's where he should go, but he won't. It's the first place we would look for him. Besides, the bounty hunter's been staying at Ms. Rochat's house."

"What do you want me to do with him when we recover him?"

"Finish him. This has gone on long enough. His little stunt tonight pushed his usefulness below his risk level. This may actually help us. Caldwell was becoming a liability. Warehousing drugs is one thing; people are a bit harder. Keep it clean though. I do not want our fingerprints on it. An overdosed drug addict is not as suspicious as a bullet through the head. You have to get to him before he makes contact with Ms. Rochat. Understand?"

"What about Rochat?"

"I'll remind you again, we're not the mob. This is business. Caldwell knew that. He called us. But the more bodies that start piling up, the harder it is to keep the police off our tail. That being said, if Ms. Rochat is going to blow the whistle, protect the business."

"Got it, boss. We're on our way."

❖

The phone woke Holt from a wonderful dream. She and Isabelle were in Tahiti, staring at the gorgeous ocean, wearing nothing but the sunshine. She was slow to let go of the fantasy.

"Lo," she said.

"Holt, he's here. Someone's here."

Isabelle was whispering, but her voice was strained and she sounded terrified. Holt was awake immediately.

"Are you at home? Can you get out like we talked about?"

Holt was throwing on clothes, shoving on shoes, and silently thanking Isabelle for calling her cell phone instead of the home phone. If she had to ask Isabelle to call her back, she might have gone insane. As it was, she was barely able to tamp down her own panic. The perfect beach scenario of her dreams was replaced by images of Isabelle lying naked on an autopsy table. Holt felt bile rise in her throat and her mouth started to water. This wasn't the time to vomit. It wouldn't do Isabelle any good. She got her body back under control.

"I'm at home. I can't get out, Holt. Lola told me to hide in the closet, but I haven't heard anything from her. I guess it's only been a couple minutes, but it feels like an hour. I'm terrified."

"I'm coming, baby. I'm on my way. I'll be there. I'll keep you safe. You stay hidden. When I get there, you tell me where you are. Don't tell me right now in case someone can hear you, or if you have to move."

"Please don't hang up." Isabelle's voice rose.

Holt was three minutes from Isabelle's house. The trip usually took fifteen minutes, but she ran four red lights and ignored every speed limit posted on her route.

She couldn't call in backup because she would have to hang up with Isabelle to do that. She hoped Lola had been able to reach someone at the office before whatever was going on at Isabelle's had started.

"I'm around the corner, Isabelle. I'm going to be there in a minute. Now I need you to tell me where you are." She could hear Isabelle's frightened breathing and it was tearing at her sanity.

"Guest bedroom closet, like you told me."

As Isabelle was relaying her location, the sound of breaking glass and shouting was painfully clear through the phone. Holt slammed the truck into park and vaulted into the night, hitting the ground at a sprint, heading for Isabelle's front door. In no other circumstance would she be this careless with her own safety, but right now, all that mattered was Isabelle.

She was mounting the front steps when gunfire registered through the phone. "Isabelle! Are you okay?" She knew she was practically shouting, but she could barely think, and every instinct she had was screaming at her to rush through the door.

"I'm frightened enough to pee my pants, but I'm still okay. Holt, put the phone away. If you're coming in here, you need both hands and all of your brain. Come and get me when you're done. And do not get shot."

Isabelle's plan made sense, but Holt was reluctant to let go of the tenuous tie she had with her beautiful, perfect Isabelle. Still, it was the only way she could ensure her safety.

"I'll be right there. Hang tight."

Once the connection was broken, Holt was able to find enough distance to think like a bounty hunter and not react in fear. The front door was open. She edged through it carefully and slipped in the house. The lights in the front of the house were out. She stuck to the shadows and moved quickly toward the bedrooms and Isabelle.

As she was creeping toward the hall, she heard Lola shout, a gunshot ring out, and Lola cry out in pain. She raced toward the noise, hoping Lola wasn't seriously wounded. She peeked around the corner and saw Lola laid out awkwardly on the floor. She wasn't moving. Two men in masks and dark clothing stood at the end of the hall. When they saw her, they opened fire.

Close quarters shooting wasn't as easy as it seemed in the movies, and composure when the crashing sound of the shots were ringing off the walls around you was something that was learned over time. These guys had obviously not learned yet. They were amateurs, and each of their shots was wilder than the one before. Although Holt knew the shot that killed you could just as easily be meant for another target, she liked her chances better knowing she was up against amateurs.

In a move she was sure the men would never have expected, she turned the corner and sprinted down the hall, directly at the men shooting at her. As she had hoped, they were stunned into momentary inaction and stopped firing. She made the first man in five long strides. He raised his pistol again, readying to take a shot at a target too close to miss, when Holt unleashed a right hook.

It was her experience that guns left people overly confident, and hardly anyone with a pistol in hand bothered to think about defending themselves. Unlike these guys, she wasn't an amateur, and criminals of a higher class than these had pointed guns in her face before. Although she was unarmed, there was plenty of room for her to maneuver her feet and use her fists. This was the kind of fighting she was best at.

When Holt's fist impacted with the man's jaw, she felt the crunch of a broken mandible. Aside from a bad shot, he was also a poor fighter and didn't know to close his mouth when getting punched.

Once his jaw was broken, he became more erratic and popped off three shots into the ceiling. Although Holt figured he had to be nearly out of ammunition, she didn't want his last shot to land in her ass. She jabbed a quick, sharp shot to his nose and followed with three lightning fast punches to his body. She didn't know if she had broken ribs. It was possible, but she did know he was done shooting for a while when he hit the ground and curled into the fetal position, his hands over his face.

While Holt was disarming the first man, the second scurried into the bedroom as he saw how things were going for his friend. Holt plucked the first man's gun from his hand as he writhed on the floor in pain and stripped it down, removing the magazine, racking the slide, checking the chamber, and removing the slide. The gun was in pieces in less than ten seconds. Just because she didn't like carrying guns didn't mean she didn't know how to use them. She pointed what was left of the weapon at the man on the floor and pulled the trigger. There was no firing mechanism or ammunition, but he flinched anyway.

She kept the clip and the slide and dropped the rest of the gun on the guy's head and carefully moved around him, setting up her entrance to the master bedroom where his accomplice had disappeared. She glanced into the room and saw the second gunman leaning over a third man sprawled on the bed in a Vitruvian Man position. Isabelle was popular tonight.

Holt yelled and ran at the second gunman, realizing who it was lying on Isabelle's bed. The gunman leapt away from the bed and looked around frantically to find an escape. He still had his gun in hand, but didn't seem to consider using it.

"He'll be dead in less than a minute if you don't do something about it," the man taunted her. "It's me or him."

"Why should I give a fuck about him?" Holt asked, not giving up the angle to the door, but keeping an eye on the man on the bed.

"He came here for a reason. There must be something he wanted to say."

"Your name is Diamond," Holt said. She was guessing because it was dark, but the voice was familiar.

The effect on Diamond was instantaneous. His shoulders slumped, then bunched in tension, and he rushed Holt and the door. She let him go. She knew who he was; he confirmed it with his reaction. She also knew where he lived. What she needed to do now was figure out how to save Representative Caldwell.

When she got to the bedside, she realized why she had so little time. An empty syringe was still in his arm, a rubber tube neatly tying off the vein just below. His breathing was shallow and he was listless. She guessed opiate overdose. She wondered if these guys had orders to make it look like an accident. That only would have worked if they could have kept him out of Isabelle's house. She didn't know why they didn't just shoot him.

The decision to try to save Caldwell before checking on Isabelle and Lola went against every instinct. She hoped she wouldn't live to regret it. She had a small hospital's worth of supplies in her truck. She was his only chance. As she ran from the room, she noticed Diamond had dragged his accomplice with him when he made his escape. They had even managed to pick up the gun pieces. She glanced at the extra bedroom as she sprinted past, but didn't want to shout to Isabelle in case there were still bad guys around. She just hoped Isabelle knew to stay hidden until she came to get her.

As she rounded the corner to the front door, she had to leapfrog Lola, who was conscious and crawling in the direction of the kitchen, bleeding from her left temple. Holt stopped her single-minded sprint, checked the wound, and saw that the bullet had only grazed Lola's head. She probably had one hell of a headache. Holt inserted her forearms under Lola's armpits and quickly dragged her back to the doorway to the extra bedroom. Lola's eyes were unfocused, and she looked in danger of nodding off, but she was a better bad guy deterrent than anything else Holt had if Diamond, et al, decided on an encore.

"Lola," Holt said, holding her face to try to force her attention. "I need you to call Moose. Tell him where we are."

"All did ready," Lola said, producing a cell phone from her tightly clenched fist.

"Good woman. I'll be right back," Holt said and again sprinted down the hall toward the door. Even if Diamond had been exaggerating, she didn't have much time to save Parker Caldwell.

On her way to her truck, she called 911, reported the emergency, a suspected overdose, and that she was beginning treatment. She hoped they would arrive in time, as she didn't have much Naloxone with her.

She retrieved the opiate antagonist from her truck, sprinted back to the house, and returned to Caldwell's side just in time for him to start seizing. He was barely breathing, and when she tried to hold down his arm, just enough to get a new needle in the vein, his skin was cold and clammy.

Holt injected a small dose of Naloxone, wanting to reverse the effects of the opiate overdose, but not wanting to send him into immediate withdrawal, which would be excruciating. From the look of his track-marked arms, he had a pretty serious habit. The first dose of Naloxone had no effect. She gave him more. His eyes shot open and he looked terrified. He grabbed her arm and pulled her down to him, whispering in her ear. She didn't know if his consciousness was a result of what she was doing, or some Herculean effort to rid himself of the dirty secret he was carrying before he died, but after he confessed, he lost consciousness again, his breathing even more shallow and labored after the exertion.

Moose bolted into the room as Holt was administering the third dose of Naloxone. "What you got, H?"

"OD, not responding very well to the counter."

"How much have you given him?" Moose stood on Caldwell's other side and checked his pupils.

"Three doses. He should be responding better." Holt was frustrated.

"They could have mixed the shit they gave him with something else, Suboxone, tranquilizers, or gotten him drunk." Moose looked disgusted. "I think he's fucked."

"Go check on Lola. She needs a Band-Aid and probably has a concussion. And please get Isabelle out of the closet, but do not let her see this."

"Max is with Lola, and I checked in with Isabelle before I came in here," Moose said. "She's on the bed in the extra bedroom, helping Max with Lola, I think. Lola had talked her out of the closet before I got here so Isabelle had already started to clean her up."

Holt pulled Caldwell to the floor and began CPR, waiting for the paramedics. She considered it a minor miracle that Caldwell was still alive when they started working on him. They carted him off to the hospital, and she was left with helpless rage—at not being able to prevent this from happening, at Caldwell, at Diamond. At feeling utterly out of control, a sensation both foreign and unwelcome. Suddenly, the only important thing in her life was seeing Isabelle's face. Just thinking of Isabelle quelled some of the fire threatening to consume her.

Isabelle was sitting alone on the bed, her arms wrapped protectively around herself, her hands and shirt red with Lola's blood, and she looked like she was losing a battle to hold back her tears. When Holt walked in, Isabelle jumped from the bed and rushed into her waiting embrace. The torment Holt felt evaporated, quickly replaced with relief that Isabelle was safe.

Isabelle had the ability to do what no other person or thing had ever done, quiet the demons lurking in Holt. She hadn't ever felt this way before. It felt nice to know someone else could calm her when she couldn't calm herself, but she wasn't used to needing anyone quite like that either.

"What took you so long?" Isabelle asked, her face buried in the comfort of Holt's neck. "You smell like sleep, and sweat, and superhero."

"Sorry, got lost on my way over," Holt said lightly. "Had to stop for some breakfast. Never good to face bad guys without a full stomach."

Isabelle punched Holt lightly in the shoulder and kissed her. The kiss felt different. It was just a little more—more intense, more passionate, more promising, just *more*.

"Do you need to stay for the police?" Isabelle looked like she didn't want to spend another minute in the house.

"Unfortunately. I don't think they'll be satisfied with catching me later at the office. They'll want to talk to you too." Isabelle started crying again. "Only if you're up for it," Holt said quickly.

"This night just kinda sucked. I'm a little overwhelmed. I'm kinda over the gunshots. Is anyone else hurt?"

Holt slid her hand from Isabelle's shoulder, and Isabelle welcomed her as their fingers intertwined. "How about tonight we stay like this and see if together we can get through whatever they throw at us?"

Isabelle nodded, and they walked hand in hand to the living room to speak with the cops.

CHAPTER TWELVE

After waiting for the police and recounting every detail of Isabelle's close call, Holt was wound tight and struggling to contain her restless energy. She was angry, frustrated, and wildly turned on. She had been living in such close proximity to Isabelle, under stressful circumstances, for over a week, and tonight she had almost lost her. She wanted to reconnect with her, check out every inch of her, make sure she was safe. She also didn't know how to get rid of the feelings tearing her up, and sex seemed far more enjoyable than hours at the boxing gym. She had been sitting with Isabelle glued to her side for two hours, holding her hand and trying to keep her from looking at the bullet holes in her walls. It was taking its toll.

"Do you mind if we go to your place?" Isabelle asked.

Isabelle seemed to be experiencing the same longing as Holt, because once in the truck, she wasn't shy about letting her hands wander all over her. She caressed Holt's thigh, smoothed her hand along Holt's abs, and ran her fingers through her hair.

"It's not generally a good idea to tease the animals," Holt said. "You're driving me a little crazy here."

"Good," Isabelle said. "I know we're not supposed to be going there, and I'm sure it's the adrenaline and trauma, but I really want you—need you—right now."

Not knowing if it was a good idea, but too tired to care, Holt said, "I'm all yours."

When they skidded to a halt in front of Holt's building, Holt leapt from the truck and ran around to open Isabelle's door. Isabelle sprang into her arms and Holt held her, feet off the ground, kissing her senseless. With one foot, Holt kicked the truck door closed and Isabelle wrapped her legs around Holt's waist.

There was nothing they could say to each other to make the trauma they had suffered any less, but they could share the emotions with touch, kiss, and passion. It felt like they were trying to explain what they were feeling with each kiss. They kissed frantically, passing the tension back and forth until it was less terrifying and felt more manageable.

They stumbled up the outside stairs, leading to the private entrance to the third floor, neither relinquishing the other's mouth. When Holt glanced away from Isabelle long enough to punch in her personal code to open the door, Isabelle latched on to her lip and gave a less than gentle tug. The door clicked open and they fell through, landing in a heap of tangled limbs in the entryway.

Isabelle was on top and took full advantage of her position. Holt's shirt was off and discarded, hitting the door that one of them had managed to kick shut. The sight of Holt's exposed breasts sent Isabelle over the edge. She was straddling Holt's hips and working on tracing yet another one of her tattoos when she looked Holt over and stopped what she was doing.

"Do you even know the meaning of the word cheeseburger? Muscles and tattoos, God, you're sexy. If you take your pants off, I'll probably explode."

Holt enjoyed the scrutiny of her upper body. Isabelle's stare was primal and her hunger apparent. She could feel the heat travel across her skin, following the path of Isabelle's attention. Before Isabelle recovered fully and could begin working on her pants, Holt turned the tables. She pumped her hips once, throwing Isabelle off balance. In a fluid motion of a much repeated sit-up movement, Holt sat up and caught Isabelle against her. She raised her knees slightly, allowing a measure of support to Isabelle so she could remove her shirt.

Isabelle's nipples tightened against the cool air and in anticipation of things to come. Holt pulled Isabelle to her, raising her knees higher, forcing Isabelle's smaller frame tighter to her body. Their kiss wasn't gentle or tentative. The night had been too emotional and stressful. The need between them pulsed in the still air.

"You said you had a bed?" Isabelle asked.

When Holt nodded and pointed, Isabelle sucked Holt's lower lip into her mouth and tugged. Holt was forced to follow Isabelle's lead or lose her lip, and ended up flat on her stomach on the floor of her entryway when Isabelle abruptly let go and moved away. Isabelle was playfully sashaying to the bed, probably making sure Holt was getting the full effect of her impressive ass. Holt executed a push-up a Navy SEAL would have been proud of and set off in pursuit.

They collided in a tangle as they reached the bed, and Holt's momentum sent them tumbling onto the soft comforter. This time Holt ended up on top, and she didn't waste the opportunity. Before she streamed a line of kisses along the long, elegant neck below her, she pinned Isabelle's hands above her head and held them there. At the base of her neck, Holt bit down, eliciting a tiny scream from Isabelle.

Trusting Isabelle to leave her hands where they were, Holt traced the curve of Isabelle's breasts with one hand, using the other to unbutton Isabelle's pants. With only minimal help, Isabelle shimmied out of her jeans and everything underneath. Holt's head spun. She felt drunk taking her first look at Isabelle's beautifully naked body. Although she had slept with plenty of women in her time, nothing had prepared her for this.

She let her body lead the way, since her brain was useless, and she followed her instincts. Replacing her hand with her mouth, she worked her way around Isabelle's breast, not quite touching her nipples. She used her hand to do the same to Isabelle's other breast. One whimper from Isabelle was all the encouragement Holt needed. She sucked one rock hard nipple into her mouth and bit down gently. Isabelle moaned and held Holt's head tight to her, arching off the bed, encouraging her to take more. Holt did, switching her attention between one and then the other. She briefly wondered if she could make Isabelle come like this. It seemed like a possibility.

Isabelle slipped her hand down Holt's torso and swiftly unbuttoned her jeans.

"No underwear. I like it," Isabelle said.

"I didn't have time earlier. I wanted to get to you." Holt briefly felt the vulnerability of earlier, but drove it away.

Isabelle continued her exploration. Holt was wet and hard and shuddered at her touch. As Isabelle stroked harder along Holt's already erect clit, Holt growled and pushed her knee between Isabelle's, forcing her legs apart and spreading her own in the process.

Holt pulled herself back up Isabelle's body far enough to have access to her mouth and also make it easier for Isabelle to enter her. Nearly ready to come from the few strokes already delivered, she wanted them to get off together. She smoothed her hand down Isabelle's body, feeling the tight peak of a hardened nipple, the fluttering of her stomach as her breath increased its pace, and the silky hairs meeting between her legs. She was wet and just as hard as Holt.

They joined first lips and then bodies as each drove into the other. Isabelle arched up as Holt slumped lower, connecting their bodies along their entire frames. Holt tried to block out the rushing in her ears and head as she struggled not to come. She wanted to wait, and most importantly, she wanted to please Isabelle. Their moans mixed with fierce kisses as they drove each other closer to the edge. Holt pumped her hand faster, matching the rhythm of Isabelle's hips, feeling the muscles around her fingers contracting in the first waves of orgasm. Isabelle pushed deeper into Holt and they came hard and loudly, calling out their pleasure.

Holt lowered herself onto her side, but didn't remove her fingers. She rubbed her thumb across Isabelle's clit and was rewarded with a swift intake of breath and the immediate rise of her hips. She came quickly and seemed to melt into the bed, looking supremely happy. Holt had never seen someone so sexy or so beautiful. Seeing Isabelle without fear or paranoia in her eyes was a gift so precious, Holt was willing to work forever to keep her happy. She had a feeling it was going to be a long night.

CHAPTER THIRTEEN

Isabelle didn't wake until late in the morning. When she and Holt had finally fallen asleep, the sun was just sliding over the horizon welcoming a new day. Despite the attack in her home the previous night, she felt relaxed and happy. Sex with Holt was good like that.

Isabelle could tell Holt was agitated, though she was clearly trying to hold still. Even though she hadn't let go of Isabelle all night, her arms were vibrating with tension, and she didn't look like she'd just woken up.

"How long have you been awake?" Isabelle asked, leaning her head back and kissing Holt.

"A little while. Just doing some thinking," Holt said. "I think it's too much of a coincidence that one of your clients owns a methadone clinic and Diamond had all those bottles in his apartment. I need to follow up."

"Aren't bounty hunters the action type? Shouldn't you be kicking in a door or something?"

"I can't reach the door from the bed," Holt said, smoothing Isabelle's hair and kissing the top of her head, pulling her closer as she did. "I didn't want you to be freaked out when you woke up. I didn't want you to be alone this morning, and I didn't want you to jump to conclusions about last night, so I stayed. I'm sure my crew can keep things running without me today. Lola called in sick for you too. I hope I didn't overstep by asking her to do that."

"I know what last night meant, Holt," Isabelle said, but even as she did, she wasn't sure it was the truth. She had expected to still feel unsafe this morning, but in Holt's arms, she didn't. She had also been counting on one night being all she needed to get Holt out of her system. If possible, she wanted her even more this morning.

"That's good," Holt said, "because I don't have a fucking clue."

"I don't either," Isabelle said. "I really like having sex with you. That I'm sure about. But your job, my past, last night. I still don't know, Holt. I wish I did. I thought I would."

Holt held Isabelle a little tighter. "I really like having sex with you too. At least we can agree on that. I still have to protect you. I still have to find who is chasing you. I honestly don't know if I can do that if we're sleeping together every night. Usually, I count on a certain level of detachment."

"You can't keep running yourself ragged," Isabelle said. "Can you let someone else take over at my house every night?" Isabelle didn't like the thought at all.

"No way. I barely survived tonight. I trust everyone I work with, but not with your life." Holt looked queasy.

"Where does that leave us?" Isabelle asked.

"Horny and exactly where we were yesterday morning, I think," Holt said, apology in her eyes.

"Fine, then tell me a story to distract me. Why do you do this job?" Isabelle asked. "And I don't mean why are you okay with the violence, or what motivates you to come to work every day. Tell me why you started this company. Tell me why you do what you do. I'm so anxious all the time, and you and your people are so competent, but I think it would help me to understand you better." Holt had rejected her request for this story once before, but knowing more about Holt seemed more important. How could she decide if she was okay with what Holt did without knowing why she did what she did?

Holt tensed, not a lot, but enough for Isabelle to notice.

"I mostly became a bounty hunter to piss off my parents. And it turns out I'm pretty good at it," Holt said. "You have to go back much further to get the full story though. Jose, Lola, and Moose are all involved. I've known Jose since childhood and Moose from middle school. Lola joined the team later."

"But there's more to it than that, right?"

"Moose, Jose, and I were best friends in middle school and high school. There was a fourth guy, George, who was part of our group. Then it all came apart."

Now Holt was wound tight, her body a coiled, vibrating ball of tension.

"You don't have to tell me—"

"I want you to know," Holt said, seeming to make a conscious effort to relax. "I told you how Moose got his nickname. His motorcycle accident that led to his opiate addiction."

It seemed like Holt was on a roll, and Isabelle didn't know what to say anyway, so she stayed quiet and waited for Holt to continue.

"Moose started to drift away from the group. Jose, George, and I were still tight though. George was the only one who really understood why Moose wasn't around too much. I don't know for sure, but I think George was mixed up with some of the crowd that supplied Moose's habit. We were young and he wanted so badly to be cool and tough. One of the dopes he hung out with convinced him to get a gun for protection, and to make him look like hot shit."

Isabelle rolled onto her back and pulled Holt into her arms, her heart hurting in response to Holt's trembling voice. It felt good to hold all that raw emotion and power and know it was where Holt wanted to be.

"I was boxing then, mostly just to piss off my mom, so I wasn't as involved in George's day-to-day shit. Jose hung with me at the gym. Neither one of us knew the mess George had himself in. I still don't have a fucking clue what the whole story is, but he slept with the wrong girl, or threatened the wrong dude, or just mouthed off at the wrong time. I don't know. We were walking home from the gym one day because he decided he should learn to fight, so I was teaching him, and he had that fucking gun tucked in the front of his pants. We both felt like that made us invincible. No one would mess with us if he was carrying. No one except the guy George had pissed off. He walked up, pulled the gun from George's pants, shot him in the head, pointed it at me, laughed, and walked away. It's like he wanted me to know how dumb I was for thinking that a gun made me safe."

"Oh my God," Isabelle said, pulling Holt into a crushing hug. "You were a kid. No wonder you don't carry a gun for work. How do you get over something like that?"

"You don't. I still see his face as he got shot sometimes. I held him in my arms for the few minutes it took him to die," Holt said, almost whispering. "Moose heard and really freaked out. He started using more and more. I tried to talk to him, but he was like a different person. It was just me and Jose for a while, and then Lola came along."

"How does she fit in the picture? Girlfriend?"

"No, she's George's baby sister."

"She didn't blame you did she?" Isabelle was beginning to see why Holt was so maniacal about protecting her and catching her tormenter. It must tear Holt apart when she can't right a cosmic wrong. Isabelle wondered if constantly chasing those who deserved it was a way for Holt to work off her guilt at not saving her friend. Isabelle wasn't sure she would have survived a trauma like that. Her childhood had marked her in ways she was still discovering, but everyone had come out alive.

"No, I don't think she ever thought I could have done anything different. We just felt like we owed each other something. I don't know when that debt will be paid on either side. I was glad to have her around though, because about a year later, shit got really hairy." Holt sighed heavily and shifted in Isabelle's arms before continuing. "I didn't know at the time, but the cops had a video of George getting shot. The guy who did the deed was a big time drug dealer with ties to a major cartel. He was on the FBI's ten most wanted list. When the feds got a lead on him, they came knocking at my door asking me to testify against him."

"How old were you?"

"Eighteen. Jose was seventeen and Lola was sixteen." Holt shook her head like she couldn't believe she was ever that young. "I said I would. I felt like I owed it to George. The next day, the US Marshalls showed up at my door and said if I was testifying, the only way to stay alive was witness protection, for me and my family."

"That's what? New life, new name, no contact with your old friends?" Isabelle couldn't imagine giving up everything she had ever known.

"Yeah, you can't even keep pictures or mementos of your old life. Anything that could tie you to your old life has to be left behind. I was on my way to a Golden Gloves championship at that point. I didn't want to give up my boxing career. I would have, though, except my parents flatly refused to join the program. They said it would have been too much of a sacrifice to give up their charity work, their foundation, their friends, their connections, all because their daughter happened to see a drug dealer kill another lowlife."

"They actually said that? Your parents refused to let you join witness protection because it interfered with their social calendar? And they called your friend a lowlife?" Isabelle was beyond outraged. She sat up so quickly she unceremoniously dumped Holt off her chest and onto the bed.

"Hey," Holt complained, "bring back my pillows."

"Sorry," Isabelle said, resuming her reclined position but retaining her rage.

"They couldn't forbid me to do it. I was eighteen. I could have gone if I wanted. But I didn't want to give up boxing, and if I wasn't safe, Jose and Lola probably weren't either. The US Marshalls weren't going to offer protection to them, but if anyone had been watching me the year prior, they knew who I was spending all my time with. I made the stupid decision to forgo the protection and testify, identity intact. I moved out of my parents' house. For a while, I was bouncing around between friends' houses, the boxing gym, and other less pleasant locations. Just my luck the guy who killed George escaped the FBI's custody. He had been implicated in lots of shit before, but nothing ever stuck. That's why the FBI was so excited about me. I was an extraordinary eyewitness. Three guesses where it was rumored Mr. Murderer was headed once the feds lost him."

"I think I see where this is going," Isabelle said, kissing Holt before letting her continue.

"When I heard the trouble I was in, I moved full-time to the streets. I didn't want to risk any of my friends' safety. Jose still hasn't forgiven me for going it alone, but I sidelined him. He's not a fighter, and for a while, I was better on my own. Eventually, though, I needed help. That's when I looked up Moose. We had lost touch because of the drugs, the trial."

"Do I even want to know where you were living?" Isabelle asked. Holt shook her head and Isabelle left it alone.

"Moose was rotting in jail when I finally found him. He described to you the torture I put him through. I was too young to know better. I needed him and I needed him clean. I don't know why, but it worked. He never touched smack again. We both know how extremely rare his story is. That's just not how recovery is usually done, but that time together is the bond that keeps us tighter than family now."

"The two of you tracked down one of the FBI's most wanted? By yourselves, at eighteen?" Isabelle wasn't sure why she was so shocked. She hadn't observed anything to suggest Holt wasn't up to such a preposterous task, but it seemed shocking all the same.

"Took us six months, but we found him."

"Where is he now?"

"In the ground," Holt said grimly. "The second meeting, he had the gun and the overconfidence, and I had my wits. He chased me blindly through an abandoned mill building and was too busy lining up his shot to notice the stairs were broken. He fell six stories." Holt sighed. "Moose and I were famous for a little while, and we started the business. We've been tracking people ever since. Lola joined as soon as she was eighteen."

"I don't know how you're still emotionally in one piece," Isabelle said. She had always suspected Holt's backstory was complicated, but she couldn't have guessed this kind of horror.

"It's funny, but until I met you, I would have said I was doing just fine, thank you," Holt said. "Now I wonder how true that is. I suppose that's not a pain you get over quickly, and I realize I would do anything to protect you. I wonder what that means about me sometimes."

"It means you're wonderful and about the most principled, dedicated person I have ever met. But don't worry. If you step over the line, I'll bring you back," Isabelle said, feeling like it was the least she could do.

❖

"Diamond's freaking out, Decker. I'm not sure how useful he's going to be for a little while," Gary said, not making eye contact with him. "Our two weeks are almost here. What do you want me to do with the supply?"

Decker was having trouble deciding how to react to the latest development in the mess that his prize operation had dissolved into. Parker Caldwell was dead, an unfortunate necessity since the man had outlived his usefulness and become a headache, but Diamond had been sloppy, and the bounty hunter had recognized him. If Decker could keep his link to the heroin addict hidden, the supply was fairly protected.

"Proceed on schedule. Don't let Diamond anywhere near the supply in case Lasher is watching him. You stay away from him too. I don't want his name linked to mine."

"I'm a little worried this is going to set him off. He's been on the edge of relapsing for weeks. He's got a big mouth when he's using."

"Well, make sure he stays quiet then. Get him in rehab and remind him of the consequences of being too talkative." Decker didn't like to inflict pain personally, but the power of being able to order it done intoxicated him. "I'm going out of town for a few days. You'll have to get by without me."

"Business or pleasure?" Holt asked from the doorway, looking too relaxed for Decker's liking.

Decker was disgusted to see Gary flinch. For the hundredth time this week, he reminded himself of the pitfalls of working with idiots.

"Holt Lasher, what a pleasure," Decker said, taking in the foe filling his doorway.

"I'm sure," Holt said, her face neutral, but her eyes burning with rage. "I don't think we have ever been introduced."

"What do you want?" Gary asked rudely.

Decker inwardly cringed and wished there was a way to dump Gary through a hole in the floor, although he wasn't happy to see Holt Lasher either. There was a semi-automatic pistol in his top right desk drawer. He took a moment to imagine what it would feel like to pull the trigger and the thrill he would get seeing the bullet slice through Holt's body. He wondered if he could hit her between the eyes. But he was trying to lessen his complications, not increase them. Having to hide a body, install new carpet, and find a therapist for Gary would be a headache. His moment of fun wasn't worth it.

"Please forgive my colleague for his rudeness. This is my accountant, Gary. He's a numbers man, if you follow my meaning.

Usually, I only allow him to talk to himself. I've heard of your reputation as a bounty hunter, Lasher, but you're right; we've never formally met. I think we would get along well, however. We have a lot in common."

"I'm not sure about that," Holt said, "Where are you escaping to?"

If Holt's question had a hidden accusation, Decker couldn't detect it in her voice, which was calm, almost lazy, and because Gary's rudeness had backed him into a corner, he had to answer. She wasn't accusing them of anything and so far had been pleasant. If he followed Gary's lead and was rude, it would give her more reason to be suspicious and poke around. In all honesty, it didn't seem like the woman needed much of a reason to be nosy.

"Colorado. A friend is loaning me their house for the week."

"Abandoned his ski house for the summer, huh? Such a shame. It's beautiful in the mountains this time of year."

"A common misperception," Decker said, not sure what Holt was getting at. "Not all of Colorado is mountainous."

Holt was looking around Decker's office and seemed to be paying particular attention to Gary. She was physically intimidating, but her expression, piercing yet devoid of any specific emotion, was obviously making Gary twitchy. She looked like a very large dog locked on to an unsuspecting squirrel. Given the way Gary had conducted himself over the last six months, Decker was uncomfortable with her scrutiny.

"May I help you with something?" Decker asked. "I was just finishing up a few business matters with Gary before heading home to pack."

Holt looked Decker in the eye, her gaze unflinching and aggressive. She stepped forward a foot, using her powerful frame to fill Decker's line of sight. On a lesser man, the intimidation probably would have worked. Gary would be scared dead by now, but Decker was powerful himself, although not nearly as physically endowed. He didn't appreciate being bullied in his office and stepped forward.

They were only a few inches apart in height, and were no less than a yard from each other. Decker matched Holt's stare and was impressed that she seemed amused by the fact he stood his ground instead of being cowed.

"I was in the neighborhood. I came to offer my condolences on the death of Parker Caldwell. I hear you were friends."

"Casual acquaintances. We traveled in the same social circle," Decker said, "I heard about his death this morning on the news. Terrible tragedy."

"Casual acquaintance? That wasn't how he told it. He raved about your close personal and business relationship. He would be so hurt to hear you say you shared little more than crudités."

Decker wasn't sure how well he managed to hide his surprise. He glanced at Gary, who was standing with his mouth open in shock. When he looked back to Holt, she was gone. She had left as quietly and suddenly as she had appeared.

"Fuck."

❖

"Okay," Holt said, her mind clear and sharply focused. "I'm in a piss poor mood, and we have one too few bad guys in the can. Time to go hunting."

Holt's employees were lined up, standing at attention in the main room of the bounty hunting office. Holt hadn't asked them to drop everything and focus on catching Isabelle's tormentor, but here they all were. Moose stood perpendicular to the line, looking like a drill sergeant observing his recruits. Max was the first in line, closest to Moose, a position usually taken by the highest ranking of Holt's employees.

"Where's Isabelle?" Jose asked. He didn't need to be part of this show of support, since he worked outside the office, but the fact that he was there meant a lot to Holt. He was slightly out of line, and no marine would have admired his posture, but the look in his eyes was all Holt cared about.

"She's in my office. She's working from here today. Probably the next few days."

"Let's get this bastard, boss lady," Moose said.

"We all take exception to you getting shot at," Max said.

"I'm not a huge fan myself," Holt said. "I'm sure Lola wasn't thrilled with the experience either. And I won't stand for Isabelle to continue being tormented."

"We all like Isabelle," Jose said, finally looking around and seeing how the rest of the group was standing and correcting his own stance and posture.

"Okay, then let's get to work," Holt said, "Before he died, Caldwell told me to 'follow his votes.' I'm guessing that means his work as a representative. I want to know his stance on every issue."

"On it, boss," two employees said, peeling out of line and jogging to their computers.

"I also want deep background on Decker Pence. I chatted with him this morning, and I think he's a first-rate asshole. He's vacationing in Colorado this week. Max, I want to know everything, right down to what kind of underwear he likes. I'm sure he's the lynchpin here. Everyone else, pick up the extra cases. Business runs as usual."

With her employees dutifully carrying out her orders, Holt found herself with little to do. She wanted to stand over Max's shoulder and hurry her along in her computer search, but she had been told many times that wasn't actually helpful.

Instead of hovering, or losing her temper at the slow pace, something she was finding easier and easier to do, she opened the door to her office, stepped inside, and the world was new again. Isabelle was resting her head on one hand, her hair less than perfectly styled and her shoulders hunched with stress. Holt had never seen anyone so beautiful.

"Can I do anything?" Holt asked, wrapping her arms around Isabelle's shoulders, engulfing her in a protective hug from behind.

"Catch the person doing this to us?" Isabelle said.

Even though Holt wasn't directly under attack, Isabelle knew the toll this ordeal was taking on her. While someone was trying to destroy Isabelle, Holt was working hard to prevent it. This was affecting both of them. On top of that, there could be no true "us" until the mess was sorted out. Isabelle refused to build a relationship as a damsel in distress. She was leaning more and more toward at least giving "us" a shot, but her thinking was so ass-backward right now, she didn't know. Not having Holt in her life was unacceptable at this point. Holt had given too much of herself on Isabelle's behalf, and on top of that, she was funny, kind, and really nice to look at. It seemed weird to suggest they should just be friends after they had been in two shoot-outs, been stalked and chased, and had slept together. Some couples never face the amount of adversity she and Holt had already dealt with together. On the other hand, she felt like she was living in constant fight-or-flight mode, which didn't feel like the way to make long-term life decisions, just the way to stay alive.

"What are we doing?" Isabelle asked. She could tell by the way Holt twitched that the question had caught her off guard.

"Can I have a little context? Do you mean right now? This weekend? The rest of our lives?"

"I don't know what I mean. This is really messing me up, Holt." Isabelle stood and flung herself into Holt's arms.

She didn't know what she wanted, or what she was feeling, but she did know Holt felt safe. Her usual rock solid self-control abandoned her, and no matter how much she tried to keep the tears away, they streamed down her face.

Holt kissed her wet cheek and used her thumb to wipe away some of Isabelle's tears.

"Right now," she said, "we are standing in my office, crying and hugging, and you are looking achingly beautiful."

A tiny sliver of Holt's words broke through the fear, and Isabelle's heart fluttered briefly.

"This weekend, I have no plans, but in two weeks, I would like to take you to a fundraising benefit. As for the rest? The present feels almost too complicated to fathom right now, so why muddy it up with long-term plans?"

Isabelle didn't know if Holt's answer helped. She didn't know if she expected it to. Did Holt not want a future with her? Was she also too fucking stressed to think about more than an hour from now? Isabelle kissed Holt, a long, slow, kiss. At least that always felt nice.

"Isabelle," Holt murmured against her lips, "I think I—"

"Holy shit. Sorry, boss lady. I'll, uh, I guess, um, later."

Holt moved away from Isabelle just far enough to catch the back of Max's shirt before she was able to scamper back out the door.

"Speak."

"Um, okay, so I was looking up Pence. Going to talk to Isabelle about…You know what, I should have knocked. I'll come back later," Max said, looking like she was waiting for Holt to spontaneously combust.

"You're here now," Holt said.

Isabelle was intrigued by what Holt was going to say, but felt relief as well. It was nice to take a break from feelings and hear some bad guy catching news. She didn't know if she was ready to hear what Holt had to say, and if Holt said it, she had no idea how she'd react to whatever it was. At least the bad guys were something tangible, something to focus on that didn't include her own emotional roller coaster.

"Um, right."

"Oh, for God's sake, Max. I won't let her bite you. She was kissing me, something she can resume when we're done. What did you want to talk to me about?" Isabelle couldn't help laughing. Max was so easily put off by Holt.

Max didn't look convinced, but she carried on. "I wanted to get your sense of Decker Pence. I want to focus my initial search if possible, to save time. I didn't know if you had any ideas."

"Well, now that you mention it, I've got something maybe you can help me figure out." Isabelle walked back to the computer screen she had been staring at before Holt distracted her. "This spreadsheet has been bothering me since I got it. Decker Pence said it was just a training file, but I can't let it go."

"This is that crazy file you mentioned on your list of potential threats? There are really line items for gas bubbles?" Max asked, laughing.

"And soap bubbles, air bubbles, the Washington Nationals, Florida Marlins, Texas Rangers, a fox, a lion, and a weasel, and I found one mention of a Los Angeles rapper. It makes no sense," Isabelle said. "But look at the bubbles, all varieties. Those are really large numbers, and there are only five of them. Looks like you could get a pretty decent house for those amounts of money, or a lot of jewelry, or a really fancy car. Maybe you could start there?"

Max looked ridiculously excited. "Can I have a copy of this file?" Max asked. When Isabelle nodded, she quickly made a copy and ran from Holt's office.

"That went well," Holt said.

Isabelle slipped back into her arms and kissed her again. "Tell me more about this benefit that is at the very end of your future vision."

"Well, it's for the same charity that Max won a bunch of money for by beating me in the run. It's the only time I have to see my parents each year, and I think it's the only thing left in the world we agree on. Not long after I started this business, I also started the charity and the gala benefits. It's fun. Everyone around here takes the black tie dress code very seriously and scrubs up well."

"Black tie you say? Then I have the perfect time killer until we find a bad guy. Sitting around your office isn't really distracting me. I haven't gotten any work done today, and I've already beaten the three games I have on my phone. Only logical thing to do is go shopping for this benefit of yours. Come with me?"

The pained look on Holt's face suggested that shopping wasn't her thing.

"Shopping sounds great."

"Not willing to let me out of your sight? Even if you have to go to the mall?"

"How did you know the smell of new clothes makes me twitch?"

"You need a better poker face," Isabelle said.

When Holt insisted Lola come along on the shopping trip so she didn't have to go in every store with her, Isabelle didn't argue. However, when Lola insisted Jose accompany them, Holt took issue. She argued he wasn't trained, and despite his good intentions, would be a liability to her and one more person to protect, but Lola stood firm. If it was fashion they were after, then Jose had to go with them. Lola seemed to be making sure the bandaged side of her head was always facing Holt during the argument. Hard to argue when your friend just got shot.

"He has to go," Lola said, grabbing a tappet wrench from Jose's tool belt, which he had removed in preparation for shopping, and slipping it in his back pocket. She untucked his greasy work shirt and pulled the shirt tail down to cover the wrench.

"Now he's armed," she said, looking for Holt's approval.

Isabelle thought Holt was amused, but she didn't let on. She linked arms with Isabelle and led her out of the office, indicating Lola and Jose should follow. As they walked out, Isabelle heard Lola whispering to Jose behind them.

"If you use that thing to hit anyone I don't tell you to whack, I'm going to use it on your skull, you understand?"

"I'd like to buy you your party clothes, if you'll let me," Holt said. "It's the least I can do since you'll have to meet my mother."

Isabelle didn't know how to respond to Holt's request. It felt like a more concrete step toward a relationship than sex. She wasn't sure if she was ready for that. On the other hand, having someone care enough about her to buy her a pretty dress felt nice. Who didn't like to wear clothes someone else had bought just for you?

"I'll consider it if you stop teasing me about your mother and actually tell me about her."

Lola and Jose snorted behind them.

"They don't like her much," Holt said, glaring at her friends. Holt looked like she was unsure where to begin.

"I told you about my dad. I understand nasty parents."

"Well, my mother has certainly never raised a hand to me, to a dirty dish, an aversive task, you get the idea. I'm an only child and a huge disappointment. She wanted a daughter. My father wanted a son. Neither got their wish."

"That woman would only have been happy if you had come out of her as a china doll," Jose said. He didn't seem to try to hide his disgust.

"And that's enough for the moment. Let's go shopping." Holt ushered them all out the door.

When they got to the mall, Jose and Lola entertained themselves for the first twenty minutes picking out evening gowns for her that would make Holt's mother happy. It gave Isabelle quite a bit of insight into the woman who, at the very least, gave birth to Holt, and she couldn't wait to meet her. However, she could see that Lola and Jose's teasing was starting to annoy Holt. She understood. She could call her father every name in the book, but she still cringed a little when other people joined in.

"Are you two knuckleheads interested in finding me something that doesn't make me look like I grew up in the Hamptons getting my hiney wiped with hundred dollar bills?"

"My mother isn't going to leave you alone," Holt said. "She's been harassing me about bringing a date to this gala for years. In the interest of full disclosure."

Isabelle figured she could handle it. Holt's mother sounded like a stereotypical wealthy woman. She dealt with rich people every day at work. She did wonder just how much money Holt came from though. On the scale of evening gowns, Lola and Jose had been picking out some styles favored by the super rich.

It turned out when Lola and Jose focused, they were the dynamic duo of shopping. Isabelle forgot about the craziness of her life for a while as she slipped in and out of fancy clothes, pranced out of the dressing room, and struck her best pose, soaking in Holt's admiring looks. It felt so normal and domestic and nice. Her entourage was a little abnormal, but with the way her life had been the last few weeks, even that seemed comfortable and perfect.

Once the gala clothes, and a few others that Jose and Lola insisted Isabelle couldn't live without, were purchased, they returned to Holt's lair.

"You didn't have to pay for all that," Isabelle said. Holt had asked again so earnestly if she could pay that Isabelle had caved. She didn't know how she felt about being treated to fancy clothes by Holt. For so many years, she had prided herself on her financial independence, and now she was holding shopping bags of items she realistically couldn't have afforded. It made her feel very well cared for and also a little cheap. She wasn't sure she should have agreed so easily, but Lola and Jose had been there and she didn't want to argue with Holt in front of everyone.

"Consider it an apology for not protecting you better. For not yet catching this bastard."

Isabelle could hear the guilt in Holt's voice and see it in her eyes. Isabelle liked to jokingly imbue Holt with the same superhero morals that she thought only existed in the pages of the comic books Holt said she liked so much. Apparently, Holt actually thought like Captain America.

"Holt Lasher, we need to talk, right now." Isabelle grabbed Holt by her shirt front and dragged her to her office. She pushed Holt gently into her desk chair.

"Holt, when comic book writers imagine their protagonists, they couldn't imagine anything quite as remarkable as you. Your honor, courage, morals are impeccable and noble. It's one of the things I love about you, but it doesn't leave much room for me to be your equal. Don't buy me clothes because you haven't protected me well enough. First, that's ridiculous, but more importantly, that's not a relationship. If we're going to have one of those, you're going to have to come up with other reasons to treat me well."

When Holt began to protest, Isabelle kissed her quiet, and continued. "Not yet, Holt. I don't want you to buy me things out of guilt. I can't be someone you think always needs protecting and be your partner. Some women may be okay with both roles, but I'm not. If you want to buy me things, do it because you are wildly, madly in love with me and can't stand for a second that I don't own whatever it is. I can't go through life as a woman incapable of influencing her own life, and you deserve better than someone who can."

Holt stood and moved into Isabelle's personal space. She cupped her hands around Isabelle's lower back and pulled her in close. "I want to be, you know."

"You want to be what?" It was hard not to want Holt to be her superhuman savior when she was this deliciously close.

"Madly and wildly in love with you. I want to let myself just let go and see just how wild you make me, but I've got to be honest, you terrify the hell out of me. I would rather run through a brick wall than lose you, but I'd also prefer that brick wall than falling for you and having you say you're not interested. And I'm worried about how I feel, and about losing you, and for someone who doesn't deal with emotions regularly, that's quite a combo. I'm a little thickheaded sometimes because I've never had to share this part of myself, and no case has ever meant this much."

"You know it's not you, right? If you were a lawyer, we'd probably already be married," Isabelle said, realizing for the first time how true that was. Holt was wonderful, but separating Holt from the world she lived in was impossible. It was everything that came with Holt that Isabelle was hesitant about.

"If I were a lawyer, I wouldn't be me," Holt said. "I know it's always been my job, but despite all evidence to the contrary, my job is usually not that exciting. But it does come with me. I've thought of going back to school. I could maybe see if I'm good at something else—"

"Holt Lasher, don't you dare," Isabelle said. "You are not giving up who you are for me. That's not okay." Despite her quick reaction, Isabelle really wanted Holt to become a marine biologist, or a pharmacist, or join Jose in his shop.

"Why not? I'm asking you to do that for me. I'm asking you to leave what is comfortable and safe and return to a life of stress and danger on the off chance this might work out. How is that different?"

Isabelle felt like she was standing in a stream of pure electricity. Her stomach was jumpy and her skin tingly. She didn't know what this conversation meant. Were they breaking up? Could you break up before you were together? Were they laying a foundation? Was it all supposed to be so hard?

"I don't think this is something we can solve right now," Holt said. "At least I can't. It's probably not the best time to be making major decisions like this anyway. We have a little added stress, and I don't think clearly when that's the case, but I'm glad we're talking. I care about you so much. You are more beautiful to me every time I see you, and never more than when you were just yelling at me for being a sexist pig."

"Holt, please don't think I don't care about you. I can't imagine you not in my life right now. I'm just—" Isabelle was cut off by a kiss from Holt.

"Everything I need right now is in how you make me feel and how you smile with your whole face when I walk in a room," Holt said. "As fair warning, I've been on my own a long time. You'll probably need to have a few more of these chats with me until I'm properly molded, so you might want to reserve all praise and adulation until you see the final product. We have plenty of time to mull over our feelings and figure out what we want from each other. Why don't you and Max go chase a bad guy through the exciting world of gas bubbles, and when you need someone to kick in a door, just holler. I'll be polishing my boots."

CHAPTER FOURTEEN

After three days of compiling everything they could on Decker Pence, Max and Isabelle found the break they had been searching for. After an initial search of real estate in Rhode Island and the rest of New England turned up only two buildings owned by him, they found a listing owned by his wife. The purchase price was identical to one of the bubble entries and had been bought in the past year. The building was a vacation house in Narragansett, a small beach community in the southern part of the state.

Holt looked thrilled with the news. She'd been pacing the office like a caged tiger, making everyone else irritable too. Their nightly love making at Holt's house had a razor sharp edge of anger and frustration. They had reneged on their decision to not sleep together again almost immediately, but the longer the chase continued, the happier Isabelle was that they had. Aside from providing them with a way of connecting with each other and feeling safe at the end of the day, it seemed to be the only time Holt thought about something other than work.

"Can you check the properties in Colorado? I have a feeling one of those bubbles will match wherever it is Pence has holed up."

Max searched public records of housing sales in Colorado, and thirty minutes later pulled up seven listings purchased for prices that exactly matched one of the bubble entries. Holt looked over the list, four in Denver, one in Aspen, one in Boulder, and one in Cheyenne Wells, near the eastern border Colorado shares with Kansas.

Even seven seemed like an impossibly large number to Isabelle. She couldn't see a way they could know for sure one of these belonged to Decker.

"That's the one," Holt said. "The only one not in the mountains."

"Why would anyone go to Colorado and not stay in the mountains?" Max asked. "What's in Cheyenne Wells?"

"No clue," Holt said. "I'm sure you'll let me know soon, but that's where he is. He mentioned the house wasn't in the ski areas when I spoke to him."

"Just when did you speak to him?" Isabelle asked, suddenly feeling unsteady. The hunt was thrilling and also terrifying. The spreadsheet had always been a nagging annoyance, but now, as they slowly started to unlock the puzzle, the whole situation seemed far less theoretical. A client she had known for years was buying properties she had no idea about, and in all likelihood had been terrorizing her off and on for months. She was frustrated with the steady diet of helplessness and fear.

"I dropped by his office. I needed to see if he's our guy, and I needed him to know I'm watching him."

Holt looked so gallant and steady, Isabelle wanted to drag her back home and lose a month in Holt's bed. How much easier would it be if she had fallen for Jose? The thought was so ridiculous it made her smile.

"Holt?"

"Yes, love?" Holt replied, still staring at Max's computer screen.

Isabelle noticed how quickly a few heads turned at Holt's endearment, but she didn't care who heard. Holt had just publically called her love. She hadn't expected it to feel so wonderful. Remarkably, Holt didn't seem to have noticed. That felt nice too, as if it was the most natural thing in the world. Her own jumbled feelings for Holt had to wait, as something more pressing had just occurred to her.

"Even if Decker Pence is the guy after me, how do we get him? Can you arrest him? What can we prove?"

Everyone shifted uncomfortably, and the tension in the office rose perceptibly.

"It's possible his simply knowing that we know what we know will be enough to keep him away," Holt said. "Although I'm not really comfortable with that kind of stalemate."

"Or you need him to come after me again," Isabelle said. "You need me as bait."

Holt looked like she could vomit.

Isabelle laughed. It felt like a strange reaction, but the expression on Holt's face was funny. As a child, she had reacted to some of her father's more violent moments with laughter too. It seemed to be an extreme coping mechanism.

"Sorry. It's a stress response," Isabelle said.

"With all due respect, Isabelle," Moose said. "I don't know that you would be very attractive bait anyway."

"Moose, leave it," Holt said.

"You don't think she can handle all this, H?" Moose asked, looking first at Holt, then directly at Isabelle. "Isabelle, you seem like the kind of woman who wants to be in charge of her own fate. If I'm wrong, then I suggest you wait in Holt's office because your boy Decker, if he's the one, is a bad SOB. I know Holt doesn't want to scare you, but I'm thinking not knowing is worse."

"Awesome. Make me look like the insensitive asshole," Holt said.

Isabelle moved so she was next to Holt and tucked herself under Holt's arm. She wrapped her arm around Holt's waist and squeezed gently. Holt wasn't insensitive from trying to protect her from all of this. She was working her tail off trying to keep her safe, emotionally and physically. Moose was right, though. She wanted to be part of the solution.

Holt sighed. "Moose is right. You're probably not very inviting bait. Although that was never an option," she added quickly. "If he wanted you dead, he probably would have done it already. This new development with the file might tip him over the edge, but with me involved now, I just don't see it."

Isabelle caught the quick but meaningful look that passed between Holt and Moose. She replayed Holt's last phrase "with me involved now."

"Well, I sure as hell don't like the idea of you using yourself as bait," Isabelle said, trying not to panic. "There has to be a better way."

"We're bond enforcement, not the police. Our ability to really get him is limited without further action on his part. So we need to force his hand."

"So get the police involved. Your cousin is a cop." Isabelle's mind was racing.

"That seems to be a non-starter. Danny said the investigation into the break-in at your office had a really bad smell to it. If Decker has even one cop who owes him a favor and is positioned well, we're screwed."

"We could probably get Diamond on the home invasion," Moose said, "but that would never get us Decker."

"He wouldn't rat on his boss?" Jose asked.

"Doubt he knows enough," Holt said, "and even if he did, he's not a reliable witness. Not against someone like Decker Pence."

"So how do we help you convince him to come after you and not get you killed in the process?" Isabelle asked, trying desperately to keep her voice from shaking as she said the words that, if they came true, would ruin her life.

"Kill?" Jose said, his eyes as large as saucers. "Just why do you want that psycho to try to kill you?"

"Decker Pence is a well-respected businessman. We can't just go to the police and say what we suspect. Even if we unlock this spreadsheet, gas bubbles and baseball teams aren't enough to put him away. Diamond doesn't work because his word isn't powerful enough to go against Decker's," Moose explained.

"But there are very few people in Rhode Island that have more sway than Holt," Jose said, understanding spreading across his face.

Holt looked grim but determined as she nodded confirmation to Jose's hypothesis.

"Okay," Jose said, "like Isabelle said, how do we get him to go after you? Are you going to convince him to put a hit on you?"

"If it comes to that," Holt said. Everyone seemed to think it would. "I need information overload," she said. "If he feels like I'm inside his head, or always watching him, it'll make him paranoid. Paranoid people don't act rationally, especially panicky, paranoid people."

Isabelle knew the feeling.

"Max, Isabelle, can you crack the spreadsheet? It would be nice to know what he's hiding. Even if it's just information on the people that work for him, like Diamond or Gary, his bookkeeper. Max, pull every record, background detail, and scrap of intel you can on this guy. The little things are what matter, where he bought coffee yesterday, who his mother is and where she lives. We have to scare the shit out of him. That gives us the advantage."

"Does this need to be aboveboard, boss?" Max asked, taking notes while she waited for Holt's answer.

"I know it's not our usual protocol, but we're not building a case for the police. Get me the background information I need any way you can."

"Hack it up, kid," Moose said.

Despite her whirring emotions and jumble of thoughts about this new plan of attack, Isabelle wanted to get to work.

"Let's go back to the bubbles," she said. "Can you search for houses purchased for the exact amounts listed as each of these?" She pointed to the remaining bubble amounts. "Let's start in Rhode Island."

After a few minutes of searching, Max found one hundred properties purchased for the prices listed on the spreadsheet. "Look at that," Max said. "That's the address of the house Holt broke into. The house Diamond lives in and Gary Capelletti owns. Soap bubbles number two."

"Good work, guys," Holt said, patting Max on the shoulder and kissing Isabelle.

"You got the raw end of that congratulations, kid," Jose said.

When Max turned bright red, the entire room cut up.

"That's the first real evidence that links Diamond to Decker, although it could all be circumstantial. This is Rhode Island, after all."

"Assuming Decker funded all these housing purchases, I don't understand where the hell he's getting all this money," Isabelle said. "None of this went on his tax returns."

"Let's find out," Max said, a flicker of excitement in her eyes.

At the end of the long day, Isabelle didn't even pretend she wasn't going home with Holt. They had talked about sleeping arrangements the last few nights, although she had always ended up with Holt. Tonight, she knew they both needed the closeness, and she didn't want to spend the night alone and afraid in a hotel room. Besides, Holt never would have let her stay anywhere by herself, so it made more sense for them to both be comfortable in Holt's loft.

It was well after midnight when they crawled into bed together, and Isabelle was almost desperate for the escape she knew Holt's body would provide. Unfortunately, when she thought about sleeping with Holt, it felt disingenuous. They were enjoying each other, and it was wonderful, but there was so much emotion left unsaid or unexplored. Holt was risking her life for her, and neither one of them could say for sure how they felt about the other. And then Holt had called her "love" this afternoon and Isabelle had liked it. It was enough to make her nuts.

Isabelle floated the idea that they should just sleep now that they were in bed. Holt reacted to the news exactly as Isabelle expected she would.

"I've got plenty of feelings to keep us busy without ever having to worry about you and me, and us, and relationships, and a white picket fence," Holt said.

"Not gonna happen, stud," Isabelle said, confident in her decision, but still wishing she didn't have to be so rational.

"What happens if Decker comes after me and I'm maimed for life? We wouldn't want to miss out on a night of mind-blowing sex, would we?"

Isabelle figured she must have turned white, or green, at the mention of what could possibly happen to Holt because she quickly changed tactics.

"I've gotta be on top of my game if I'm going to keep myself safe. You don't want me to be distracted by wanting you so badly I can't walk comfortably, right? What if I have to run away from a bad guy and am so hard all I can do is waddle?"

"Last time I inventoried, you've got two hands. Make use of them."

Holt laughed and pulled Isabelle close. "I love that you're looking out for me, and even though it will make me crazy, you might be right about not sleeping with me. Boxers don't have sex for weeks before a big fight. I'll just pretend that's why I have to lie next to you wearing nothing but my T-shirt tonight without touching."

"I only grabbed one pair of pajamas," Isabelle said, pretending to be offended by the implication that she was a tease. "I need to do laundry. The last time I was home, people were shooting at us, remember?" Did she mind that the T-shirt just barely covered her ass, and when she moved around the loft it was obvious she wasn't wearing anything underneath? Not at all, but she didn't need to confirm Holt's suspicions.

"Are you nervous?" Isabelle asked, snuggling in tight to Holt's warm, solid form.

"Terrified," Holt said. "There have been times when I couldn't find a person I was looking for. Sometimes bad things resulted, but that's part of the job, unfortunately. If that happened this time, I don't think I could live with myself. Not being good enough scares me."

"Aren't you worried that you'll get hurt?"

"No, not really," Holt said. "Moose and Lola will protect me. Hell, even Jose could do damage if properly motivated. I have good friends."

"What about your parents? You've only told me little bits about them. Will they be worried about you risking your life for me?"

"Oh, I won't tell them about this. I hardly ever talk to them anyway. We never had a particularly warm relationship," Holt said. "It went downhill after George died and I moved out. Like I told you, testifying in court was a patriotic duty, but testifying against a drug dealer charged with murder was a blight on the family. What kind of people know anyone who would get themselves killed by a drug dealer? The Lasher legacy couldn't be burdened with that ugliness. I can hear my mother's screechy voice now." Holt sounded mildly amused.

"Wait a minute," Isabelle said, connecting the dots for the first time. "You're from *that* Lasher family? The Lasher family that owns half of New England? But their child is Emily or Emma or Amanda, something like that," Isabelle said, confused.

"Not just from it, the living heir," Holt said, now definitely amused. "My legal name is Holt Lasher. My birth certificate tells a different story. But one of the perks of being eighteen when you find out what big assholes your parents are is you don't have to keep the name they gave you. Now you see why I'm a much better witness against Decker Pence than Diamond would be."

"I guess so. Decker should be shaking in his Colorado ski boots," Isabelle said. "So if you're so filthy rich, why didn't you pack Lola,

Jose, and Moose up and get the hell out of Rhode Island after the bad guy came after you?"

"My parents would have loved that. It would have fit perfectly with the rest of their friends shipping their kids off to parts unknown. I couldn't do it, though. I couldn't stand the thought of George's killer walking free. Besides, if I could find him at eighteen with no training or skill, how long before he found me? It never would have ended."

Not to mention you never walk away from a challenge, Isabelle thought.

"My parents tried to insist on paying the startup costs for this business, but there was a fairly sizable reward for capturing the baddie, so I declined. I didn't want their money then, and I don't need it now. The only money I've taken from them since is for a foundation I started five years ago. The gala I invited you to is to support that foundation. It's the only thing my mother and I agree on. I let her plan it, actually. She's better at it than I am, and she really enjoys doing it. And, of course, annoying me as much as possible in the process."

"Is your father going to be there too?" Isabelle asked, hoping she would be able to contain her desire to throttle Holt's parents.

"They'll both be there. They seem incapable of having anything else to do that weekend."

"I think I might hate them," Isabelle said, then placed her hand over her mouth. "Sorry, that popped out. They're your parents. I shouldn't hate them."

Holt laughed. "I never mind a strong sexy woman defending my honor. Unfortunately, though, you'll have to get in a long line if you're considering slapping them. Jose leads the parade every year."

"I guess I'll just have to settle for being on the arm of the hottest woman at the party."

Holt nuzzled into Isabelle's neck and started kissing the sensitive skin. Isabelle pushed her away playfully.

"I don't think so, hot stuff. I haven't changed my mind just because you're irresistible."

"Not that irresistible, apparently. You must have loins of steel," Holt grumbled.

They both laughed and Holt pulled Isabelle into a tight embrace. It was going to be a long night for both of them.

CHAPTER FIFTEEN

"Good morning, boss," Max said as Holt walked into the office. Isabelle grinned and went straight to Holt's office.

"Debatable." She hadn't slept at all after telling Isabelle her story. She had visions of Decker Pence and George running through her head as she had when she first told Isabelle about George. On top of that, she was so horny, just looking at Isabelle this morning was almost enough to make her explode.

"Um, okay," Max said, looking unsure.

Max still looked unkempt and like she hadn't slept enough in months. Holt had been trying to respect Max and let her come talk to her when she was ready, but Max didn't seem to be in a rush to come and chat. She was looking worse and worse, and Holt couldn't stand it anymore. If she slept any less, Holt was worried Max would start doing serious damage to her health.

"Oh," Holt said. "Isabelle said you needed to talk to me about something. Are those the same clothes you had on last night?"

"Fine, yes," Max said, frustration and anger clear in her voice. "Why does everyone keep asking me about my damn clothes? I got kicked out of my house. Who cares? It doesn't affect my work here."

"That been building for a while?" Holt asked. She crossed her arms and leaned against the desk, an eyebrow raised.

"Guess so," Max said. "Sorry."

"Why did you get kicked out?" Holt asked.

"No offense, ma'am, but I've got a lot to tell you, and I don't really want to talk about it right now."

"Fair," Holt said. "Answer me one thing and then I'll remove myself from your business. Where are you sleeping if you can't go home?"

"Um, here, mostly. The storage closet, extra offices, my desk. Sometimes the street." Max looked uncomfortable.

"Not anymore. Understand?" She held up her hand to stop Max's argument. "There are three studio apartments upstairs. Moose has one, Lola sometimes uses a second when her lady kicks her out, and the third is empty. It's yours as long as you need it, and if I hear you're not using it, I'll kick your ass. Talk to Lola or Moose about where to get sheets, towels, toilet paper, etc. Now, what do you have to tell me?" Holt couldn't believe Moose hadn't already gotten Max into one of those apartments, although she had hidden this from her pretty well too. Holt felt bad she hadn't noticed or pushed Max sooner.

Max provided Holt with an outline of the fruits of her nightlong computer search. Most of it was aboveboard and came from various public records. Credit card statements and other key information were obtained slightly less benignly. Max didn't seem particularly worried about getting caught. She was confident in her abilities as a hacker.

"This is great, Max," Holt said, finally feeling some forward progress. "Isabelle is in my office. She said something about comparing the file to Decker's actual records. You want to check in with her? I'm going to make a phone call."

Holt dialed the number Max said was associated with Decker's Colorado house. The trick was going to be to steer their conversation to areas Holt had fairly reliable information on. She wanted to scare Decker and make him paranoid. Having to do too much guessing would weaken her in his eyes.

When a man answered the phone, Holt recognized his voice. "May I please speak to the owner of this property?" she asked.

"Speaking," Decker responded, sounding wary.

"Hello, Decker Pence. May I call you DP? I think I'm going to. You have one of those names that just begs for you to say the first and last every time, but frankly, it's just too long. So, DP, how's your vacation going? Must be nice to own the only completely worthless ski house in Colorado. What exactly is in Cheyenne Wells?"

"Who is this?" Decker asked.

"I'm hurt you don't recognize my voice. We spoke last week. I intimidated you, you lied to me, I thought we hit it off pretty well." Holt was enjoying herself.

"Holt Lasher," Decker said, all friendliness gone from his voice. "As I told you, I'm not in Colorado for the skiing."

"I do remember you mentioning that. Also that the house was being loaned to you by a friend. I think I'm going to insist all my friends change their names to my name too. Then I only have to remember one."

"My grandmother owned the house. She willed it to me when she died," Decker responded, his voice getting more agitated.

"Eh eh," Holt said. "Don't lie to me, little man. Your grandmother's name is probably not Ernest Richard Stewart, the previous owner. Besides, your paternal grandmother lived her entire life in California, and Marie Decker Jones is alive and well, tucked away with your mom in Bumblefuck, Florida."

"What the fuck do you want?" Decker asked, his voice once again calm, eerily calm. It gave Holt the creeps, and she lost her sense of humor.

"I would very much like you to work out some better lies while you sit on your window stool at Java Madness tomorrow morning. We'll be in touch."

Holt hung up before the profanity on the other end really got going. Max had been thorough in her search and had even called the café where Decker had used a credit card the day before and got information on where he had been sitting. Despite being a regular, Holt was hoping he wouldn't be returning to Java Madness. It would be a small litmus test of the affect of her phone call.

She toyed with the idea of sending someone to Colorado to torment him in person, but it wasn't worth the risk. She wanted him focused solely on her, and she refused to leave Isabelle here without her. She also had better protection here in Rhode Island, both from her crew and the authorities. She wasn't naïve enough to think Decker Pence didn't have friends in high places, but she was banking on her friends being a few steps higher on the social ladder. To keep Isabelle safe, she was happy to exploit the trappings of a wealthy upbringing and a recognizable last name.

With Isabelle on her mind, she headed toward her office. She found her days now revolved around ways of being close to Isabelle. She didn't need to always be physically present, but Holt craved the connection, something she had never experienced, nor ever desired.

Max and Isabelle were huddled around the laptop on Holt's desk when she entered. Neither seemed to notice Holt's entrance, and neither flinched at all when she took up residence in the visitor's chair next to the desk.

"Oh," Max said excitedly, "another one there, one hundred fifty-six thousand, twenty-two, in two thousand and six."

"What the fuck?" Isabelle said, anger infusing her voice. "This ledger is insane. Where is all this money coming from?"

"Please tell me you cracked that thing," Holt said, making them jump.

"You're kinda sneaky, boss," Max said. "You should have knocked or cleared your throat or something."

"It is my office," Holt said, amused at the change in Max's demeanor over the past few months. Gone were the days of Max cowering in anxiety and fear. Holt could still scare the hell out of her, but that was true with everyone. When she wasn't tired, she was confident and contributing.

"I think you have a few years before you should be thinking of staging a coup, hotshot," Isabelle said, bumping shoulders with Max.

Before Max could defend herself, or get more embarrassed, Isabelle launched into an explanation of what they had found.

"We started by comparing the legitimate paperwork I have for Decker's businesses with this funky spreadsheet. Max noticed, quite brilliantly I think, that the numbers don't add up on the weird spreadsheet."

Max jumped in. "But then Isabelle noticed, even more brilliantly, that if you add in the legitimate income from the methadone clinic for the past six years to each yearly total of baseball, bubbles, and circus animals, you get the grand total noted for each year. Down to the penny."

"Whatever Decker is doing illegally, it's happening at the methadone clinic," Isabelle finished.

"So what do all the other things mean? The baseball teams? The animals?"

"Hey," Isabelle said, "Decker owns multiple businesses. We just narrowed it down to one. It's not even lunch yet and we know what some of the bubbles are and where the shady stuff is happening."

"Oops," Holt said, enjoying Isabelle's teasing annoyance. "My apologies. I didn't realize the level of brilliance I was witnessing. I'll step outside to not get in the way of the victory lap."

"It's a good thing you're cute," Isabelle said with a smile. "Otherwise, you would be an insufferable wiseass."

❖

Three days later, Holt decided to turn up the heat on Decker's supporting cast. She had hassled Decker into an early return from vacation, but without more ammo, she was really just harassing him. Max and Isabelle swore they were close to having more information for her. Lola had been working on Parker Caldwell's record in the House of Representatives, and for the past twenty-four hours, all three of them had been holed up in Holt's office barely allowing anyone in.

"I think we need to implement the 'general can't trust his troops' plan," Moose said, ambling up to Holt who was at loose ends. Everyone else was working hard. "I don't know if we're going to get anything from the Three Musketeers in there. It's a lot to ask in a really quick timeframe."

"As usual, you were reading my mind," Holt said. "I was going to pay a visit to Diamond and Gary Cappelletti. It would be really fantastic if one of them actually turned on Decker though."

"It would speed up the process of pissing off the boss man, but you don't need them to turn to make it work. As long as it looks like he can't trust them, you're golden."

"What are you thinking?" Holt asked. She wanted to punch Diamond in the face until he told her anything she wanted to hear. She probably wouldn't ever do something like that, but it didn't make her want it less.

"Can you get Gary or Diamond to send you some e-mails or call you? We need some way of making it look like they're buddy-buddy with you."

"Can you get someone close enough to take some pictures without being seen? That might be a nice touch."

"I like the picture idea. I'll see who I can pull in. But, H, don't lose focus on this one. I know it means more, but it's not worth throwing out the rules of engagement here. You getting yourself killed won't do shit to protect Isabelle."

"Speaking of which, I was thinking the gala might be the time to make myself baitish," Holt said. "We can control the conditions a little better there while still making me look nice and tasty."

"That's reasonable. Going to take a lot of setup. We've got less than a week."

"Then get the camera ready, call Danny, and find Diamond. It would be nice to set up Gary and Diamond, but we have to go after the weaker of the two. We don't have time to delay this. If you can find him now, I'm ready to roll out the door." Holt ignored Moose's warning. He was right; this one did mean more, and if she needed to rewrite the rules a little, she was going to do it.

❖

"Where have you been?" Isabelle asked. She realized she hadn't seen Holt in a while. Usually, she seemed to find a reason to be close to Isabelle every half hour or so.

Holt kissed her quickly. "I was out taking some photos with my new BFF Diamond. Speaking of which..." Holt looked around, clearly looking for someone. When she spotted Moose, her eyes lit up. "Did you get them? Did you get the pictures?"

There was a frenetic energy in the room that was making the otherwise bland office space buzz with intensity. It was heady and distracting. Holt looked unfocused, which wasn't like her.

"Boss," Max said, "Isabelle, Lola, and I found something."

"Sweetheart?" Isabelle said.

Just like that, Holt was back, looking at Isabelle with a mixture of concern, tenderness, and lust.

"Are you okay?" Isabelle asked.

"Just waiting for an answer from Moose," Holt said. "I'm hoping we have some more leverage to use against Decker Pence. Did Max just say something about you guys finding something?" Isabelle could tell Holt was trying to replay the last minute of conversation to catch up.

"Superheroes don't always have great hearing," Moose said.

"Probably from banging their heads through walls going after the bad guys," Isabelle said. "It's a flaw I can live with."

Uncharacteristically, Holt's face reddened. "What did you find, baby?"

"Have a seat. Max has something put together on the screen."

"Okay. Before we start, Moose, tell me you got some good shots?"

"Looks like you guys are two old friends yucking it up," Moose said. "The arm around his shoulders was a nice touch. In the still shot you can't tell he's shaking out of his boots."

"Sweet," Holt said. "Okay, start the show. Who has the popcorn?"

Much to Isabelle's amazement, ten seconds later, Jose came hurtling around the corner from the kitchenette carrying two large microwave popcorn bags. They weren't watching a movie; they were talking about life-or-death scenarios, but here they were eating popcorn. These guys really were cool under pressure. Everyone plopped down in nearby chairs, and Isabelle chose Holt's lap as there was a shortage of seating, and Max began her presentation.

"As you all know, Decker Pence is a real asshole," Max started, putting up Decker's driver's license picture and running through an exhaustive list of his vital statistics, most of which she had already shared with Holt and Isabelle.

"He owns businesses all over Rhode Island and property all over the state. Through some accounting mumbo jumbo, no offense to our genius Isabelle, our group figured out two important things about Decker Pence's business dealings. First..." Max changed the view on the screen to show the ridiculous spreadsheet. "The bubbles are all properties bought in the past two years. When you take those out of the equation..." Max animated the screen and removed the bubble accounting entries. "And if you remove all these baseball teams and animals..." Max pressed another button on her remote, and the silly entries evaporated. "You are left with this total for the past six years. Now, if you bring up his so-called legitimate accounting records that Isabelle had access to, does anyone see something that looks familiar?"

"I think Max has a future as a tour guide," Jose said, popping some more popcorn in his mouth. "She seems to be enjoying the spotlight."

"Okay, I see the reported profits from the methadone clinic line up with what's left over on the childish sheet. You told me that already, Max. What's new?" Holt asked.

"Getting to that, boss," Max said. "Lola has been looking at Rep. Caldwell's record in office for the past six years, the time that lines up with this spreadsheet. There are thousands of motions, votes, and bits of legislation that he had a hand in during that time. However, once we knew to focus on the methadone clinic, this pattern emerged."

Max clicked again, and a history of methadone related public records attached to Parker Caldwell's time in office jumped onto the screen. Starting about a year and a half ago, Parker Caldwell seemed to have developed a keen interest in methadone despite not having a single clinic in his district, and never having shown much affinity for substance use issues in the past.

Holt nearly dumped Isabelle off her lap she was so excited.

"Does this mean more to you than it does to me, boss?" Max asked.

Everyone looked at Holt, hoping she could see the hidden thread they were missing.

"Moose could probably explain it better, with actual numbers, prices, and profits, but yes. Looks like Decker has a pretty sweet racket going. My best guess as to what he's up to is this. Parker Caldwell was bribed, probably with money or drugs, to send as many state-funded methadone slots to Decker's clinic. Look at the pattern of funding on the screen. Almost all of the money the state is willing to pay for people's treatment goes to Decker, but it's supposed to be spread out among the various clinics in the state. I'm willing to bet that money never makes it to deserving people. This will nail Decker. Great, great work, you three."

"Methadone, called 'Done' on the streets, is a flat fee for your dose each week when you get it from the clinic," Moose jumped in. "Whether you're on thirty milligrams a day or three hundred milligrams a day, you would pay the same. That's not true on the street."

"Right," Holt said, her voice animated. It was obvious the hunt excited her. "You can get a lot more on the streets."

"'Done' can sell for as high as a dollar per milligram. People are desperate right now with the economy, and legit methadone maintenance is expensive, sometimes more expensive than heroin."

"I've helped him get away with this for years," Isabelle said, horrified. "No wonder he has so much extra money I couldn't account for. This is why he's been after me, isn't it? One stupid file and I was given the whole key to his operation. No wonder he wanted me intimidated, or dead."

"You didn't do any of this, love. He's a criminal. They lie. It's part of the gig. But I do take exception with him making your life miserable, and taking services away from people who need it."

"That lying, money laundering, piece of shit, asshole." She looked Holt in the eye and pointed her finger in Holt's face. "You get him. Get him however you have to. I don't like being played, and I really don't like cheaters. I'd get him myself, but I don't know how to kick ass. It makes me sick to think of all the innocent people he's hurt."

"Amen, Isabelle," Jose said. Moose patted her on the shoulder.

"I'm gonna nail him to the wall, love."

"Uh, boss, if we know what this spreadsheet means, can't we just drop it off for the police?" Max asked.

"Probably, kid," Moose said. "But cases like this are hard to prove. The guy at the top is usually pretty well insulated. Attempted murder is a bit more black-and-white. Besides, I don't want to try to explain gas bubbles to the cops."

"There's a pretty good bet one of these unaccounted for expenditures is to pay off a few of Rhode Island's finest. Ninety-nine percent of them are stand-up men and women, but all it takes is a couple," Holt said.

"What's the next move?" Isabelle asked.

"Next, we make this the worst week of Decker's life," Holt said. "Knowing what this means doesn't guarantee anything, but it gives us the best shot. We need to make him angry enough to want to kill me himself."

CHAPTER SIXTEEN

Decker was jumpy. Despite his best efforts to shake off Holt Lasher, she was starting to get to him. She had called or stopped by every day for the past week, and every day she seemed to know more and more about him. He knew very little about her. It was driving him crazy. Something had to be done. To make matters worse, Diamond had disappeared just when they were ready to repackage and sell the latest batch of Done. He had to admire her tenacity. He had been harassing Isabelle Rochat for quite a while.

The knock on the door startled him, and he jumped, which really pissed him off. Whoever walked by was going to get an earful. Hopefully, it was someone other than Gary, who had been getting more and more twitchy. Decker wasn't sure how much longer he could hold out against the pressure.

"Decker Pence, boy, do you have yourself a shit pile of trouble about to land on your head."

Decker looked over the good-looking Latino man standing in his doorway. He was dressed in work clothes, and the grease stains on his hands were apparent even from a distance.

"Who are you?" Decker asked.

"Just a guy who has a problem with the same scum you do."

"I can't imagine what you're talking about," Decker said, trying to get a read on him.

"Of course not. How about I tell you a little of my troubles and you can tell me a little of yours? I've got a bounty hunter that thinks she owns this town and me. I'm a mechanic in a building she owns. You think I can make a decent wage though? Fuck no. She takes eighty percent from me. *Eighty percent.* I'm about ready for that shit to stop. And I happen to know she's getting pretty tired of you and your gas bubbles, baseball teams, and Done ruining this town. I figure we can help each other."

Decker's heart skipped a beat at the mention of Gary's moronic spreadsheet and Done, but there was no way this guy could know anything about his business, right? "I still don't know what you are talking about, young man. I think you have the wrong guy."

"Right, there are so many Decker Pences in the phone book who own methadone clinics and launder money. Whatever, man. When you wise up, call me. Number's on the back. Check out the photography. I did it myself."

The man dropped a manila envelope on the floor of Decker's office, just inside the door and turned and walked out. Decker thought about calling him back and making him sorry he didn't show a little more respect, but it wasn't worth it. The mystery mechanic obviously knew who Decker was, and apparently, a lot more about Decker's business than he wanted to be public knowledge.

When he opened the envelope, three eight-by-ten black-and-white glossy photos landed on his desk. The pictures barely made a sound as they came to rest. Decker's ears rang with the sounds of panic as he took in the images.

Decker picked up the phone and dialed Gary. It was time for Diamond to be located. The phone rang twice before a woman's voice came on the line.

"DP, hey, buddy, how's it going? Gary and I were just having a nice chat about the weather, baseball, and our favorite state representatives. Your employee has very good political sense. You must be so proud."

Holt Lasher's voice on Gary's phone was more than Decker could handle. He threw his phone against the nearest wall, and then had the humiliating task of walking across the room to disconnect the call, as the wall hadn't done that for him. Holt's laughter taunted him until he hit "end call."

"Fuck." He didn't even want to think of the ways Holt had for getting people to talk to her. Her success tracking criminals couldn't all be legitimately earned. "He better keep his trap shut."

Decker considered the idea that Gary might be Holt's willing guest. He looked at the photographs of Holt with Diamond, her arm around his shoulders, for fuck's sake. Decker didn't stop to think; he picked up his phone and dialed the number on the back of the envelope.

❖

"Is this plan going to work, Holt?" Isabelle asked. She had finally convinced Holt to leave the office, and she was sitting at the breakfast bar in Holt's condo worrying. Holt was making dinner, looking quite sexy in a white T-shirt, camo shorts, and an apron that said "Grill Sergeant." She was whistling while she worked, and it occurred to Isabelle that Holt's demeanor had changed significantly since they started unraveling the mystery of Decker's business practices and Holt started annoying him.

"It's not foolproof," Holt said. "But I like it a whole lot more than the other possibilities on the table. We're forcing the issue to keep Decker off guard. I don't want him to have enough time to check Jose's background, or think rationally. Sometimes, irrational can be predictable."

"You like being the one he's focusing on don't you? Being the one in danger." Isabelle was curious about this side of Holt. It was the part of Holt's job that she liked least, and scared her the most. The time she had been in danger was the worst of her life, and she couldn't understand how someone could thrive under that stress.

"Like? No, I don't like it much at all," Holt said, looking thoughtful. She held Isabelle's eyes and continued. "It's never comfortable knowing someone wants you dead. I'm realistic, though. It's part of my job, people hating me. We all know that. I don't like the idea of Decker scheming to kill me, but if I had a choice of you or me as the focus of his wrath, I would choose me every time. Same goes for my team. I would rather they stay safe, even if it means more danger for me."

"Do you ever get used to it?" Isabelle asked, trying to see the ugly parts of Holt's job in a slightly more noble light. She supposed someone had to do Holt's job, as long as there were people who broke the law and declined their invitation to court. If she were the victim of a crime, and the offender skipped out on justice, she would want someone as capable and upstanding as Holt responsible for bringing them in. She couldn't imagine anyone else protecting her all this time. Maybe everyone else deserved the same.

"Nope," Holt said. "I've been at this for ten years, and it's still weird to me. Still scares me sometimes. The saving grace is that in ten years, I've only tried to bait one other person into coming after me. It's not part of my day-to-day work. Mostly, we're staring at computer screens, combing through police reports, and making phone calls. That's true of me even more than the others. I have to run the business side of things as well. My ass is going to start looking like my office chair pretty soon."

"Your ass looks pretty good from where I'm sitting."

"You could see it without my jeans or boxers. Just say the word."

"The word is still no, baby. After Decker's in jail, we'll stay in bed naked for days. Just catch him first."

"You do know how to provide motivation."

❖

Decker waited anxiously in the back booth of the all-night slots casino where he had asked the mystery mechanic to meet him. It was three thirty in the morning, and he hadn't slept in over twenty-four hours. Thoughts of the pictures of Holt Lasher with Diamond, looking friendly and conspiratorial, were consuming him.

He berated himself again for being stupid enough to trust one of the most important parts of his scam to a barely sober drug addict. Diamond was a friend of Gary's, and he had all the right connections on the street that they needed to move the Done. If Diamond was in bed with Holt, there was no telling who he could trust. Gary was the wild card. They were the only three who knew the scope of the Done operation. Holt answering Gary's phone had him spooked. He hoped meeting Holt's turncoat buddy would ease his mind. Decker didn't deal well when things didn't go his way.

"You liked my pictures I take it," Jose said, sliding into the booth across from Decker.

"No, I didn't like them, you stupid fuck, but you knew I wouldn't. What do you want from me?"

"You okay, man? You look a little strung out. I'm not into doing business with a junkie. Too hard to trust."

"I'm clean," Decker said, not hiding the hostility in his voice. "What do you want?"

"I figured we could help each other," Jose said. "I've got a problem with Holt, and you've got a bigger problem with her. I want my fair shake on my business dealings, and you, well, you're screwed if she goes to the cops."

"Fuck the cops," Decker said, "I've got myself well protected."

"Not against someone like Holt. You do know who her parents are, right? Shit, the whole city would throw her a parade even if she arrested every member of the Red Sox. You think your little pissant payoffs are going to be enough to keep you out of the pokey? Please."

Decker hadn't considered how Holt's clout in the state matched up to his. He was a businessman and used to getting his way based on his reputation and presence. This mechanic was right, though. He was no match for Holt Lasher.

"What does she have on me?"

"You saw the pictures. How much does your boy Diamond know about your state funding and Done redistribution?" Jose asked. "I can't get too close during her meetings, but they've been poring over a spreadsheet with all sorts of weird shit on it for weeks. Three days ago, her whole team was toasting and drinking champagne, saying stuff about finally breaking the code. They don't pay attention to me because I'm just a lowly mechanic, you know?"

"That stupid fuck Gary," Decker said. "I told him his dumb code wasn't a security system. My whole operation is on those spreadsheets." Decker was furious, panicking, and talking to himself. He had almost forgotten he was entertaining a visitor.

"What about Gary?"

"What do you mean what about Gary?" Decker asked.

"Can you trust him? I know Holt. That's her next stop on the way to the top. You took a shot at her girlfriend. Bad move, partner. She's coming for you, and she's gonna go through him."

"I didn't take a shot at that accountant. That was Gary's idea. He sent the wrong file to her for my taxes and I told him to fix it. That was his solution. None of this would be happening right now if he hadn't overreacted. Fuck. What do we do?" Decker knew he shouldn't be telling all this to a stranger, but he was tired and afraid.

"I just want my share of my business. Can you get some guys to rough her up a little? Maybe force her to sell you the mechanic's shop?"

"She's a golden gloves boxing champion, you idiot. My roughing her up will end with me getting my ass kicked."

"You've got guys, right? Send them. Make it an ambush."

"No way. I'm not getting more people involved. She's like a damn octopus, tentacles everywhere. Besides, roughing her up isn't going to keep her from talking. It's not good to kick a dragon. How do you know all this stuff about my business?"

"My shop's right next to Holt's office. We share a bathroom. I see shit on my way to the can. She trusts everyone she works with, including me, so she usually doesn't cover up what she's working on. Besides, you pissed her off so the entire team is working on catching your ass. Now, you're the boss here. You tell me what we should do," Jose said, leaning in, waiting for Decker's response.

Decker thought for a while and ran option after option over in his head. He wanted to have the solution be as simple as Jose had implied. Just teach her a lesson. But he knew about Holt Lasher. He knew her past. The only way he was going to avoid everything she knew being made public was to silence her for good. As he mulled over the thought, his excitement grew. He had never killed anyone before. Holt Lasher seemed like a worthy victim for his first time. He debated whether he should trust this stranger after such a short time, but he was in no position to bargain. He would protect himself, and hopefully take out Holt while making a new friend. Maybe the Done business was over, but there was good money in cars too.

"We kill her," Decker said. "Get some papers drawn up saying in the event of her death, you get the shop. Don't go to a cut-rate forger either. Make it legit."

"Who you gonna get to do the hit?" Jose asked.

"No one. We do this ourselves. Nice and clean. No loose ends. You good?" Decker asked.

"Shit, man." Jose looked hesitant. "This the only way?"

"You said I'm the boss, so trust me. I'm a hell of a lot better at being an asshole than you are. This is the only way." All Decker needed to do was convince this guy to help him carry out the murder. If this guy even looked at him funny, Decker planned on killing him too and framing him for the job. That way he was home free. Cut off the head of the snake and the rest dies too. Holt's team would never bother him again.

"I don't know," Jose said.

Decker pulled a pistol out of his pocket and laid it on the table. "You were the one who stuck your nose in my business." Jose looked panicked, exactly the reaction Decker wanted.

"Okay. I'm in."

Holt sighed, ran her fingers through her hair, and looked around her loft. She felt helpless. She didn't like leaving the most important details of her plan to get Decker Pence up to Jose, but she didn't have much choice. If she really thought about it, she didn't like much of this plan at all, but it didn't seem like she had many options.

She was a woman of action, and turning over the silly spreadsheet to the police, telling them of her suspicions, and waiting for months, only to see the case thrown out of court was more than she could stomach. She was in the shitty position of knowing what Decker was up to but not being able to nail him for it. Unfortunately, Isabelle also knew what Decker was doing, and her being in danger was enough to push Holt to a risky plan she normally wouldn't even consider.

Sometimes, her life was crazier than a comic book plot. Although she couldn't remember Batman sitting in his living room, waiting for his friend/untrained accomplice to return from carrying out the most important part of the grand plan. Isabelle was asleep in the other room, and Holt hadn't turned on the living room lights so as not to wake her. She was restless and moody, and sitting in the dark seemed appropriate.

Two quick knocks, followed by Jose peeking his head in her front door, finally ended the interminable wait.

"Moose cleared you?" Holt asked from the couch.

"I would never put you in that kind of shit," Jose said, sounding offended. "We drove around a while. No tail. That's what took so long. The meeting was fucking quick."

Holt didn't say anything. She waited while Jose picked his way through the dark and sat on the couch next to her. She could tell he wanted to turn on a light, but she didn't, so they sat in the dark.

"He went for it," Jose said.

"Already?" Holt was surprised. This was only the first meeting. It was only supposed to set up Jose and Decker as a team. Jose was trying to build trust and subtly suggest options.

"Yeah, almost immediately. We went from 'hey, maybe you can send a guy over to rough her up a little' to 'we kill her' in about five minutes. This dude is scary, Holt. You sure you know what you're doing?"

"Oh sure," Holt said, too strung out emotionally to hide her sarcasm. Jose would have been able to call her bullshit anyway, so she was saving them both time. "I have a good plan for tricking a psychopath into trying to kill me without him actually succeeding."

"Does Isabelle know this has you wound so tight?"

Holt sighed. "I don't know. I've been trying to keep some of the stress from her, but she's pretty good at seeing right through me. She's freaked out enough without me dropping my shit on her too. She asked me if I was sure this was going to work. I really have no fucking idea."

"Did you tell her that?"

"Hell no. I didn't want to make her more nervous."

"I've got three things to tell you, and then I'm going out to find a fruity drink and a cute boy to flirt with. I can't stand all this anxiety."

"Will you just ask Moose out already?" Holt said, knowing Jose had been in love with him since high school.

"One," Jose said pointedly, making his view of Holt's suggestion clear, "you need to tell Isabelle how you're feeling. That woman is the best thing that ever happened to you, and you won't keep her by treating her like a porcelain doll. If you get yourself killed and she doesn't know that's a possibility, she's gonna reincarnate your ass so she can give you a piece of her mind. And then she's gonna do you in."

"Jose—"

"Shut up, Holt. I'm only on point number one."

With anyone else, Holt would have been angry. But she and Jose were long past that.

"Two, Decker agreed way too easily. Either he's a world class creepy dude, or he's got other plans. I don't know if they involve me ending up dead next to you, or he's going to string me along and then run his own game, but he came up with this plan too quick. So point number three is, call Bogota. You need a new tux."

"I'm not getting a new tux. The one I have is fine. You think that won't scare Isabelle?"

"I don't give a shit, Holt. She's going to freak out no matter what you do, but a new tux might help a little bit. And I'm not above getting your whole team to nag you."

"Are you trying to blackmail me?" Holt asked, her voice rising a little as she tried to control her temper. Jose could get away with a lot, but he was pushing it.

"Why is Jose blackmailing you, baby, and why are you both sitting in the dark yelling at each other?" Isabelle asked, appearing from behind the partition separating the bedroom from the rest of the loft.

"It's nothing, sweetheart," Holt said, jumping up to walk Isabelle back to bed. She didn't disagree with Jose that Isabelle should know about the plan, the danger, and their progress, but it was the middle of the night.

Isabelle and Jose however, had other plans.

"I'm up now and I don't believe it's nothing," Isabelle said, turning on a light and flopping sleepily on the couch between Jose and where Holt had been sitting. "Jose, what's going on?"

"Jose," Holt halfheartedly warned him. She knew he would ignore her and tell Isabelle everything.

"Decker Pence is a bad scary dude," Jose said, waving his hands dramatically, "and he agreed to our plan in about thirty seconds. I don't trust him and I was trying to suggest that your beautiful lady over there take every precaution to keep her fine form bullet free."

"He wants me to wear a bulletproof tuxedo to the gala," Holt said. "Occasionally, I wear bulletproof clothing if the situation is really dicey. In this case, I would prefer not to because there is some limitation on movement and I would really rather be fully mobile."

"You make it sound like you're going to be in an armored tank. Your vital organs will be protected. It's not exactly a straightjacket."

"You can really order a bulletproof tuxedo?" Isabelle asked.

"From a designer in Columbia. Rumor has it he suited President Obama for his inauguration," Jose said. "Every employee and customer has to be shot while wearing one of his designs so they trust what they are wearing or selling. Totally freaking awesome, and crazy."

Holt didn't need to hear Isabelle's measured, highly organized, logical plea. She just needed to see the fear in Isabelle's eyes, and know that it mirrored her own internal anxiety. Jose was trying to protect her. If it gave both of them a measure of security, she would go shopping.

"Fine," Holt said. "Call Bogota. They should still have my measurements. They've gotten suits to me in less than a week before. I know you think my job is crazy, but those dudes make bulletproof clothing and shoot people. I don't even carry a gun."

"You let someone shoot you?" Isabelle asked.

"Hey, the suit works. Only one way to find that out. Best marketing gimmick ever."

❖

"Is this the rehearsal dinner?" Holt asked when she walked into the main room of her offices. "Leftover pizza is the best you could do for the eve of my big day?"

Everyone had been practically living at the office the past week. Except Jose, who worked as usual, in case Decker was watching. It was the night before the gala, and Holt looked like her nerves and emotions were settling into pre-chase mode.

Isabelle, on the other hand, was getting more anxious as the big day approached. It didn't matter that her only job at the gala was to have a good time and stay with Holt until the final moments. How was she supposed to have a good time when her date was wearing a bulletproof tuxedo?

She studied the blueprints of the building where the gala was being held, taking in the labels for each door. The door they were to enter at the beginning of the evening was D North. Every other door was labeled based on that premise.

Even though Jose and Decker had been in constant contact planning this event, the details of what was actually going to happen still seemed far too sketchy to Isabelle. Holt's life was on the line and they were using words like "hopefully" and "just in case."

"Go over it one more time, Jose," Holt said. Isabelle felt like she might vomit if she had to hear this plan, and all the ways it could go wrong, one more time.

"There is an alleyway behind D South. It's dark, secluded, and there are no video monitoring devices in a one hundred foot section that is approximately three hundred feet from D South. My job is going to be convincing you to follow me to the alley. Decker will be waiting there, along with two other men he recruited. Once I get you to the agreed upon spot, I will retreat behind Decker and get out of there as fast as I can.

"You have to keep Decker talking long enough to explain his intention to kill you. Moose set up the surveillance devices himself. When Decker speaks, it will be recorded. Lola and Max collected and printed a pretty good set of bread crumbs back to what Decker's been up to the past few years, but the more you get in his own words, the better."

"The nine one one call to police will be made as soon as I see you leaving with Jose," Moose said. "Your cousin Danny will already be at the party and is ready to come aid the damsel in distress."

Holt didn't seem to like being called a damsel and she glared at Moose. "I can't believe after planning this obsessively, this is the best we could come up with."

"It's Decker," Jose said. "Man's a bad dude, but he's got no imagination. He looked at the area, saw an alley, and figures it always works in the movies. He's a little bit of a control freak. I can't suggest too much without him flipping out about who's running the show. I don't think he's ever done anything like this before."

"All right," Holt said, "the plan is the best we can do. You all go home, get some sleep, get dolled up tomorrow, and have a good time.

Remember, the gala is actually for a good cause. Our favorite juvenile delinquent is joining the program. Peanut deserves our full attention. See you all in the morning."

Holt thought about what a fuckshow this had all turned into. She also missed Isabelle who had opted to stay at Holt's loft with Lola providing security outside. For the first time in ten years of doing this job, Holt felt truly vulnerable. She had something to lose now, something more valuable to her than her own life. She couldn't afford to mess this up, but in truth, this plan sucked.

Even if she somehow pulled it off, got Decker to admit to what he had done, and didn't get shot in the head, this was pretty much Isabelle's worst case scenario when it came to her job. She had no idea what would stop her from walking out the door once she was safe again. She thought about talking to Moose or Jose about what she was feeling, but she knew they would just worry. Everyone was already anxious enough. She was just going to have to fake her usual confidence and hope everything went well. She knew she needed to focus on what needed to be done tomorrow, but Isabelle was, more and more, constantly on her mind. If Isabelle walked away when it was done, she'd have to deal with it, although she had no idea how.

❖

Isabelle paced Holt's living room. She had wanted to attend the final planning meeting with Holt and the crew, wanted to ask questions, lots of questions, like what was to stop Decker from killing her the minute he saw her instead of getting chatty, but she knew what the responses would be. Holt had to play to his ego and hope he wanted to show off his superiority before he squashed his enemy. If not, Holt had to fight her way out of the situation. It sounded ludicrous to Isabelle. She had decided hearing it again wasn't going to make her feel any better about it. Now she wasn't sure if she made the right decision. Being home alone, worrying by herself, was miserable. What if Holt died? What if Decker got away? What if, what if, what if?

If anyone had told her six months ago she would be helping plan something like this, she would have had them committed to the loony bin. Perhaps the most unsettling part of the entire plan was that, since she met Holt, a scenario exactly like this one was what she feared. Holt in danger, chasing a bad guy, maybe never coming home. She hadn't wanted to get involved because she didn't like Holt's job and what it could entail. Now, faced with her worst-case scenario, she was less inclined to leave, felt more for Holt, and wanted to play an active part in saving Holt's hide.

She knew, even if she walked away right now, Holt would go through with this scheme. Isabelle didn't need to have any part of it or Holt and her danger. It was the fact that, despite all that, Isabelle didn't want to be anywhere else. It didn't seem like it had been long enough to be brainwashed, or to be in love, but she couldn't deny how she felt. Holt Lasher, every last dangerous, unsavory, noble part of her, was the one Isabelle wanted. It sucked to finally figure that out the night before a psycho tried to kill her.

"Decker, it's me, Gary. I think something's happening with my phone and I can't find Diamond. I'm freaking out a little here."

Gary was standing in front of Decker's house speaking into the security screen. He looked slightly crazed.

"What do you mean something's happening with your phone?" Decker asked. He had a sinking feeling.

"I don't know. I hadn't gotten a call in ten days, and then I tried to call it and no one answered, but it never rang. Diamond's gone and I couldn't find you."

Decker buzzed the gate open.

"Get up here, Gary. I think we've been played."

CHAPTER SEVENTEEN

Holt felt like she was waiting on her prom date. Isabelle was finishing getting ready for the gala and Holt was sitting on the couch, replaying the plan one last time. Amy was with her. They had gone together every year, although as her mother was fond of pointing out, since they were just friends, Amy didn't count as a date. No sense breaking tradition now, even if it meant Holt showing up with a woman on each arm.

"I can't believe that cockamamie scheme is the best you could come up with," Amy said for the umpteenth time.

Holt shrugged. It wasn't perfect, but she was done second-guessing. The plan was in place; she had to perform. "I need your help tonight," Holt said, her voice low so Isabelle couldn't hear her from the bathroom. "Tonight, everyone is going to be so damn worried about keeping me from becoming Swiss cheese that no one is going to be watching Isabelle. Once this goes down, she's vulnerable. Will you keep your eyes on her all night?"

"Why not have one of your team watch her? I don't know what I'm doing. Not that watching your girlfriend all night isn't going to be an enjoyable task."

"I want you to keep Isabelle safe because you'll still have a job if I'm dead, so you can focus a bit better than the others, and you're my friend and I'm begging. You know what she means to me."

"That I do, kid," Amy said, standing up and kissing Holt on the top of the head.

They were spared any more talk of the anxiety-provoking part of the evening by Isabelle's entrance. Holt was speechless. Isabelle was always beautiful, but tonight she looked radiant.

A one-shouldered black cocktail dress fit her as if it had been custom sewn. Her blond hair was off her neck in an elegant updo, and her sexy heels did everything they were supposed to do to accentuate her beautiful legs.

"Hello, beautiful," Holt said, not sure how she had managed to get Isabelle to agree to be in the same room with her, let alone as her date. "You look amazing."

"You're looking pretty good yourself," Isabelle said, taking in Holt's black three-piece tuxedo. Even if the vest and jacket were designed to stop bullets, the tailoring accentuated all of Holt's finest features and didn't look in the least bit like the usual bulletproof vests law enforcement wore. "I like your cuff links," Isabelle teased her, admiring the pinup girls that adorned each of Holt's cuffs.

"I thought my mother would like them."

They were silent on the ride to the gala. Holt held tightly to Isabelle's hand, and Isabelle prayed it wouldn't be the last time.

The gala was held in a hotel ballroom, and when they arrived, it was already quite full. Balloons bobbed festively at each table, and the space looked like a perfect setting for a party. A band was setting up at the front of the room, just off the large dance floor, and a silent auction was being held in the smaller room next door. One wall was covered with pictures of smiling teenagers.

Isabelle dragged Holt over to them. Peanut was one of the kids looking out from a picture, dressed in a shirt and tie in the photo and looking almost nothing like the kid she had seen in her pool.

"You said Peanut was joining the program. What does that mean? Who are these kids?"

"Well, this gala is a fundraiser for a charity that I started a while ago. The running that you saw at the boxing gym was too. This is really the only way my parents and I still interact. I've chased quite a few of these kids after they get themselves in trouble and don't know how to get out. I've got a deal worked out with the judges here. If the kids agree to join my program, they can avoid jail, but in return, they have to make good grades, stay out of trouble, be involved in a sport, after school tutoring, and when they graduate from high school, college tuition is paid if they want to go. My parents get to put their name on the program and brag about all the good work they do."

"Ugh," Isabelle said. "How is it that I hated you and your job, and now neither is true? Is this brainwashing? Stockholm Syndrome? Are you too good to be true?"

Holt looked uncomfortable, and Isabelle put her out of her misery by kissing her and grabbing her ass subtly under her jacket tails.

"Emily," someone said a little too loudly. Isabelle wouldn't have reacted except for the full body cringe she felt from Holt. She spun around and came very close to knocking a full glass of champagne into the woman who looked like an older, more feminine, more pretentious version of Holt.

"That hasn't been my name since I was eighteen," Holt said angrily.

"Oh, dear, why do you insist on constantly bringing up the past? I see you listened to my request and brought a date. It will look so much better for me and your father to have you finally be seen with someone. Now, we'll have to get you two over to the press so you can get your picture taken. It will be in all the papers."

"I don't think so," Holt said.

"May I steal you away a moment please, ma'am?" Jose asked Isabelle, suddenly by her side. He didn't let her answer before leading her off, away from Holt and her mother.

"She asked me to keep that woman away from you. She'll try to claim victory for Holt having a date, and if anything could drive you away from our lovely superhero, that creature is the thing."

"I'm not going anywhere," Isabelle said. "Holt knows that. She was pretty horrible, though, and she was only talking for thirty seconds. What about Holt? Will she be okay?"

"She's had years of practice getting out of those tentacles," Jose said. "Shall I leave you safely with Amy? We decided last night I should be as visible as possible tonight so Decker can find me if he's here. And Holt wants me to stay away from you, except to rescue you from her mother."

Almost as soon as Jose disappeared back into the crowd, Isabelle lost sight of Holt as well. She could still see Holt's mother, looking annoyed and perplexed, but Holt was nowhere to be seen. She followed the horrible woman's gaze just in time to see Holt ducking out one of the side doors, D East.

"Shit, where does she think she's going?" Isabelle muttered, not hesitating as she scooted after her. She was pretty sure that wasn't part of the plan. She looked for someone to tell, but there were no recognizable faces nearby. She didn't want to distract Holt or put herself in danger, but if Holt was in trouble, it didn't look like anyone else saw her leave.

"Isabelle, wait up," Amy said, coming after Isabelle.

They hit D East at a good clip, and Isabelle pushed out into the night with Amy hot on her heels. They stopped outside the door, looking both ways. Holt was nowhere in sight.

"What's that?" Amy asked. "Can you hear that? That sounded like someone in pain."

"Come on," Isabelle said, her heart pounding. She took off toward the noise Amy had heard. It sounded like Holt, and she didn't sound good.

"Should we get someone?" Amy asked, following behind Isabelle.

"No time. I'm sure someone saw us leave. If we go back in now, we'll lose them. I'm pretty sure my running through an alley after Holt because I heard her cry out in pain wasn't part of the master plan. Seems like the plan is fucked. I wasn't supposed to be part of the plan."

When they neared the end of the building, Isabelle slowed and cautiously stuck her head around the corner. The hotel where the gala was being held was in downtown Providence. Despite the improvements to the city, there was a violent underbelly that persisted, and sketchy buildings and dodgy alleys weren't difficult to come by. Ahead of her stretched just such a location with Holt a terrifying focal point.

"Oh my God," Isabelle said, pulling back, tears running down her face. She was terrified.

"There were three guys. They were dragging Holt. I don't think she's conscious. You don't think they—"

"No," Amy said forcefully. "I don't. But let's go make sure. Seems like we might be the only chance that idiot has of getting out of this mess. What the hell was she thinking?"

"She was trying to save me," Isabelle said, the full horror of what could happen hitting her like a baseball bat to the gut.

"Shit. I know that, Isabelle. What do you say we return the favor?"

Isabelle nodded, and this time they both peeked around the corner. The coast was clear. Isabelle pointed at one of the buildings and they took off toward it. Although Amy was wearing a suit and sensible shoes, Isabelle wasn't dressed for running down alleys. She ditched the high heels, said a prayer that she wouldn't step on anything too gross or incapacitating, and carried on.

Just outside the door to the building Isabelle saw Holt being dragged into, Amy stepped on Holt's cell phone.

"Must have fallen out of her pocket," Amy said.

"That's good," Isabelle said. "Holt showed me an app Max made, kinda like a panic button. Once we find her, all we have to do is push the button and wait for help to arrive. Everyone has their phones with them tonight."

"Push the button now. Why wait?" Amy said.

Isabelle opened the app and hit the big red panic button in the middle of the screen. Max apparently didn't believe in subtle. "If we lose signal, they won't be able to track us, so keep an eye on the bars in the corner."

Cautiously, they pulled the door open and slipped inside. They were in an abandoned warehouse type building littered with junk, rotten furniture, and debris.

"This is just the kind of building movie bad guys bring their victims to," Amy said.

Isabelle shuddered. She had instinctively followed Holt, hoping to protect her. But now that she was supposed to be the superhero, she was more than a little freaked out. There was junk all over the floor. She had no shoes. She had no weapons. What was she going to do once she actually found Holt? She saw the same questions in Amy's eyes. It was too late to go back, so they pressed on. Hopefully, help would arrive soon.

They stayed out of sight as much as possible, ducking behind any cover they could find. As they moved further into the building, muffled conversation became audible. It sounded like someone was very, very angry.

Isabelle stopped abruptly, and Amy ran into her back. A man screamed with rage. He sounded very close. They inched forward, counted to three, and dared to look around a large filing cabinet shielding them. Fifteen feet in front of them, surrounded by a ring of portable lights, sat Holt, her face bloodied, her hands and feet tied to the chair she sat on.

Decker Pence walked into the light, cocked his fist, and punched Holt hard in the face. Isabelle fought the urge to charge at the man and beat him silly. She had once cowered in fear at an angry voice and a raised fist. Now she surprised herself with her strength. Amy must have sensed her desire because she put a steadying hand on her shoulder and held her in place.

Aside from the gun Decker was waving in his non-punching hand, Isabelle didn't know who else was in the building, and she wasn't much of a fighter.

"You know," Holt said to Decker, "you really are a crappy host. No one has offered me anything to drink. This chair really should have an ottoman, and blood doesn't go with my fucking suit. Do you know what this is going to cost to dry-clean?"

Holt looked calm, much calmer than Isabelle was feeling. From her body language and tone, Holt seemed to be under the impression she was in charge of the encounter.

"Do you think I won't fucking kill you, bitch?" Decker yelled, waving his gun in Holt's face. "After what you've done to me? You think you've got the moral high ground? We're not different. You and I are the same."

Holt still looked unimpressed. Isabelle didn't know how she could stay so calm. Her own teeth were clacking together, and she couldn't stop the flow of tears.

Amy pointed at Holt's cell phone. "No signal. Unfucking believable. Hopefully, the signal we sent in the alley was enough."

Decker yelled more insults at Holt and punched her again. She spit in his face, which he didn't seem to take kindly to. He aimed the gun at Holt's chest and pulled the trigger. Isabelle screamed.

A vacuum seemed to have been formed in the building. Isabelle couldn't hear anything. She could barely see. Her legs felt too weak to hold her, or she would have run to Holt. People didn't survive getting shot in the chest.

"Ouch," Holt said sarcastically.

Holt's voice cut through Isabelle's fog. It took a few seconds to register, but then she almost laughed with relief. The tuxedo. Wondrous, amazing Jose had just bought Holt more time. She poked her head around the cabinet a fraction.

"Decker, she's not bleeding or dead or anything," a second man said nervously.

"Shut up, Gary. She's obviously got a vest on under the suit," Decker said, looking around the room suspiciously. "Did you hear that? Could have been a scream."

"Wouldn't it have been her?" Gary asked, pointing at Holt.

Holt smiled at Gary and blew him a kiss.

"I said shut up, Gary. Take your gun and the rest of the group and search this place. Top to bottom. If someone is in here, they better be tied to a chair next to this piece of trash in five minutes."

"I think that's our cue to leave," Amy said. "We need to get back outside to get a signal anyway."

"You go. I'm staying here. I think I can make their search a little harder. Make sure the rest of the group gets over here fast." Now she felt calm too. Her head was clear, and she had a plan. Holt had cheated death once, but Isabelle didn't want her to have to a second time. Holt needed her. It was time to step up.

Amy looked unsure, but when Isabelle nudged her toward the door, she started to pick her way back the way they had come.

"Oh," Isabelle said quietly. "If you can find a way to turn off these lights, do it."

Amy nodded and was gone.

Isabelle looked back out at Holt and Decker. She couldn't see Gary, but she could hear him on the other side of the circle.

"Since we have a few minutes before you try again to kill me and whoever you're hallucinating is out there," Holt said, shifting her weight on the chair and looking like she was trying to get comfy, "I have a couple questions for you."

Isabelle was amazed at Holt's bravery. In the last half hour, she had been knocked unconscious, beaten, and shot in the chest, and even with the protection, she had to be hurting, but she was sticking to the plan and trying to get Decker to talk.

Suddenly, much to her horror, Isabelle realized the recording equipment wasn't in this building. Even if Decker spilled his guts and Holt lived, it would be his word against hers. She had to record; she was the only one who could.

Isabelle took her cell phone out of her pocket and kissed it for good luck. All she could do was pray that the microphone was good enough to pick up Decker's confession. There was a pile of boxes five feet to her right and three feet closer to Holt. She could hide her phone to record much better there, but she risked exposure if she moved.

When Gary reappeared in the circle of lights to briefly talk to Decker, and they conveniently turned their backs to where Isabelle hid, she made her move. She slid in behind the boxes with barely a sound and nestled her phone safely out of direct sight of the circle, but hopefully close enough to pick up the conversation. Once that was done, she waited.

Gary moved off shortly, still far enough away from Isabelle that she didn't feel like she needed to move. Holt was looking intently at Decker. Isabelle thought she might be daring him to talk to her.

"You know how easy it was for me to get Parker Caldwell in my pocket?" Decker asked, taking Holt's dare.

"Drugs?" Holt asked.

"We started him off small. Just a little here and there. But pretty soon, there was no way he could ever live without me. I had one of my guys, a patient at my clinic, provide anything Caldwell wanted. Customer service is the key to any successful business."

"Of course. How'd you get him to buy into your methadone plan?"

"The clinic was too fucking easy. Money like you have no idea. It happened accidentally at first. A patient died, but the paperwork didn't get processed quickly. The state never caught on. They kept funding his slot. I kept filling out all the correct paperwork and upped his dose to two hundred fifty milligrams. We thought about just keeping the money and not buying the methadone, but that was too risky. People pay attention to what you buy and what you dispense. But if a person's not taking the methadone, you can get rid of it on your own. If we had tablets, we really could have made a killing, but we thin out the Done and my guy sells it on the street. All cash transactions. Can't really put that kind of money in the bank. It's not like I pay taxes on money earned cheating the government."

"That's where the real estate comes in, right?" Holt asked.

"Sure. I have a few people I trust. We buy stuff in my name, their names. We create companies and charities and funnel the money through those. Anything to clean it up."

"Where does Isabelle Rochat come in to all this?" Holt asked.

"She wouldn't have been involved in this mess at all if Gary hadn't sent her this dumb bookkeeping record he uses to keep track of our under the table business. She's been my accountant for years and never knew any of the illegal stuff. She was completely ignorant. Until Gary sent her that stupid spreadsheet. I told him to leave it alone, but he wouldn't listen. He and a buddy hatched a plan to scare her into not saying anything about what she had received. They got shotguns and ski masks and blasted away at her siding. I guess you know that; you were in her pool."

"Not too pleased to be shot at either."

"She kept asking questions, and you stuck around longer than I wanted, so we broke into her office. Just to send a message to both of you."

"You dumb bastard," Holt said, laughing, "she wasn't even speaking to me until you tossed her office. That freaked her out enough that she gave me another chance. You were home free until that point."

Isabelle found the conversation disconcerting. The recounting of the past few months of her life was too clinical, too casual, too unemotional. Imagining not speaking to Holt now seemed ridiculous and she could barely remember why she had been so stubborn. It felt comical that Decker Pence, a nasty criminal, was detailing her courtship with the amazing Holt Lasher. When telling the story, they would certainly leave out his matchmaking.

Decker brought her back to the moment.

"Well, we scared you both when I had Caldwell killed in Isabelle's house. He got frisky and snuck out. I knew he would head for Rochat's house. He had been eavesdropping a little too often. My employees were careless. He knew she was in trouble, and I guess the only remaining good left in him felt like warning her that she was in deep shit with me. You broke four ribs and the jaw of one of my guys. I was impressed with you. Not so much with my employee. That's a body that will probably never be found. Along with my stupid secretary who sent Rochat the file in the first place, of course."

Isabelle shivered. Thank God she'd hidden in the closet like Holt had told her to. She moved into the shadows to continue setting up her plan.

"And now here we are," Holt said, seeming unaffected by Decker's admission.

"You tried to play me. Did you really think I wouldn't figure out that you had control of Gary's cell phone? What did you do with Diamond? The pictures were a nice touch. Had me going for a while. But I'm not stupid."

"Let's agree to disagree on that one. Now that we're all caught up, what are we going to do with the rest of the evening?"

Decker paced in front of her, clearly working up his nerve again.

Holt wasn't sure how she was going to work her way out of her current jam. She was trying to buy as much time as possible. Her chest was killing her where Decker had shot her, but she wasn't about to complain since she was still breathing, albeit a little shallowly from the pain.

She had heard the same scream Decker had when he shot her. It sounded like a woman. She prayed it wasn't Isabelle. Since no one had come in guns blazing, she had to assume her team didn't know where she was. Whoever was out there might be the only thing she could count on for help, but the thought it might be Isabelle, putting herself in the line of fire they'd been trying to keep her from all this time, made her nauseous.

As Holt was plotting how to disable Decker and free herself from the chair, three things happened. First, the lights in the entire building cut out, plunging everyone in the warehouse into darkness. Second, firecrackers, the kind set off in the driveways of millions of homes on the Fourth of July, started spinning, exploding, sparkling, and popping in seemingly every direction. Finally, Decker fired off two shots straight into the air. Holt had no idea why he started popping his gun off. She hoped it was a sign of panic.

Holt thrived in these conditions. The fireworks were providing enough noise, distraction, and light that she could hop her chair over to where one of the spotlights stood, now dark. Decker's random gunshots had allowed her to keep tabs on his location. The intermittent fireworks kept him in view. He didn't seem interested in anything except who or what was attacking the warehouse. He was yelling, but even as close as Holt was, she couldn't hear anything he said because of the noise, which was really quite overwhelming.

When she reached the light, she ran the chair into it, knocking it over. As she hoped, the glass on the light broke. She took a deep breath, purposefully tipped her chair over, and exhaled on the descent and landing. Her already sore chest screamed in protest, but four inches from her face was the object of her quest. A glass shard, roughly six inches long, and narrow enough to fit in her hand without completely destroying the skin, had come loose from the light face. She hoped it was all she needed to get out of there alive.

Someday, bad guys would learn to use handcuffs or something that wasn't easily cut with objects lying around their evil lairs, but for now, Holt was happy Decker was an amateur. She used her knee, which was in contact with the ground, to spin the chair around until her hands were where her face had been. It took a few tries to locate the piece of glass in the dark, since the fireworks were beginning to fizzle out. Getting it to her hands in any useful manner was no picnic either. The ropes were tied tightly.

As she finally maneuvered the glass shard where she wanted it, the warehouse went silent and dark once again. Decker raged, sounding feral and desperate. Holt worked her glass piece faster, less cautious about keeping her hands from getting cut. She needed to get free. Decker was more dangerous now than he had been at any other point. She had seen men in his situation, a perfect plan gone south, trapped, and seemingly no solution. This was when people became reckless, desperate, and deadly.

Decker fired another wild shot, this time at the floor. It hit the cement floor five feet from Holt's head. Her adrenaline was really pumping now. Unfortunately, the shot had provided just enough light for Decker to see Holt.

"You think you can get away with this?" Decker yelled, getting nearer as he spoke.

Holt worked the rope. She was almost free. Decker fired another shot, this one too close for comfort. She wouldn't survive another, since he seemed to have figured out the bulletproof tux didn't cover her head.

"Light, please," Holt yelled, hoping those fireworks hadn't been the grand finale.

On cue, a sparkler shot into the circle. Decker was almost on top of her. The little light projectiles licked the ground around them like welding sparks. Decker raised his gun as Holt freed her hands.

Her feet were still tied to the chair so she couldn't stand and fight. Instead, she planted her palms on the floor, ignoring the shards of glass that shredded her hands, pushed herself into a tucked handstand, and whirled her lower body at Decker's legs.

The chair hit him first, then her body mass. He went down in a heap, the shot meant for Holt's brain hitting the ceiling. As he landed, the gun slid out of his hand and skidded five feet away. Decker cursed and grabbed his knee.

The force of Holt's swing had twisted the chair from under her body. She was able to sit up and easily cut the ropes around her ankles. She was back to full strength.

So was Decker. As Holt hopped to her feet, so did Decker. The last few sparkles sputtered from the stick a few feet from them as they squared off. The room was once again pitch-black and silent as Decker swung at Holt.

She sensed the blow, aimed at the left side of her head, and batted it away with her left hand. The body to body contact gave her a measure of how far away Decker was and at what angle his body was positioned from Holt. She threw a jab to where she expected his torso to be and was rewarded with a grunt. The punch wasn't hard enough to do damage. It was an information gathering expedition and was followed by a lightning quick combination of left punch, right hook.

Decker fell forward into Holt and grabbed her shoulders to regain his balance and to keep her from getting in any more serious punches.

"Decker," Gary yelled from close by.

"Over here," Decker wheezed, still locked with Holt. "Get me out of this mess."

Holt tried to extract herself from Decker's grip, but he had his arms wrapped around her torso, pinning her arms at her sides. She was moving her feet quickly, and he was having trouble keeping up. At times, she felt his feet come completely off the ground, but he wasn't letting go. He was also throwing a shoulder into her throbbing chest as often as he could and trying to bite her shoulder. Luckily, the tuxedo also seemed capable of deflecting oral assaults, but Holt was annoyed she couldn't get free, and the pain was wearing her down.

Suddenly, the lights were restored. Doors all around them burst open, and Holt's team and members of the Providence Police Department rushed in. Holt used the distraction to fling Decker off her. Gary was running at them, gun waving wildly. When Holt stepped toward Decker, Gary fired three shots. Two missed completely, but the third lodged in Decker's left shoulder.

"You fucking ass, you shot me," Decker screamed as he and Gary were surrounded by police officers and arrested.

Holt saw her team looking her over anxiously, but she didn't see the only person she had any interest in being with right now. Luckily, she didn't have to wait long for Isabelle to fly from behind a pile of boxes nearby and propel herself into Holt's arms. The force caught Holt off guard and they both stumbled backward, arms clutching, lips meeting. Holt's heart was pounding.

Even though they were surrounded by police officers and just about everyone who worked for her, Holt didn't want to stop kissing Isabelle. They weren't gentle, loving kisses, but the kind you give someone after you thought you would never get the chance to do it again. Isabelle buried her face in Holt's neck and squeezed her tightly. Holt realized Isabelle's legs were wrapped around her waist, and you couldn't fit a playing card between their bodies. Her chest hurt, but not only from the force of the gunshot. She really hadn't known if she would see Isabelle again.

"Uh, boss?" Lola had apparently lost the game of rock-paper-scissors her team often played to determine who had to do a particularly unpleasant task.

"Yes, Lola?" Holt was in no mood to be angry with anyone, not with the woman she loved in her arms and the greatest threat to both of them lying angry, bleeding, and handcuffed on the floor.

"The police have a few questions, and, well, so do we."

"Oh, wait," Isabelle said, disentangling herself from Holt's grasp and bouncing toward the pile of boxes she had emerged from earlier. She pulled out her cell phone and beelined for Moose and the police officer who looked like he was in charge. Holt followed.

"What's that?" Holt asked.

"Decker's confession," Isabelle said. "Since you went a little off the rails with what was my understanding of the plan, I thought we should improvise."

"He Tasered me and dragged me to this stupid building," Holt said, feeling a little defensive. She was embarrassed she had been so easily trapped.

"I saw you getting dragged down here. Amy and I came after you."

"I have an entire army of highly trained ass kickers, and you're the one who swoops in to save my biscuits."

"I have more invested in the biscuits than the others," Isabelle said, touching Holt's chest gently. "Are you okay?"

"Was it you who screamed?" Holt asked, already knowing the answer.

"I saw him shooting you and I couldn't help it. How did you stay so calm?"

Holt was aware the whole room was watching their conversation, their heads going back and forth like they were watching a tennis match, but she didn't care. The only one in the room that mattered was the one who needed questions answered immediately. Everyone else could wait.

"I had to. It's part of the job. People do dumb things when they're stressed or angry or agitated. Staying calm can save your life. And bulletproof tuxedos."

"The dry-cleaning is going to be a nightmare," Isabelle said.

"Do you happen to know who unleashed pyrotechnic hell in here?" Holt asked, trying to suppress a smile.

"I did," Isabelle said. "Those boxes are full of them. Gary was looking all over for me. I didn't want him to find me, and I figured you needed Decker distracted. I asked Amy to cut the lights when she left to get the ass kickers, so when the lights went out, I thought it was time to liven things up. There were a couple wheely cart things so I loaded them up, lit the fuses, and shoved them off. The smaller ones I lit and threw. It was actually kinda fun."

"Where did you get the lighter?" Holt asked, not sure why she cared about the tiny detail.

"I had it in my purse. One of those just in case things that got thrown in. Now I know what the 'case' was that I needed it for. Setting off fireworks to save you from a madman."

"You don't have any shoes on, and your purse is the size of an eye patch, but you had a lighter in there?" Holt was amazed. "What else do you have 'just in case'?"

"Wouldn't you like to know?" Isabelle said before kissing her again.

"My girlfriend is fucking awesome," Holt said.

"Your girlfriend, huh?" Isabelle asked, looking quite happy.

"Is that presumptuous?" Holt asked, realizing she was making assumptions. She also realized she hadn't followed Jose's advice about telling Isabelle how she felt, and the worst had almost come true. She didn't want to go another minute without telling her. "'Cause I almost died, and all I could think about was that I never worked up the courage to tell you that I love you."

"I love you too, Holt. I think I've known it for a while but was too terrified to admit it. Before I met you, I couldn't have done what I just did. I might not love your job, but I'm a stronger, more confident person when I'm with you. And at the end of the day, anyone who's been a victim of a crime deserves a hero like you on their side. God, I love you."

Holt felt like she was floating. Despite all the shit she had just been through, she had never been happier. She kissed Isabelle. They were really getting going again when Moose tapped Holt on the shoulder.

"Why don't you and Isabelle get on home? I'll take care of the paperwork here and the police can interview you both tomorrow. You don't need the emergency room, right?"

"Not tonight," Holt said, putting an arm around Isabelle's waist. Every one of Holt's team shook her hand on the way out the door. Each expressed in their own way how happy they were she and Isabelle were okay. Amy and Jose were last in line. They didn't have to say anything. Holt could tell she was going to get an earful from her friends.

"It's not going to be tonight," Amy started, "But you are going to have to promise us a few things before you go out and make stupid plans like the one you had going on tonight. Got it? Isabelle won't be around every time to save your ass."

Holt laughed and nodded. She kissed Amy on the lips, Jose on the cheek, and finally pushed open the warehouse door. She and Isabelle stepped into the Providence night.

"My car keys don't happen to be in that amazing purse of yours do they?" Holt asked, feeling euphoric and exhausted after the wild evening.

Isabelle dangled the keys in front of Holt's face. "Take me home, sweetheart."

CHAPTER EIGHTEEN

"Thank you for saving my ass tonight," Holt said. "I can't believe Decker caught me so easily."

Isabelle couldn't believe Holt was thanking her. "I seem to remember you being the one risking your life for me. I don't think you need to thank me. Now that it's over, what did you think the odds were that the plan was going to work? Be honest with me."

"Oh, probably about fifty-fifty," Holt said, smiling slightly. "It was a shit plan."

"Then why did you go with it?" Isabelle was pretty sure she knew the answer, but she needed Holt to tell her. If they were going to be a team going forward, they had to be open and honest with each other.

"Because the alternative wasn't an option," Holt said. "And before you ask me to, no, I won't promise to never do it again. If your life is in danger, I'm going to do whatever I can to protect you. I guess Decker Pence was right about that. We'll both do whatever it takes to get what we want when it matters enough."

"You are nothing like Decker Pence, my love." Isabelle was horrified Holt even entertained the thought.

"We might be similar, but I have you. If I ever consider crossing a line, or going too far, you're my guiding light. God, I'm glad you are willing to take a chance on me."

"You're worth the chance. And I won't ask you not to protect me because I know that's like talking to a brick wall, but promise me you won't take unnecessary chances. I've let you in, and now I don't know how I would live without you in my life. Don't you dare do anything that would make my happily ever after impossible."

"Yes, ma'am," Holt said, kissing her. "Shower with me? I smell like fear, and I've got bloody bits to wash off."

They undressed each other and Holt adjusted the water. She wrapped her arms around Isabelle from behind. Isabelle felt like she was experiencing everything in amplified, exquisite detail. Holt's touch ignited her in ways no one ever had. She wanted to kiss her slowly all night and be devoured quickly at the same time.

Her breath caught as Holt ran her hands from her stomach up and across each breast. Her nipples jumped to attention and her clit throbbed hopefully.

"Holt, baby, I know you can see the size of the bruise on your chest." Holt seemed to have no sense of concern about her own vulnerabilities.

"I'm fine," Holt said against Isabelle's back. Holt's breath against Isabelle's wet skin was making rational thought difficult.

"Let me clean you up," Isabelle said. She took Holt's hands in hers and washed the cuts and scrapes carefully. She wiped the blood off her face and carefully soaped around the giant black and blue spot spreading across Holt's chest. She shampooed Holt's hair and let her hands wander along Holt's tattoos as she rinsed her hair.

"Go get ready, love. I'll be right in," Isabelle said, suddenly unable to keep her body under control.

Holt shot out of the shower. Isabelle laughed as Holt toweled off quickly and hustled into the bedroom. No one had ever been able to explain to her what true love felt like in a way that made her believe it existed. Now she knew why. How could she tell someone that true, deep, real love was a naked ass hopping through the bedroom toweling off wet feet? Some things were best discovered on your own.

"Help me with this?" Holt asked, lying on the bed trying to get her towel from underneath her.

She was moving with more stiffness than Isabelle guessed she wanted her to see. Gently, Isabelle pulled the towel from under Holt. "You stay there, baby. Don't move."

Isabelle dropped the towel by the side of the bed and started slowly marking a trail of kisses across Holt's body. She moved from

Holt's lips to nibble on her ears, then down her neck to her chest. She lingered a breath away from each breast but didn't touch either. Holt's nipples were hard, but she stayed just away. When it looked like Holt was in physical pain, Isabelle relented and sucked one hard nipple in her mouth while massaging the other breast with her hand. She was careful to avoid the expanding bruise in the middle of Holt's chest.

"God, you feel good, baby," Isabelle said, marveling at the hard planes and soft skin.

"I'm wound a little tight here, Isabelle. You've been making me crazy for weeks."

Isabelle toyed with Holt until she knew she was close to coming, and then worked lower, across the rippled abs and down to the tender skin where stomach meets hip. Holt's breathing was irregular, and she was squirming. She tried to get her hands on Isabelle, but Isabelle redirected them above her head.

"You are so sexy," Isabelle said.

She moved back to Holt's mouth and kissed her deeply, a kiss of ownership and commitment. She straddled Holt's stomach and leaned over her, putting her breasts within reach of Holt's mouth. This time, Holt didn't leave her hands above her head but pulled Isabelle closer, taking each breast in turn, into her mouth.

"Please, baby," Isabelle whispered, her breath hitched.

Holt pulled Isabelle's hips forward until she was gently resting over her face. "Your chest…"

Holt licked Isabelle's clit, and Isabelle forgot her worries. Holt drew her closer still and sucked her clit into her mouth, running her tongue over the sensitive skin.

Isabelle leaned forward over Holt's head, steadying herself against the back of the bed. Holt looked mesmerized.

"Be careful, baby," Isabelle said between gasped breaths. "I'm really close."

"That's okay. I'm done teasing you," Holt said, increasing the speed of her attentions.

"Kiss me. Don't stop kissing me. Show me you're real," Isabelle said.

Holt kissed her clit, then drew Isabelle fully into her mouth. Isabelle felt herself swell and she pumped her hips against Holt's mouth. She came with a shudder and slid back down Holt's body.

She wanted full body contact, the kind that spoke more about feelings and promises than words were capable of describing. She started rubbing circles across Holt's stomach and quickly worked her way lower.

"I'm happy to just hold you," Holt said.

"Oh no," Isabelle said, dipping her fingers into Holt's wetness. "We're done with the days of you sacrificing everything for me. Okay by you?"

"Don't stop what you're doing," Holt said, gasping.

Isabelle slid through Holt's arousal and slipped inside with two fingers. Holt nearly came off the bed as she sunk deep. Isabelle kissed her and bit her lip hard.

"I'm coming," Holt said, her body tensing in pleasure.

Holt shuddered as Isabelle pulled her fingers out. She collapsed against Holt and they held each other tightly.

"This has been one hell of a day," Holt said, kissing the top of Isabelle's head.

"One hell of a courtship. You sure do know how to show a girl a good time."

"What do you mean? Holt said, laughing. "We hung out by the pool, you invited me to your office party, we had hot wieners, I took you to a party, we got a fireworks show. I am a good fucking time."

"I love you," Isabelle said. "Let's just love each other tonight. We can figure out the rest of it in the morning."

"That is the best plan I've heard in months," Holt said, gently rolling herself on top of Isabelle. "I can handle anything tomorrow brings, as long as every tonight includes you."

❖

After the best night in Holt's memory, she wasn't happy to be woken by her cell phone at five a.m. She was even less amused when Lola informed her she was outside and needed to talk.

"I'll be right back, baby," she said, kissing Isabelle when she grunted her sleepy protest to Holt leaving their cozy bed.

Holt padded to the door. Lola was lucky Holt had boxers and a T-shirt on. Isabelle was only wearing a T-shirt when she followed Holt to the door.

"What trouble is knocking at the door now? Do I need pants?"

"Depends on how you feel about Lola seeing your cute butt," Holt said.

She was concerned that Lola was here at this hour, especially after the night they had all had. She pulled the door open and Lola stumbled in looking like she hadn't slept since they had parted ways at the warehouse.

"Hi, Isabelle, H. I'm sorry to bother you, but I think we have a problem."

"Holy hell," Isabelle said. "This looks like it's going to require pants." She ducked behind the screen and hollered back to Lola, "When was the last time you ate anything? You look like hell. Never mind. Don't answer. I'm hungry. I'm cooking you breakfast. Holt, you better have food in that enormous stainless steel fridge."

"What's up, Lola?" Holt asked, getting Lola settled on the couch.

"Well, I think someone stole your truck, based on the glass in your driveway, and there's this," Lola said, holding up a small piece of plastic.

"Is that a pregnancy test?" Isabelle asked from the kitchen, looking shocked.

Lola nodded.

"It was taped to the door when I got home last night. My girlfriend is gone, and I've been looking for her ever since," Lola said.

"And someone stole my truck?" Holt asked. "Well, that's the shit. Looks like I might need pants now too."

"I thought you said your job was boring," Isabelle said. "I think I've been bamboozled. It's a good thing I love you."

About the Author

Jesse Thoma splits her professional time between graduate school and work. She is a project manager in a clinical research lab and spends a good amount of time in methadone clinics and prisons collecting data and talking to people.

Jesse grew up in Northern California but headed east for college. She never looked back, although her baseball allegiance is still loyally with the San Francisco Giants. She has lived in New England for ten years and has finally learned to leave extra time in the morning to scrape snow off the car. Jesse is blissfully married and is happiest when she is out for a walk with her wife and their dog, pretending she still has the soccer skills she had as an eighteen-year-old, eating anything her wife bakes, or sitting at the computer to write a few lines.

Books Available from Bold Strokes Books

The Princess Affair by Nell Stark. Rhodes Scholar Kerry Donovan arrives at Oxford ready to focus on her studies, but her life and her priorities are thrown into chaos when she catches the eye of Her Royal Highness Princess Sasha. (978-1-60282-858-2)

The Chase by Jesse J. Thoma. When Isabelle Rochat's life is threatened, she receives the unwelcome protection and attention of bounty hunter Holt Lasher who vows to keep Isabelle safe at all costs. (978-1-60282-859-9)

The Lone Hunt by L.L. Raand. In a world where humans and praeterns conspire for the ultimate power, violence is a way of life… and death. A Midnight Hunters novel. (978-1-60282-860-5)

The Supernatural Detective by Crin Claxton. Tony Carson sees dead people. With a drag queen for a spirit guide and a devastatingly attractive herbalist for a client, she's about to discover the spirit world can be a very dangerous world indeed. (978-1-60282-861-2)

Beloved Gomorrah by Justine Saracen. Undersea artists creating their own City on the Plain uncover the truth about Sodom and Gomorrah, whose "one righteous man" is a murderer, rapist, and conspirator in genocide. (978-1-60282-862-9)

Cut to the Chase by Lisa Girolami. Careful and methodical author Paige Cornish falls for brash and wild Hollywood actress, Avalon Randolph, but can these opposites find a happy middle ground in a town that never lives in the middle? (978-1-60282-783-7)

More Than Friends by Erin Dutton. Evelyn Fisher thinks she has the perfect role model for a long-term relationship, until her best friends, Kendall and Melanie, split up and all three women must reevaluate their lives and their relationships. (978-1-60282-784-4)

Every Second Counts by D. Jackson Leigh. Every second counts in Bridgette LeRoy's desperate mission to protect her heart and stop Marc Ryder's suicidal return to riding rodeo bulls. (978-1-60282-785-1)

Dirty Money by Ashley Bartlett. Vivian Cooper and Reese DiGiovanni just found out that falling in love is hard. It's even harder when you're running for your life. (978-1-60282-786-8)

Sea Glass Inn by Karis Walsh. When Melinda Andrews commissions a series of paintings by Pamela Whitford for her new inn, she doesn't expect to be more captivated by the artist than by the paintings. (978-1-60282-771-4)

The Awakening: A Sisters of Spirits novel by Yvonne Heidt. Sunny Skye has interacted with spirits her entire life, but when she runs into Officer Jordan Lawson during a ghost investigation, she discovers more than just facts in a missing girl's cold case file. (978-1-60282-772-1)

Murphy's Law by Yolanda Wallace. No matter how high you climb, you can't escape your past. (978-1-60282-773-8)

Blacker Than Blue by Rebekah Weatherspoon. Threatened with losing her first love to a powerful demon, vampire Cleo Jones is willing to break the ultimate law of the undead to rebuild the family she has lost. (978-1-60282-774-5)

Another 365 Days by KE Payne. Clemmie Atkins is back, and her life is more complicated than ever! Still madly in love with her girlfriend, Clemmie suddenly finds her life turned upside down with distractions, confessions, and the return of a familiar face... (978-1-60282-775-2)

Silver Collar by Gill McKnight. Werewolf Luc Garoul is outlawed and out of control, but can her family track her down before a sinister predator gets there first? Fourth in the Garoul series. (978-1-60282-764-6)

The Dragon Tree Legacy by Ali Vali. For Aubrey Tarver time hasn't dulled the pain of losing her first love Wiley Gremillion, but she has to set that aside when her choices put her life and her family's lives in real danger. (978-1-60282-765-3)

The Midnight Room by Ronica Black. After a chance encounter with the mysterious and brooding Lillian Gray in the "midnight room" of The Griffin, a local lesbian bar, confident and gorgeous Audrey McCarthy learns that her bad-girl behavior isn't bulletproof. (978-1-60282-766-0)

Dirty Sex by Ashley Bartlett. Vivian Cooper and twins Reese and Ryan DiGiovanni stole a lot of money and the guy they took it from wants it back. Like now. (978-1-60282-767-7)

The Storm by Shelley Thrasher. Rural East Texas. 1918. War-weary Jaq Bergeron and marriage-scarred musician Molly Russell try to salvage love from the devastation of the war abroad and natural disasters at home. (978-1-60282-780-6)

Crossroads by Radclyffe. Dr. Hollis Monroe specializes in short-term relationships but when she meets pregnant mother-to-be Annie Colfax, fate brings them together at a crossroads that will change their lives forever. (978-1-60282-756-1)

Beyond Innocence by Carsen Taite. When a life is on the line, love has to wait. Doesn't it? (978-1-60282-757-8)

Heart Block by Melissa Brayden. Socialite Emory Owen and struggling single mom Sarah Matamoros are perfectly suited for each other but face a difficult time when trying to merge their contrasting worlds and the people in them. If love truly exists, can it find a way? (978-1-60282-758-5)

Pride and Joy by M.L. Rice. Perfect Bryce Montgomery is her parents' pride and joy, but when they discover that their daughter is a lesbian, her world changes forever. (978-1-60282-759-2)

Ladyfish by Andrea Bramhall. Finn's escape to the Florida Keys leads her straight into the arms of scuba diving instructor Oz as she fights for her freedom, their blossoming love...and her life! (978-1-60282-747-9)

Spanish Heart by Rachel Spangler. While on a mission to find herself in Spain, Ren Molson runs the risk of losing her heart to her tour guide, Lina Montero. (978-1-60282-748-6)

Love Match by Ali Vali. When Parker "Kong" King, the number one tennis player in the world, meets commercial pilot Captain Sydney Parish, sparks fly—but not from attraction. They have the summer to see if they have a love match. (978-1-60282-749-3)

One Touch by L.T. Marie. A romance writer and a travel agent come together at their high school reunion, only to find out that the memory of that one touch never fades. (978-1-60282-750-9)

The Raid by Lee Lynch. Before Stonewall, having a drink with friends or your girl could mean jail. Would these women and men still have family, a job, a place to live after...The Raid? (978-1-60282-753-0)

The You Know Who Girls: Freshman Year by Annameekee Hesik. As they begin freshman year, Abbey Brooks and her best friend, Kate, pinkie swear they'll keep away from the lesbians in Gila High, but Abbey already suspects she's one of those you-know-who girls herself and slowly learns who her true friends really are. (978-1-60282-754-7)

Month of Sundays by Yolanda Wallace. Love doesn't always happen overnight; sometimes it takes a month of Sundays. (978-1-60282-739-4)

Jacob's War by C.P. Rowlands. ATF Special Agent Allison Jacob's task force is in the middle of an all-out war, from the streets to the boardrooms of America. Small business owner Katie Blackburn is the latest victim who accidentally breaks it wide open, but she may break AJ's heart at the same time. (978-1-60282-740-0)

The Pyramid Waltz by Barbara Ann Wright. Princess Katya Nar Umbriel wants a perfect romance, but her Fiendish nature and duties to the crown mean she can never tell the truth—until she meets Starbride, a woman who gets to the heart of every secret, even if it will be the death of her. (978-1-60282-741-7)

The Secret of Othello by Sam Cameron. Florida teen detectives Steven and Denny risk their lives to search for a sunken NASA satellite—but under the waves, no one can hear you scream... (978-1-60282-742-4)

Finding Bluefield by Elan Barnehama. Set in the backdrop of Virginia and New York and spanning the years 1960–1982, *Finding Bluefield* chronicles the lives of Nicky Stewart, Barbara Philips, and their son, Paul, as they struggle to define themselves as a family. (978-1-60282-744-8)